Star

'Liberty is never unalie
the blood of patriots or
natural human rights that have ever been invented, liberty is least likely to be cheap and is never free of cost.'

About the Author

Robert Anson Heinlein (1907 – 1988) was one of the greatest and most decorated science fiction writers of the twentieth century. He remains the only author to have won four Hugo awards.

Also published by Hodder & Stoughton

Stranger in a Strange Land

The Moon is a Harsh Mistress

ROBERT A. HEINLEIN

Starship Troopers

The science fiction classic

HODDER

First published in the USA in 1959 by GP Putman's Sons, New York
First published in Great Britain by New English Library,
a division of Hodder & Stoughton, in 1960
This edition published by Hodder & Stoughton,
An Hachette UK Company

First published in abridged form as a serial novel in
The Magazine of Fantasy & Science Fiction in 1959

A CIP catalogue record for this title is available from the British Library

ISBN 978 1 473 61611 0
Ebook ISBN 978 1 848 94878 5

Printed and bound by Clays Ltd, St Ives plc

Hodder & Stoughton policy is to use papers that are natural,
renewable and recyclable products and made from wood grown
in sustainable forests. The logging and manufacturing processes
are expected to conform to the environmental regulations
of the country of origin.

Hodder & Stoughton Ltd
Carmelite House
50 Victoria Embankment
London EC4Y 0DZ

www.hodder.co.uk

To 'Sarge' Arthur George Smith –
Soldier, Citizen, Scientist
– and to all sergeants anywhere
who have labored to make men
out of boys

R.A.H.

Acknowledgements

The stanza from 'The 'Eathen' by Rudyard Kipling, at the head of Chapter VII, is used by permission of Mr Kipling's estate; Quotations from the lyrics of the ballad 'Rodger Young' are used by permission of the author, Frank Loesser.

Chapter 1

Come on, you apes! You wanta live forever?

– Unknown platoon sergeant, 1918

I always get the shakes before a drop. I've had the injections, of course, and hypnotic preparation, and it stands to reason that I can't really be afraid. The ship's psychiatrist has checked my brain waves and asked me silly questions while I was asleep and he tells me that it isn't fear, it isn't anything important – it's just like the trembling of an eager race horse in the starting gate.

I couldn't say about that; I've never been a race horse. But the fact is: I'm scared silly, every time.

At D-minus-thirty, after we had mustered in the drop room of the *Rodger Young*, our platoon leader inspected us. He wasn't our regular platoon leader, because Lieutenant Rasczak had bought it on our last drop; he was really the platoon sergeant, Career Ship's Sergeant Jelal. Jelly was a Finno-Turk from Iskander around Proxima – a swarthy little man who looked like a clerk, but I've seen him tackle two berserk privates so big he had to reach up to grab them, crack their heads together like coconuts, step back out of the way while they fell.

Off duty he wasn't bad – for a sergeant. You could even call him 'Jelly' to his face. Not recruits, of course, but anybody who had made at least one combat drop.

But right now he was on duty. We had all each inspected our combat equipment (look, it's your own neck – see?), the acting platoon sergeant had gone over us carefully after he mustered us, and now Jelly went over us again, his face mean, his eyes missing nothing. He stopped by the man in front of me, pressed the button on his belt that gave readings on his physicals. 'Fall out!'

'But, Sarge, it's just a cold! The Surgeon said—'

Jelly interrupted. '"But Sarge!"' he snapped. 'The Surgeon ain't making no drop – and neither are you, with a degree and a half of fever. You think I got time to chat with you, just before a drop? *Fall out!*'

Jenkins left us, looking sad and mad – and I felt bad, too. Because of the Lieutenant buying it, last drop, and people moving up, I was assistant section leader, second section, this drop, and now I was going to have a hole in my section and no way to fill it. That's not good; it means a man can run into something sticky, call for help and have nobody to help him.

Jelly didn't downcheck anybody else. Presently he stepped out in front of us, looked us over and shook his head sadly. 'What a gang of apes!' he growled. 'Maybe if you'd all buy it this drop, they could start over and build the kind of outfit the Lieutenant expected you to be. But probably not – with the sort of recruits we get these days.' He suddenly straightened up, shouted, 'I just want to remind you apes that each and every one of you has cost the gov'ment, counting weapons, armor, ammo, instrumentation, and training, everything, including the way you overeat – has cost, on the hoof, better'n half a million. Add in the thirty cents you are actually worth and that runs to quite a sum.' He glared at us. 'So bring it back! We can spare you, but we can't spare that fancy suit you're wearing. I don't want any heroes in this outfit; the Lieutenant wouldn't like it. You got a job to do, you go down, you do it, you keep your ears open for recall, you show up for retrieval on the bounce and by the numbers. Get me?'

He glared again. 'You're supposed to know the plan. But some of you ain't got any minds to hypnotize so I'll sketch it out. You'll be dropped in two skirmish lines, calculated two-thousand-yard intervals. Get your bearing on me as soon as you hit, get your bearing and distance on your squad mates, both sides, while you take cover. You've wasted ten seconds already, so you smash-and-destroy whatever's at hand until the flankers hit dirt.' (He was talking about me – as assistant section leader I was going to be left flanker, with nobody at my elbow. I began to tremble.)

'Once they hit – straighten out those lines! – equalize those intervals! Drop what you're doing and do it! Twelve seconds. Then advance by leapfrog, odd and even, assistant section leaders minding the count and guiding the envelopment.' He looked at me. 'If you've done this thing properly – which I doubt – the flanks will make contact as recall sounds . . . at which time, home you go. Any questions?'

There weren't any; there never were. He went on, 'One more word – This is just a raid, not a battle. It's a demonstration of firepower and frightfulness. Our mission is to let the enemy know that we could have destroyed their city – but didn't – but that they aren't safe even though we refrain from total bombing. You'll take no prisoners. You'll kill only when you can't help it. But the entire area we hit is to be smashed. I don't want to see any of you loafers back aboard here with unexpended bombs. Get me?' He glanced at the time. 'Rasczak's Roughnecks have got a reputation to uphold. The Lieutenant told me before he bought it to tell *you* that he will always have his eye on you every minute . . . and that he expects your names to *shine!*'

Jelly glanced over at Sergeant Migliaccio, first section leader. 'Five minutes for the Padre.' he stated. Some of the boys dropped out of ranks, went over and knelt in front of Migliaccio, and not necessarily those of his creed, either

– Moslems, Christians, Gnostics, Jews, whoever wanted a word with him before a drop, he was there. I've heard tell that there used to be military outfits whose chaplains did not fight alongside the others, but I've never been able to see how that could work. I mean, how can a chaplain bless anything he's not willing to do himself? In any case, in the Mobile Infantry, *everybody* drops and *everybody* fights – chaplain and cook and the Old Man's writer. Once we went down the tube there wouldn't be a Roughneck left aboard – except Jenkins, of course, and that was not his fault.

I didn't go over. I was always afraid somebody would see me shake if I did, and, anyhow, the Padre could bless me just as handily from where he was. But he came over to me as the last stragglers stood up and pressed his helmet against mine to speak privately. 'Johnnie,' he said quietly, 'this is your first drop as a non-com.'

'Yeah.' I wasn't really a non-com, any more than Jelly was really an officer.

'Just this, Johnnie. Don't buy a farm. You know your job; do it. Just do it. Don't try to win a medal.'

'Uh, thanks, Padre. I shan't.'

He added something in a language I don't know, patted me on the shoulder, and hurried back to his section. Jelly called out, 'Tenn . . . *shut!*' and we all snapped to.

'Pla*toon!*'

'*Section!*' Migliaccio and Johnson echoed.

'By sections – port and starboard – prepare for drop!'

'Sec*tion!* Man your capsules! *Move!*'

'Squad!' – I had to wait while squads four and five manned their capsules and moved on down the firing tube before my capsule showed up on the port track and I could climb into it. I wondered if those old-timers got the shakes as they climbed into the Trojan Horse? Or was it just me? Jelly checked each man as he was sealed in and he sealed me in himself. As he did so, he leaned toward me and said, 'Don't goof off, Johnnie. This is just like a drill.'

The top closed on me and I was alone. 'Just like a drill,' he says! I began to shake uncontrollably.

Then, in my earphones, I heard Jelly from the center-line tube: 'Bridge! Rasczak's Roughnecks . . . ready for drop!'

'Seventeen seconds, Lieutenant!' I heard the ship captain's cheerful contralto replying – and resented her calling Jelly 'Lieutenant.' To be sure, our lieutenant was dead and maybe Jelly would get his commission . . . but we were still 'Rasczak's Roughnecks.'

She added, 'Good luck, boys!'

'Thanks, Captain.'

'Brace yourselves! Five seconds.'

I was strapped all over – belly, forehead, shins. But I shook worse than ever.

It's better after you unload. Until you do, you sit there in total darkness, wrapped like a mummy against the accelerations, barely able to breathe – and knowing that there is just nitrogen around you in the capsule even if you could get your helmet open, which you can't – and knowing that the capsule is surrounded by the firing tube anyhow and if the ship gets hit before they fire you, you haven't got a prayer, you'll just die there, unable to move, helpless. It's that endless wait in the dark that causes the shakes – thinking that they've forgotten you . . . the ship has been hulled and stayed in orbit, dead, and soon you'll buy it, too, unable to move, choking. Or it's a crash orbit and you'll buy it that way, if you don't roast on the way down.

Then the ship's braking program hit us and I stopped shaking. Eight gees, I would say, or maybe ten. When a female pilot handles a ship there is nothing comfortable about it; you're going to have bruises every place you're strapped. Yes,

yes, I know they make better pilots than men do; their reactions are faster and they can tolerate more gee. They can get in faster, get out faster, and thereby improve everybody's chances, yours as well as theirs. But that still doesn't make it fun to be slammed against your spine at ten times your proper weight.

But I must admit that Captain Deladrier knows her trade. There was no fiddling around once the *Rodger Young* stopped braking. At once I heard her snap, 'Center-line tube . . . *fire!*' and there were two recoil bumps as Jelly and his acting platoon sergeant unloaded – and immediately: 'Port and starboard tubes – *automatic fire*!' and the rest of us started to unload.

Bump! and your capsule jerks ahead one place – *bump!* and it jerks again, precisely like cartridges feeding into the chamber of an old-style automatic weapon. Well, that's just what we were . . . only the barrels of the gun were twin launching tubes built into a spaceship troop carrier and each cartridge was a capsule big enough (just barely) to hold an infantryman with all field equipment.

Bump! – I was used to number three spot, out early; now I was Tail-End Charlie, last out after three squads. It makes a tedious wait, even with a capsule being fired every second; I tried to count the bumps – *bump!* (twelve) *bump!* (thirteen, *bump!* (fourteen – with an odd sound to it, the empty one Jenkins should have been in) *bump!* –

And *clang!* – it's my turn as my capsule slams into the firing chamber – then WHAMBO! the explosion hits with a force that makes the Captain's braking manoeuver feel like a love tap.

Then suddenly nothing.

Nothing at all. No sound, no pressure, no weight. Floating in darkness . . . free fall, maybe thirty miles up, above the effective atmosphere, falling weightlessly toward the surface of a planet you've never seen. But I'm not shaking now; it's the wait beforehand that wears. Once you unload, you can't get hurt – because if anything goes wrong it will happen so fast that you'll buy it without noticing that you're dead, hardly.

Almost at once I felt the capsule twist and sway, then steady down so that my weight was on my back . . . weight that built up quickly until I was at my full weight (0.87 gee, we had been told) for that planet as the capsule reached terminal velocity for the thin upper atmosphere. A pilot who is a real artist (and the Captain was) will approach and brake so that your launching speed as you shoot out of the tube places you just dead in space relative to the rotational speed of the planet at that latitude. The loaded capsules are heavy; they punch through the high, thin winds of the upper atmosphere without being blown too far out of position – but just the same a platoon is bound to disperse on the way down, lose some of the perfect formation in which it unloads. A sloppy pilot can make this still worse, scatter a strike group over so much terrain that it can't make rendezvous for retrieval, much less carry out its mission. An infantryman can fight only if somebody else delivers him to his zone; in a way I suppose pilots are just as essential as we are.

I could tell from the gentle way my capsule entered the atmosphere that the Captain had laid us down with as near zero lateral vector as you could ask for. I felt happy – not only a tight formation when we hit and no time wasted, but also a pilot who puts you down properly is a pilot who is smart and precise on retrieval.

The outer shell burned away and sloughed off – unevenly, for I tumbled. Then the rest of it went and I straightened out. The turbulence brakes of the second shell bit in and the ride got rough . . . and still rougher as they burned off one at a time and the second shell began to go to pieces. One of the things that helps a capsule trooper to live long enough to draw a pension is that the skins peeling off his capsule not only slow him down, they also fill the sky over the target area with so much junk that radar picks up reflections from dozens of targets for each man in the drop, any one of which could be a man, or a bomb, or anything. It's enough to give a ballistic computer nervous breakdowns – and does.

To add to the fun your ship lays a series of dummy eggs in the seconds immediately following your drop, dummies that will fall faster because they don't slough. They get under you, explode, throw out 'window,' even operate as transponders, rocket sideways, and do other things to add to the confusion of your reception committee on the ground.

In the meantime your ship is locked firmly on the directional beacon of your platoon leader, ignoring the radar 'noise' it has created and following you in, computing your impact for future use.

When the second shell was gone, the third shell automatically opened my first ribbon chute. It didn't last long but it wasn't expected to; one good, hard jerk at several gee and it went its way and I went mine. The second chute lasted a little bit longer and the third chute lasted quite a while; it began to be rather too warm inside the capsule and I started thinking about landing.

The third shell peeled off when its last chute was gone and now I had nothing around me but my suit armor and a plastic egg. I was still strapped inside it, unable to move; it was time to decide how and where I was going to ground. Without moving my arms (I couldn't) I thumbed the switch for a proximity reading and read it when it flashed on in the instrument reflector inside my helmet in front of my forehead.

A mile and eight-tenths – a little closer than I liked, especially without company. The inner egg had reached steady speed, no more help to be gained by staying inside it, and its skin temperature indicated that it would not open automatically for a while yet – so I flipped a switch with my other thumb and got rid of it.

The first charge cut all the straps; the second charge exploded the plastic egg away from me in eight separate pieces – and I was outdoors, sitting on air, and could *see!* Better still, the eight discarded pieces were metal-coated (except for the small bit I had taken proximity reading through) and would give back the same reflection as an armored man. Any radar viewer, alive or cybernetic, would now have a sad time sorting me out from the junk nearest me, not to mention the thousands of other bits and pieces for miles on each side, above, and below me. Part of a mobile infantryman's training is to let him see, from the ground and both by eye and by radar, just how confusing a drop is to the forces on the ground – because you feel awful naked up there. It is easy to panic and either open a chute too soon and become a sitting duck (do ducks really sit? – if so, why?) or fail to open it and break your ankles, likewise backbone and skull.

So I stretched, getting the kinks out, and looked around . . . then doubled up again and straightened out in a swan dive face down and took a good look. It was night down there, as planned, but infrared snoopers let you size up terrain quite well after you are used to them. The river that cut diagonally through the city was almost below me and coming up fast, shining out clearly with a higher temperature than the land. I didn't care which side of it I landed on but I didn't want to land in it; it would slow me down.

I noticed a flash off to the right at about my altitude; some unfriendly native down below had burned what was probably a piece of my egg. So I fired my first chute at once, intending if possible to jerk myself right off his screen as he followed the targets down in closing range. I braced for the shock, rode it, then floated down for about twenty seconds before unloading the chute – not wishing to call attention to myself in still another way by not falling at the speed of the other stuff around me.

It must have worked; I wasn't burned.

About six hundred feet up I shot the second chute . . . saw very quickly that I was being carried over into the river, found that I was going to pass about a hundred feet up over a flatroofed warehouse or some such by the river . . . blew the chute free and came in for a good enough if rather bouncy landing on the roof by means of the suit's jump jets. I was scanning for Sergeant Jelal's beacon as I hit.

And found that I was on the wrong side of the river; Jelly's start showed up on the compass ring inside my helmet far south of where it should have been – I was too far north. I trotted toward the river side of the roof as I took a range and bearing on the squad leader next to me, found that he was over a mile out of position, called, 'Ace! dress your line,' tossed a bomb behind me as I stepped off the building and across the river. Ace answered as I could have expected – Ace should have had my spot but he didn't want to give up his squad; neverthless he didn't fancy taking orders from me.

The warehouse went up behind me and the blast hit me while I was still over the river, instead of being shielded by the buildings on the far side as I should have been. It darn near tumbled my gyros and I came close to tumbling myself. I had set that bomb for fifteen seconds . . . or had I? I suddenly realized that I had let myself get excited, the worst thing you can do once you're on the ground. 'Just like a drill,' that was the way, just as Jelly had warned me. Take your time and do it right, even if it takes another half second.

As I hit I took another reading on Ace and told him again to realign his squad. He didn't answer but he was already doing it. I let it ride. As long as Ace did his job, I could afford to swallow his surliness – for now. But back aboard ship (if

Jelly kept me on as assistant section leader) we would eventually have to pick a quiet spot and find out who was boss. He was a career corporal and I was just a term lance acting as corporal, but he was under me and you can't afford to take any lip under those circumstances. Not permanently.

But I didn't have time then to think about it; while I was jumping the river I had spotted a juicy target and I wanted to get it before somebody else noticed it – a lovely big group of what looked like public buildings on a hill. Temples, maybe . . . or a palace. They were miles outside the area we were sweeping, but one rule of a smash & run is to expend at least half your ammo outside your sweep area; that way the enemy is kept confused as to where you actually are – that and keep moving, do everything fast. You're always heavily outnumbered; surprise and speed are what saves you.

I was already loading my rocket launcher while I was checking on Ace and telling him for the second time to straighten up. Jelly's voice reached me right on top of that on the all-hands circuit: 'Pla*toon!* By leapfrog! *Forward!*'

My boss. Sergeant Johnson, echoed, 'By leapfrog! Odd numbers! *Advance!*'

That left me with nothing to worry about for twenty seconds, so I jumped on the building nearest me, raised the launcher to my shoulder, found the target and pulled the first trigger to let the rocket have a look at its target – pulled the second trigger and kissed it on its way, jumped back to the ground. 'Second section, even numbers!' I called out . . . waited for the count in my mind and ordered, '*Advance!*'

And did so myself, hopping over the next row of buildings, and, while I was in the air, fanning the first row by the river front with a hand flamer. They seemed to be wood construction and it looked like time to start a good fire – with luck, some of those warehouses would house oil products, or even explosives. As I hit, the Y-rack on my shoulders launched two small H.E. bombs a couple of hundred yards each way to my right and left flanks but I never saw what they did as just then my first rocket hit – that unmistakable (if you've ever seen one) brilliance of an atomic explosion. It was just a pee-wee, of course, less than two kilotons nominal yield, with tamper and implosion squeeze to produce results from a less-than-critical mass – but then who wants to be bunk mates with a cosmic catastrophe? It was enough to clean off that hilltop and make everybody in the city take shelter against fallout. Better still, any of the local yokels who happened to be outdoors and looking that way wouldn't be seeing anything else for a couple of hours – meaning *me*. The flash hadn't dazzled me, nor would it dazzle any of us; our face bowls are heavily leaded, we wear snoopers over our eyes – and we're trained to duck and take it on the armor if we do happen to be looking the wrong way.

So I merely blinked hard – opened my eyes and stared straight at a local citizen just coming out of an opening in the building ahead of me. He looked at me, I looked at him, and he started to raise something – a weapon, I suppose – as Jelly called out, 'Odd numbers! *Advance!*'

I didn't have time to fool with him; I was a good five hundred yards short of where I should have been by then. I still had the hand flamer in my left hand; I toasted him and jumped over the building he had been coming out of, as I started to count. A hand flamer is primarily for incendiary work but it is a good defensive anti-personnel weapon in tight quarters; you don't have to aim it much.

Between excitement and anxiety to catch up I jumped too high and too wide. It's always a temptation to get the most out of your jump gear – but *don't do it.* It leaves you hanging in the air for seconds, a big fat target. The way to advance is to skim over each building as you come to it, barely clearing it, and taking full advantage of cover while you're down – and never stay in one place more than a second or two, never give them time to target in on you. Be somewhere else, anywhere. Keep moving.

This one I goofed – too much for one row of buildings, too little for the row beyond it; I found myself coming down on a roof. But not a nice flat one where I might have tarried three seconds to launch another pee-wee A-rocket; this roof was a jungle of pipes and stanchions and assorted ironmongery – a factory maybe, or some sort of chemical works. No place to land. Worse still, half a dozen natives were up there. These geezers are humanoid, eight or nine feet tall, much skinnier than we are and with a higher body temperature; they don't wear any clothes and they stand out in a set of snoopers like a neon sign. They look still funnier in daylight with your bare eyes but I would rather fight them than the arachnids – those Bugs made me queezy.

If these laddies were up there thirty seconds earlier when my rocket hit, then they couldn't see me, or anything. But I couldn't be certain and didn't want to tangle with them in any case; it wasn't that kind of a raid. So I jumped again while I was still in the air scattering a handful of ten-second fire pills to keep them busy, grounded, jumped again at once, and called out, 'Second section! Even numbers! . . . Advance!' and kept right on going to close the gap, while trying to spot, every time I jumped, something worth expending a rocket on. I had three more of the little A-rockets and I certainly didn't intend to take any back with me. But I had had pounded into me that you *must* get your money's worth with atomic weapons – it was only the second time that I had been allowed to carry them.

Right now I was trying to spot their waterworks; a direct hit on it could make the whole city uninhabitable, force them to evacuate it without directly killing anyone – just the sort of nuisance we had been sent down to commit. It should

– according to the map we had studied under hypnosis – be about three miles upstream from where I was.

But I couldn't see it; my jumps didn't take me high enough, maybe. I was tempted to go higher but I remembered what Migliaccio had said about not trying for a medal, and stuck to doctrine. I set the Y-track launcher on automatic and let it lob a couple of little bombs every time I hit. I set fire to things more or less at random in between, and tried to find the waterworks, or some other worth-while target.

Well, there was *something* up there at the proper range – waterworks or whatever, it was big. So I hopped on top of the tallest building near me, took a bead on it, and let fly. As I bounced down I heard Jelly: 'Johnnie! Red! Start bending in the flanks.'

I acknowledged and heard Red acknowledge and switched my beacon to blinker so that Red could pick me out for certain, took a range and bearing on his blinker while I called out, 'Second Section! Curve in and envelop! Squad leaders acknowledge!'

Fourth and Fifth squads answered, 'Wilco'; Ace said, 'We're already doin' it – pick up your feet.'

Red's beacon showed the right flank to be almost ahead of me and a good fifteen miles away. Golly! Ace was right; I would have to pick up my feet or I would never close the gap in time – and me with a couple of hundredweight of ammo and sundry nastiness still on me that I just had to find time to use up. We had landed in a V formation, with Jelly at the bottom of the V and Red and myself at the ends of the two arms; now we had to close it into a circle around the retrieval rendezvous . . . which meant that Red and I each had to cover more ground than the others and still do our full share of damage.

At least the leapfrog advance was over with once we started to encircle; I could quit counting and concentrate on speed.

It was getting to be less healthy to be anywhere, even moving fast. We had started with the enormous advantage of surprise, reached the ground without being hit (at least I hoped nobody had been hit coming in), and had been rampaging in among them in a fashion that let us fire at will without fear of hitting each other while they stood a big chance of hitting their own people in shooting at us – if they could find us to shoot at, at all. (I'm no games-theory expert but I doubt if any computer could have analyzed what we were doing in time to predict where we would be next.)

Nevertheless the home defenses were beginning to fight back, co-ordinated or not. I took a couple of near misses with explosives, close enough to rattle my teeth even inside armor and once I was brushed by some sort of beam that made my hair stand on end and half paralyzed me for a moment – as if I had hit my funny bone, but all over. If the suit hadn't already been told to jump, I guess I wouldn't have got out of there.

Things like that make you pause to wonder why you ever took up soldiering – only I was too busy to pause for anything. Twice, jumping blind over buildings, I landed right in the middle of a group of them – jumped at once while fanning wildly around me with the hand flamer.

Spurred on this way, I closed about half of my share of the gap, maybe four miles, in minimum time but without doing much more than casual damage. My Y-rack had gone empty two jumps back; finding myself alone in sort of a courtyard I stopped to put my reserve H.E. bombs into it while I took a bearing on Ace – found that I was far enough out in front of the flank squad to think about expending my last two A-rockets. I jumped to the top of the tallest building in the neighborhood.

It was getting light enough to see; I flipped the snoopers up onto my forehead and made a fast scan with bare eyes, looking for anything behind us worth shooting at, anything at all; I had no time to be choosy.

There was something on the horizon in the direction of their spaceport – administration & control, maybe, or possibly even a starship. Almost in line and about half as far away was an enormous structure which I couldn't identify even that loosely. The range to the spaceport was extreme but I let the rocket see it, said, 'Go find it, baby!' and twisted its tail – slapped the last one in, sent it toward the nearer target, and jumped.

That building took a direct hit just as I left it. Either a skinny had judged (correctly) that it was worth one of their buildings to try for one of us, or one of my own mates was getting mighty careless with fireworks. Either way, I didn't want to jump from that spot, even a skimmer; I decided to go through the next couple of buildings instead of over. So I grabbed the heavy flamer off my back as I hit and flipped the snoopers down over my eyes, tackled a wall in front of me with a knife beam at full power. A section of wall fell away and I charged in.

And backed out even faster.

I didn't know what it was I had cracked open. A congregation in church – a skinny flophouse – maybe even their defense headquarters. All I knew was that it was a very big room filled with more skinnies than I wanted to see in my whole life.

Probably not a church, for somebody took a shot at me as I popped back out – just a slug that bounced off my armor, made my ears ring, and staggered me without hurting me. But it reminded me that I wasn't supposed to leave without giving them a souvenir of my visit. I grabbed the first thing on my belt and lobbed it in – and heard it start to squawk. As they keep telling you in Basic, doing something constructive at once is better than figuring out the best thing to do hours later.

By sheer chance I had done the right thing. This was a special bomb, one each issued to us for this mission with instructions to use them if we found ways to make them effective. The squawking I heard as I threw it was the bomb shouting in skinny talk (free translation): 'I'm a thirty-second bomb! I'm a thirty-second bomb! Twenty-nine! . . . twenty-eight! . . . twenty-seven!—'

It was supposed to frazzle their nerves. Maybe it did; it certainly frazzled mine. Kinder to shoot a man. I didn't wait for the countdown; I jumped, while I wondered whether they would find enough doors and windows to swarm out in time.

I got a bearing on Red's blinker at the top of the jump and one on Ace as I grounded. I was falling behind again – time to hurry.

But three minutes later we had closed the gap; I had Red on my left flank a half mile away. He reported it to Jelly. We heard Jelly's relaxed growl to the entire platoon: 'Circle is closed, but the beacon is not down yet. Move forward slowly and mill around, make a little more trouble – but mind the lad on each side of you; don't make trouble for *him*. Good job, so far – don't spoil it. Pla*toon!* By sections . . . *Muster!*'

It looked like a good job to me, too; much of the city was burning and, although it was almost full light now, it was hard to tell whether bare eyes were better than snoopers, the smoke was so thick.

Johnson, our section leader, sounded off: 'Second section, call off!'

I echoed, 'Squads four, five and six – call off and report!' The assortment of safe circuits we had available in the new model comm units certainly speeded things up; Jelly could talk to anybody or to his section leaders; a section leader could call his whole section, or his non-coms; and the platoon could muster twice as fast, when seconds matter. I listened to the fourth squad call off while I inventoried my remaining firepower and lobbed one bomb toward a skinny who poked his head round a corner. He left and so did I – 'Mill around,' the boss man had said.

The fourth squad bumbled the call off until the squad leader remembered to fill in with Jenkins' number; the fifth squad clicked off like an abacus and I began to feel good . . . when the call off stopped after number four in Ace's squad. I called out, 'Ace, where's Dizzy?'

'Shut up,' he said. 'Number six! Call off!'

'Six!' Smith answered.

'Seven!'

'Sixth squad, Flores missing,' Ace completed it. 'Squad leader out for pickup.'

'One man absent,' I reported to Johnson. 'Flores, squad six.'

'Missing or dead?'

'I don't know. Squad leader and assistant section leader dropping out for pickup.'

'Johnnie, you let Ace take it.'

But I didn't hear him, so I didn't answer. I heard him report to Jelly and I heard Jelly cuss. Now look, I wasn't bucking for a medal – it's the assistant section leader's *business* to make pickup; he's the chaser, the last man in, expendable. The squad leaders have other work to do. As you've no doubt gathered by now the assistant section leader isn't necessary as long as the section leader is alive.

Right that moment I was feeling unusually expendable, almost expended, because I was hearing the sweetest sound in the universe, the beacon the retrieval boat would land on, sounding our recall. The beacon is a robot rocket, fired ahead of the retrieval boat, just a spike that buries itself in the ground and starts broadcasting that welcome, welcome music. The retrieval boat homes in on it automatically three minutes later and you had better be on hand, because the bus can't wait and there won't be another one along.

But don't you walk away on another cap trooper, not while there's a chance he's still alive – not in Rasczak's Roughnecks. Not in any outfit of the Mobile Infantry. You try to make pickup.

I heard Jelly order: 'Heads up, lads! Close to retrieval circle and interdict! On the bounce!'

And I heard the beacon's sweet voice: '*—to the everlasting glory of the infantry, shines the name, shines the name of Rodger Young!*' and I wanted to head for it so bad I could taste it.

Instead I was headed the other way, closing on Ace's beacon and expending what I had left of bombs and fire pills and anything else that would weigh me down. 'Ace! You got his beacon?'

'Yes! Go back. Useless!'

'I've got you by eye now. Where is he?'

'Right ahead of me, maybe quarter mile. Scram! He's *my* man.'

I didn't answer; I simply cut left oblique to reach Ace about where he said Dizzy was.

And found Ace standing over him, a couple of skinnies flamed down and more running away. I lit beside him. 'Let's get him out of his armor – the boat'll be down any second!'

'He's too bad hurt!'

I looked and saw that it was true – there was actually a *hole* in his armor and blood coming out. And I was stumped. To make a wounded pickup you get him out of his armor . . . then you simply pick him up in your arms – no trouble in a powered suit – and bounce away from there. A bare man weighs less than the ammo and stuff you've expended. 'What'll we *do?*'

'We carry him,' Ace said grimly. 'Grab ahold the left side of his belt.' He grabbed the right side, we manhandled Flores to his feet. 'Lock on! Now . . . by the numbers, stand by to jump – one – *two!*'

We jumped. Not far, not well. One man alone couldn't have gotten him off the ground; an armored suit is too heavy. But split it between two men and it can be done.

We jumped – and we jumped – and again, and again, with Ace calling it and both of us steadying and catching Dizzy on each grounding. His gyros seemed to be out.

We heard the beacon cut off as the retrieval boat landed on it – I saw it land . . . and it was too far away. We heard the acting platoon sergeant call out: 'In succession, prepare to embark!'

And Jelly called out, 'Belay that order!'

We broke at last into the open and saw the boat standing on its tail, heard the ululation of its take-off warning – saw the platoon still on the ground around it, in interdiction circle, crouching behind the shield they had formed.

Heard Jelly shout, 'In succession, man the boat – *move!*'

And we were *still* too far away! I could see them peel off from the first squad, swarm into the boat as the interdiction circle tightened.

And a single figure broke out of the circle, came toward us at a speed possible only to a command suit.

Jelly caught us while we were in the air, grabbed Flores by his Y-rack and helped us lift.

Three jumps got us to the boat. Everybody else was inside but the door was still open. We got him in and closed it while the boat pilot screamed that we had made her miss rendezvous and now we had *all* bought it! Jelly paid no attention to her; we laid Flores down and lay down beside him. As the blast hit us Jelly was saying to himself, 'All present, Lieutenant. Three men hurt – but all present!'

I'll say this for Captain Deladrier: they don't make any better pilots. A rendezvous, boat to ship in orbit, is precisely calculated. I don't know how, but it is, and you don't change it. You *can't*.

Only she did. She saw in her scope that the boat had failed to blast on time; she braked back, picked up speed again – and matched and took us in, just by eye and touch, no time to compute it. If the Almighty ever needs an assistant to keep the stars in their courses, I know where He can look.

Flores died on the way up.

Chapter 2

It scared me so, I hooked it off,
Nor stopped as I remember,
Nor turned about till I got home,
Locked up in mother's chamber.
Yankee Doodle, keep it up,
Yankee Doodle dandy,
Mind the music and the step,
And with the girls be handy.

I never really intended to join up.

And certainly not the infantry! Why, I would rather have taken ten lashes in the public square and have my father tell me that I was a disgrace to a proud name.

Oh, I had mentioned to my father, late in my senior year in high school, that I was thinking over the idea of volunteering for Federal Service. I suppose every kid does, when his eighteenth birthday heaves into sight – and mine was due the week I graduated. Of course most of them just think about it, toy with the idea a little, then go do something else – go to college, or get a job, or something. I suppose it would have been that way with me . . . if my best chum had not, with dead seriousness, planned to join up.

Carl and I had done everything together in high school – eyed the girls together, double-dated together, been on the debate team together, pushed electrons together in his home lab. I wasn't much on electronic theory myself, but I'm a neat hand with a soldering gun; Carl supplied the skull sweat and

I carried out his instructions. It was fun; anything we did together was fun. Carl's folks didn't have anything like the money that my father had, but it didn't matter between us. When my father bought me a Rolls copter for my fourteenth birthday, it was Carl's as much as mine; contrariwise, his basement lab was mine.

So when Carl told me that he was not going straight on with school, but serve a term first, it gave me to pause. He really meant it; he seemed to think that it was natural and right and obvious.

So I told him I was joining up, too.

He gave me an odd look. 'Your old man won't let you.'

'Huh? How can he stop me?' And of course he couldn't, not legally. It's the first completely free choice anybody gets (and maybe his last); when a boy, or a girl, reaches his or her eighteenth birthday, he or she can volunteer and nobody else has any say in the matter.

'You'll find out.' Carl changed the subject.

So I took it up with my father, tentatively, edging into it sideways.

He put down his newspaper and cigar and stared at me. 'Son, are you out of your mind?'

I muttered that I didn't think so.

'Well, it certainly sounds like it.' He sighed. 'Still . . . I should have been expecting it; it's a predictable stage in a boy's growing up. I remember when you learned to walk and weren't a baby any longer – frankly you were a little hellion for quite a while. You broke one of your mother's Ming vases – on purpose, I'm quite sure . . . but you were too young to know that it was valuable, so all you got was having your hand spatted. I recall the day you swiped one of my cigars, and how sick it made you. Your mother and I carefully avoided noticing that you couldn't eat dinner that night and I've never mentioned it to you until now – boys have to try such things and discover for themselves that men's vices are not for them. We watched when you turned the corner on adolescence and started noticing that girls were different – and wonderful.'

He sighed again. 'All normal stages. And the last one, right at the end of adolescence, is when a boy decides to join up and wear a pretty uniform. Or decides that he is in love, love such as no man ever experienced before, and that he just has to get married right away. Or both.' He smiled grimly. 'With me it was both. But I got over each of them in time not to make a fool of myself and ruin my life.'

'But, Father, I wouldn't ruin my life. Just a term of service – not a career.'

'Let's table that, shall we? Listen, and let *me* tell *you* what you are going to do – because you *want* to. In the first place this family has stayed out of politics and cultivated its own garden for over a hundred years – I see no reason for you to break that fine record. I suppose it's the influence of that fellow at your high school – what's his name? You know the one I mean.'

He meant our instructor in History and Moral Philosophy – a veteran, naturally. 'Mr. Dubois.'

'Hmmph, a silly name – it suits him. Foreigner, no doubt. It ought to be against the law to use the schools as undercover recruiting stations. I think I'm going to write a pretty sharp letter about it – a taxpayer has *some* rights!'

'But, Father, he doesn't do that at all! He—' I stopped, not knowing how to describe it. Mr. Dubois had a snotty, superior manner; he acted as if none of us was really *good* enough to volunteer for service. I didn't like him. 'Uh, if anything, he discourages it.'

'Hmmph! Do you know how to lead a pig? Never mind. When you graduate, you're going to study business at Harvard; you know that. After that, you will go on to the Sorbonne and you'll travel a bit along with it, meet some of our distributors, find out how business is done elsewhere. Then you'll come home and go to work. You'll start with the usual menial job, stock clerk or something, just for form's sake – but you'll be an executive before you can catch your breath, because I'm not getting any younger and the quicker you can pick up the load, the better. As soon as you're able and willing, you'll be boss. There! How does that strike you as a program? As compared with wasting two years of your life?'

I didn't say anything. None of it was news to me; I'd thought about it. Father stood up and put a hand on my shoulder. 'Son, don't think I don't sympathize with you; I do. But look at the real facts. If there were a war, I'd be the first to cheer you on – and to put the business on a war footing. But there isn't, and praise God there never will be again. We've outgrown wars. This planet is now peaceful and happy and we enjoy good enough relations with other planets. So what is this so-called "Federal Service'? Parasitism, pure and simple. A functionless organ, utterly obsolete, living on the taxpayers. A decidedly expensive way for inferior people who otherwise would be unemployed to live at public expense for a term of years, then give themselves airs for the rest of their lives. Is that what you want to do?'

'Carl isn't inferior!'

'Sorry. No, he's a fine boy . . . but misguided.' He frowned, and then smiled. 'Son, I had intended to keep something as a surprise for you – a graduation present. But I'm going to tell you now so that you can put this nonsense out of your mind more easily. Not that I am afraid of what you might do; I have confidence in your basic good sense, even at your tender years. But you are troubled. I know – and this will clear it away. Can you guess what it is?'

'Uh, no.'

He grinned. 'A vacation trip to Mars.'

I must have looked stunned. 'Golly, Father, I had no idea—'

'I meant to surprise you and I see I did. I know how you kids feel about travel, though it beats me what anyone sees in it after the first time out. But this is a good time for you to do it – by yourself; did I mention that? – and get it out of your system . . . because you'll be hard-pressed to get in even a week on Luna once you take up your responsibilities.' He picked up his paper. 'No, don't thank me. Just run along and let me finish my paper – I've got some gentlemen coming in this evening, shortly. Business.'

I ran along. I guess he thought that settled it . . . and I suppose I did, too. Mars! And on my own! But I didn't tell Carl about it; I had a sneaking suspicion that he would regard it as a bribe. Well, maybe it was. Instead I simply told him that my father and I seemed to have different ideas about it.

'Yeah,' he answered, 'so does mine. But it's *my* life.'

I thought about it during the last session of our class in History and Moral Philosophy. H. & M. P. was different from other courses in that everybody had to take it but nobody had to pass it – and Mr. Dubois never seemed to care whether he got through to us or not. He would just point at you with the stump of his left arm (he never bothered with names) and snap a question. Then the argument would start.

But on the last day he seemed to be trying to find out what we had learned. One girl told him bluntly: 'My mother says that violence never settles anything.'

'So?' Mr. Dubois looked at her bleakly. 'I'm sure the city fathers of Carthage would be glad to know that. Why doesn't your mother tell them so? Or why don't *you?*'

They had tangled before – since you couldn't flunk the course, it wasn't necessary to keep Mr. Dubois buttered up. She said shrilly, 'You're making fun of me! Everybody knows that Carthage was destroyed!'

'You seemed to be unaware of it,' he said grimly. 'Since you do know it, wouldn't you say that violence had settled their destinies rather thoroughly? However, I was not making fun of you personally; I was heaping scorn on an inexcusably silly idea – a practice I shall always follow. Anyone who clings to the historically untrue – and thoroughly immoral – doctrine that "violence never settles anything" I would advise to conjure up the ghosts of Napoleon Bonaparte and of the Duke of Wellington and let them debate it. The ghost of Hitler could referee, and the jury might well be the Dodo, the Great Auk and the Passenger Pigeon. Violence, naked force, has settled more issues in history than has any other factor, and the contrary opinion is wishful thinking at its worst. Breeds that forget this basic truth have always paid for it with their lives and freedoms.'

He sighed. 'Another year, another class – and, for me, another failure. One can lead a child to knowledge but one *cannot* make him think.' Suddenly he pointed his stump at me. 'You. What is the moral difference, if any, between the soldier and the civilian?'

'The difference,' I answered carefully, 'lies in the field of civic virtue. A soldier accepts personal responsibility for the safety of the body politic of which he is a member, defending it, if need be, with his life. The civilian does not.'

'The exact words of the book,' he said scornfully. 'But do you understand it? Do you *believe* it?'

'Uh, I don't know, sir.'

'Of course you don't! I doubt if any of you here would recognize "civic virtue" if it came up and barked in your face!' He glanced at his watch. 'And that is all, a final all. Perhaps we shall meet again under happier circumstances. Dismissed.'

Graduation right after that and three days later my birthday, followed in less than a week by Carl's birthday – and I still hadn't told Carl that I wasn't joining up. I'm sure he assumed that I would not, but we didn't discuss it out loud

– embarrassing. I simply arranged to meet him the day after his birthday and we went down to the recruiting office together.

On the steps of the Federal Building we ran into Carmencita Ibañez, a classmate of ours and one of the nice things about being a member of a race with two sexes. Carmen wasn't my girl – she wasn't anybody's girl; she never made two dates in a row with the same boy and treated all of us with equal sweetness and rather impersonally. But I knew her pretty well, as she often came over and used our swimming pool, because it was Olympic length – sometimes with one boy, sometimes with another. Or alone, as Mother urged her to – Mother considered her 'a good influence.' For once she was right.

She saw us and waited, dimpling. 'Hi, fellows!'

'Hello, *Ochee Chyornya*,' I answered. 'What brings you here?'

'Can't you guess? Today is my birthday.'

'Huh? Happy returns!'

'So I'm joining up.'

'Oh . . .' I think Carl was as surprised as I was. But Carmencita was like that. She never gossiped and she kept her own affairs to herself. 'No foolin''?' I added, brilliantly.

'Why should I be fooling? I'm going to be a spaceship pilot – at least I'm going to try for it.'

'No reason why you shouldn't make it,' Carl said quickly. He was right – I know now just how right he was. Carmen was small and neat, perfect health and perfect reflexes – she could make a competitive diving routine look easy – and she was quick at mathematics. Me, I tapered off with a 'C' in algebra and a 'B' in business arithmetic; she took all the math our school offered and a tutored advance course on the side. But it had never occurred to me to wonder why. Fact was, little Carmen was so ornamental that you just never thought about her being useful.

'We – Uh, I,' said Carl, 'am here to join up, too.'

'And me,' I agreed. 'Both of us.' No, I hadn't made any decision; my mouth was leading its own life.

'Oh, wonderful!'

'And I'm going to buck for space pilot, too,' I added firmly.

She didn't laugh. She answered very seriously, 'Oh, how grand! Perhaps in training we'll run into each other. I hope so.'

'Collision courses?' asked Carl. 'That's a no-good way to pilot.'

'Don't be silly, Carl. On the ground, of course. Are you going to be a pilot, too?'

'*Me?*' Carl answered. 'I'm no truck driver. You know me – Starside R&D, if they'll have me. Electronics.'

'"Truck driver" indeed! I hope they stick you out on Pluto and let you freeze. No, I don't – good luck! Let's go in, shall we?'

The recruiting station was inside a railing in the rotunda. A fleet sergeant sat at a desk there, in dress uniform, gaudy as a circus. His chest was loaded with ribbons I couldn't read. But his right arm was off so short that his tunic had been tailored without any sleeve at all . . . and, when you came up to the rail, you could see that he had no legs.

It didn't seem to bother him. Carl said, 'Good morning. I want to join up.'

'Me, too,' I added.

He ignored us. He managed to bow while sitting down and said, 'Good morning, young lady. What can I do for you?'

'I want to join up, too.'

He smiled. 'Good girl! If you'll just scoot up to room 201 and ask for Major Rojas, she'll take care of you.' He looked her up and down. 'Pilot?'

'If possible.'

'You look like one. Well, see Miss Rojas.'

She left, with thanks to him and a see-you-later to us; he turned his attention to us, sized us up with a total absence of the pleasure he had shown in little Carmen. 'So?' he said. 'For what? Labor battalions?'

'Oh, no!' I said. 'I'm going to be a pilot.'

He stared at me and simply turned his eyes away. 'You?'

'I'm interested in the Research and Development Corps,' Carl said soberly, 'especially electronics. I understand the chances are pretty good.'

'They are if you can cut it,' the Fleet Sergeant said grimly, 'and not if you don't have what it takes, both in preparation and ability. Look, boys, have you any idea why they have me out here in front?'

I didn't understand him. Carl said, 'Why?'

'Because the government doesn't care one bucket of swill whether you join or not! Because it has become stylish, with some people – too many people – to serve a term and earn a franchise and be able to wear a ribbon in your lapel which says that you're a vet'ran . . . whether you've ever seen combat or not. But if you *want* to serve and I can't talk you out of it, then we have to take you, because that's your constitutional right. It says that everybody, male or female, shall have his born right to pay his service and assume full citizenship – but the facts are that we are getting hard pushed to find things for all the volunteers to do that aren't just glorified K.P. You can't all be real military men; we don't need that many and most of the volunteers aren't number-one soldier material anyhow. Got any idea what it takes to make a soldier?'

'No,' I admitted.

'Most people think that all it takes is two hands and two feet and a stupid mind. Maybe so, for cannon fodder. Possibly that was all that Julius Caesar required. But a private soldier today is a specialist so highly skilled that he would rate "master" in any other trade; we can't afford stupid ones. So for those who insist on serving their term – but haven't got what we want and must have – we've had to think up a whole list of dirty, nasty, dangerous jobs that will either run 'em home with their tails between their legs and their terms uncompleted . . . or at least make them remember for the rest of their lives that their citizenship is valuable to them because they've paid a high price for it. Take that young lady who was here – wants to be a pilot. I hope she makes it; we always need good pilots, not enough of 'em. Maybe she will. But if she misses, she may wind up in Antarctica, her pretty eyes red from never seeing anything but artificial light and her knuckles callused from hard, dirty work.'

I wanted to tell him that the least Carmencita could get was computer programmer for the sky watch; she really was a whiz at math. But he was talking.

'So they put me out here to discourage you boys. Look at this.' He shoved his chair around to make sure that we could see that he was legless. 'Let's assume that you don't wind up digging tunnels on Luna or playing human guinea pig for new diseases through sheer lack of talent; suppose we do make a fighting man out of you. Take a look at *me* – this is what you may buy . . . If you don't buy the whole farm and cause your folks to receive a "deeply regret" telegram. Which is more likely, because these days, in training or in combat, there aren't many wounded. If you buy it at all, they likely throw in a coffin – I'm the rare exception; I was lucky . . . though maybe you wouldn't call it luck.'

He paused, then added, 'So why don't you boys go home, go to college, and then go be chemists or insurance brokers or whatever? A term of service isn't a kiddie kamp; it's either real military service, rough and dangerous even in peacetime . . . or a most unreasonable facsimile thereof. Not a vacation. Not a romantic adventure. Well?'

Carl said, 'I'm here to join up.'

'Me, too.'

'You realize that you aren't allowed to pick your service?'

Carl said, 'I thought we could state our preferences?'

'Certainly. And that's the last choice you'll make until the end of your term. The placement officer pays attention to your choice, too. First thing he does is to check whether there's any demand for left-handed glass blowers this week – that being what you think would make you happy. Having reluctantly conceded that there is a need for your choice – probably at the bottom of the Pacific – he then tests you for innate ability and preparation. About once in twenty times he is forced to admit that everything matches and you get the job . . . until some practical joker gives you dispatch orders to do something very different. But the other nineteen times he turns you down and decides that you are just what they have been needing to field-test survival equipment on Titan.' He added meditatively, 'It's chilly on Titan. And it's amazing how often experimental equipment fails to work. Have to have real field tests, though – laboratories just never get all the answers.'

'I can qualify for electronics,' Carl said firmly, 'if there are jobs open in it.'

'So? And how about you, bub?'

I hesitated – and suddenly realized that, if I didn't take a swing at it, I would wonder all my life whether I was anything but the boss's son. 'I'm going to chance it.'

'Well, you can't say I didn't try. Got your birth certificates with you? And let's see your I.D.s.'

Ten minutes later, still not sworn in, we were on the top floor being prodded and poked and fluoroscoped. I decided that the idea of a physical examination is that, if you *aren't* ill, then they do their darnedest to *make* you ill. If the attempt fails, you're in.

I asked one of the doctors what percentage of the victims

flunked the physical. He looked startled. 'Why, we *never* fail anyone. The law doesn't permit us to.'

'Huh? I mean, Excuse me, Doctor? Then what's the point of this goose-flesh parade?'

'Why, the purpose is,' he answered, hauling off and hitting me in the knee with a hammer (I kicked him, but not hard), 'to find out what duties you are physically able to perform. But if you came in here in a wheel chair and blind in both eyes and were silly enough to insist on enrolling, they would find something silly enough to match. Counting the fuzz on a caterpillar by touch, maybe. The only way you can fail is by having the psychiatrists decide that you are not able to understand the oath.'

'Oh. Uh . . . Doctor, were you already a doctor when you joined up? Or did they decide you ought to be a doctor and send you to school?'

'*Me?*' He seemed shocked. 'Youngster, do I look that silly? I'm a civilian employee.'

'Oh. Sorry, sir.'

'No offense. But military service is for ants. Believe me. I see 'em go, I see 'em come back – when they do come back. I see what it's done to them. And for what? A purely nominal political privilege that pays not one centavo and that most of them aren't competent to use wisely anyhow. Now if they would let medical men run things – but never mind that; you might think I was talking treason, free speech or not. But, youngster, if you've got savvy enough to count ten, you'll back out while you still can. Here, take these papers back to the recruiting sergeant sergeant – and remember what I said.'

I went back to the rotunda. Carl was already there. The Fleet Sergeant looked over my papers and said glumly, 'Apparently you both are almost insufferably healthy – except for holes in the head. One moment, while I get some witnesses.' He punched a button and two female clerks came out, one old battle-ax, one kind of cute.

He pointed to our physical examination forms, our birth certificates, and our I.D.s, said formally: 'I invite and require you, each and severally, to examine these exhibits, determine what they are and to determine, each independently, what relation, if any, each document bears to these two men standing here in your presence.'

They treated it as a dull routine, which I'm sure it was; nevertheless they scrutinized every document, they took our fingerprints – again! – and the cute one put a jeweler's loupe in her eye and compared prints from birth to now. She did the same with signatures. I began to doubt if I was myself.

The Fleet Sergeant added, 'Did you find exhibits relating to their present competence to take the oath of enrollment? If so, what?'

'We found,' the older one said, 'appended to each record of physical examination a duly certified conclusion by an authorized and delegated board of psychiatrists stating that each of them is mentally competent to take the oath and that neither one is under the influence of alcohol, narcotics, other disabling drugs, nor of hypnosis.'

'Very good.' He turned to us, 'Repeat after me –

'I, being of legal age, of my own free will—'

'"I,"' we each echoed, '"being of legal age, of my own free will – "'

' – without coercion, promise, or inducement of any sort, after having been duly advised and warned of the meaning and consequences of this oath –

' – do now enroll in the Federal Service of the Terran Federation for a term of not less than two years and as much longer as may be required by the needs of the Service—'

(I gulped a little over that part. I had always thought of a 'term' as two years, even though I knew better, because that's the way people talk about it. Why, we were signing up for *life*.)

'I swear to uphold and defend the Constitution of the Federation against all its enemies on or off Terra, to protect and defend the Constitutional liberties and privileges of all citizens and lawful residents of the Federation, its associated states and territories, to perform, on or off Terra, such duties of any lawful nature as may be assigned to me by lawful direct or delegated authority –

' – and to obey all lawful orders of the Commander-in-Chief of the Terran Service and of all officers or delegated persons placed over me –

' – and to require such obedience from all members of the Service or other persons or non-human beings lawfully placed under my orders –

' – and, on being honorably discharged at the completion of my full term of active service or upon being placed on inactive retired status after having completed such full term, to carry out all duties and obligations and to enjoy all privileges of Federation citizenship including but not limited to the duty, obligation and privilege of exercising sovereign franchise for the rest of my natural life unless stripped of honor by verdict, finally sustained, of court of my sovereign peers.'

(Whew!) Mr. Dubois had analyzed the Service oath for us in History and Moral Philosophy and had made us study it phrase by phrase – but you don't really feel the *size* of the thing until it comes rolling over you, all in one ungainly piece, as heavy and unstoppable as a Juggernaut's carriage.

At least it made me realize that I was no longer a civilian, with my shirttail out and nothing on my mind. I didn't know yet what I was, but I knew what I wasn't.

'So help me God!' we both ended and Carl crossed himself and so did the cute one.

After that there were more signatures and fingerprints, all

five of us, and flat colorgraphs of Carl and me were snapped then and there and embossed into our papers. The Fleet Sergeant finally looked up. 'Why, it's way past the break for lunch. Time for chow, lads.'

I swallowed hard. 'Uh . . . Sergeant?'

'Eh? Speak up.'

'Could I flash my folks from here? Tell them what I – tell them how it came out?'

'We can do better than that.'

'Sir?'

'You go on forty-eight hours leave now.' He grinned coldly. 'Do you know what happens if you don't come back?'

'Uh . . . court-martial?'

'Not a thing. Not a blessed thing. Except that your papers get marked, *Term not completed satisfactorily*, and you never, never, never get a second chance. This is our cooling-off period, during which we shake out the overgrown babies who didn't really mean it and should never have taken the oath. It saves the government money and it saves a power of grief for such kids and their parents – the neighbors needn't guess. You don't even have to tell your parents.' He shoved his chair away from his desk. 'So I'll see you at noon day after tomorrow. If I see you. Fetch your personal effects.'

It was a crumby leave. Father stormed at me, then quit speaking to me; Mother took to her bed. When I finally left, an hour earlier than I had to, nobody saw me off but the morning cook and the houseboys.

I stopped in front of the recruiting sergeant's desk, thought about saluting and decided I didn't know how. He looked up. 'Oh. Here are your papers. Take them up to room 201; they'll start you through the mill. Knock and walk in.'

Two days later I knew I was not going to be a pilot. Some of the things the examiners wrote about me were: – *insufficient intuitive grasp of spatial relationships ... insufficient mathematical talent ... deficient mathematical preparation ... reaction time adequate ... eyesight good.* I'm glad they put in those last two; I was beginning to feel that counting on my fingers was my speed.

The placement officer let me list my lesser preferences, in order, and I caught four more days of the wildest aptitude tests I've ever heard of. I mean to say, what do they find out when a stenographer jumps on her chair and screams 'Snakes!' There was no snake, just a harmless piece of plastic hose.

The written and oral tests were mostly just as silly, but they seemed happy with them, so I took them. The thing I did most carefully was to list my preferences. Naturally I listed all of the Space Navy jobs (other than pilot) at the top; whether I went as power-room technician or as cook, I knew that I preferred any Navy job to an Army job – I wanted to travel.

Next I listed Intelligence – a spy gets around, too, and I figured that it couldn't possibly be dull. (I was wrong, but never mind.) After that came a long list: psychological warfare, chemical warfare, biological warfare, combat ecology (I didn't know what it was, but it sounded interesting), logistics corps (a simple mistake; I had studied logic for the debate team and 'logistics' turns out to have two entirely separate meanings), and a dozen others. Clear at the bottom, with some hesitation, I put K-9 Corps, and Infantry.

I didn't bother to list the various non-combatant auxiliary corps because, if I wasn't picked for a combat corps, I didn't care whether they used me as an experimental animal or sent me as a laborer in the Terranizing of Venus – either one was a booby prize.

Mr. Weiss, the placement officer, sent for me a week after I was sworn in. He was actually a retired psychological-warfare major, on active duty for procurement, but he wore mufti and insisted on being called just 'Mister' and you could relax and take it easy with him. He had my list of preferences and the reports on all my tests and I saw that he was holding my high school transcript – which pleased me, for I had done all right in school; I had stood high enough without standing so high as to be marked as a greasy grind, having never flunked any courses and dropped only one, and I had been rather a big man around school otherwise: swimming team, debate team, track squad, class treasurer, silver medal in the annual literary contest, chairman of the homecoming committee, stuff like that. A well-rounded record and it's all down in the transcript.

He looked up as I came in, said, 'Sit down, Johnnie,' and looked back at the transcript, then put it down. 'You like dogs?'

'Huh? Yes, sir.'

'How well do you like them? Did your dog sleep on your bed? By the way, where is your dog now?'

'Why, I don't happen to have a dog just at present. But when I did – well, no, he didn't sleep on my bed. You see, Mother didn't allow dogs in the house.'

'But didn't you sneak him in?'

'Uh—' I thought of trying to explain Mother's not-angry-but-terribly-terribly-hurt routine when you tried to buck her on something she had her mind made up about. But I gave up. 'No, sir.'

'Mmm . . . have you ever seen a neodog?'

'Uh, once, sir. They exhibited one at the Macarthur Theater two years ago. But the S.P.C.A. made trouble for them.'

'Let me tell you how it is with a K-9 team. A neodog is not just a dog that talks.'

'I couldn't understand that neo at the Macarthur. Do they really talk?'

'They talk. You simply have to train your ear to their accent. Their mouths can't shape "b," "m," "p," or "v" and you have to get used to their equivalents – something like the handicap of a split palate but with different letters. No matter, their speech is as clear as any human speech. But a neodog is not a talking dog; he is not a dog at all, he is an artificially mutated symbiote derived from dog stock. A neo, a trained Caleb, is about six times as bright as a dog, say about as intelligent as a human moron – except that the comparison is not fair to the neo; a moron is a defective, whereas a neo is a stable genius in his own line of work.'

Mr. Weiss scowled. 'Provided, that is, that he has his symbiote. That's the rub. Mmm . . . you're too young ever to have been married but you've seen marriage, your own parents at least. Can you imagine being married to a Caleb?'

'Huh? No. No, I can't.'

'The emotional relationship between the dog-man and the man-dog in a K-9 team is a great deal closer and much more important than is the emotional relationship in most marriages. If the master is killed, we kill the neodog – at once! It is all that we can do for the poor thing. A mercy killing. If the neodog is killed . . . well, we can't kill the man even though it would be the simplest solution. Instead we restrain him and hospitalize him and slowly put him back together.' He picked up a pen, made a mark. 'I don't think we can risk assigning a boy to K-9 who didn't outwit his mother to have his dog sleep with him. So let's consider something else.'

It was not until then that I realized that I must have already flunked every choice on my list above K-9 Corps – and now I had just flunked it, too. I was so startled that I almost missed his next remark. Major Weiss said meditatively, with no expression and as if he were talking about someone else, long dead and far away: 'I was once half of a K-9 team. When my Caleb became a casualty, they kept me under sedation for six weeks, then rehabilitated me for other work. Johnnie, these courses you've taken – why didn't you study something useful?'

'Sir?'

'Too late now. Forget it. Mmm . . . your instructor in History and Moral Philosophy seems to think well of you.'

'He does?' I was surprised. 'What did he say?'

Weiss smiled. 'He says that you are not stupid, merely ignorant and prejudiced by your environment. From him that is high praise – I know him.'

It didn't sound like praise to me! That stuck-up stiff-necked old –

'And,' Weiss went on, 'a boy who gets a "C-minus" in Appreciation of Television can't be all bad. How would you like to be an infantryman?'

I came out of the Federal Building feeling subdued yet not really unhappy. At least I was a soldier; I had papers in my pocket to prove it. I hadn't been classed as too dumb and useless for anything but make-work.

It was a few minutes after the end of the working day and the building was empty save for a skeleton night staff and a few stragglers. I ran into a man in the rotunda who was just leaving; his face looked familiar but I couldn't place him.

But he caught my eye and recognized me. 'Evening!' he said briskly. 'You haven't shipped out yet?'

And then I recognized him – the Fleet Sergeant who had sworn us in. I guess my chin dropped; this man was in civilian clothes, was walking around on two legs and had two arms. 'Uh, good evening, Sergeant,' I mumbled.

He understood my expression perfectly, glanced down at himself and smiled easily. 'Relax, lad. I don't have to put on my horror show after working hours – and I don't. You haven't been placed yet?'

'I just got my orders.'

'For what?'

'Mobile Infantry.'

His face broke in a big grin of delight and he shoved out his hand. 'My outfit! Shake, son! We'll make a man of you – or kill you trying. Maybe both.'

'It's a good choice?' I said doubtfully.

'"A good choice'? Son, it's the *only* choice. The Mobile Infantry *is* the Army. All the others are either button pushers or professors, along merely to hand us the saw; *we* do the work.' He shook hands again and added, 'Drop me a card – "Fleet Sergeant Ho, Federal Building," that'll reach me. Good luck!' And he was off, shoulders back, heels clicking, head up.

I looked at my hand. The hand he had offered me was the one that wasn't there – his right hand. Yet it had felt like flesh and had shaken mine firmly. I had read about these powered prosthetics, but it is startling when you first run across them.

I went back to the hotel where recruits were temporarily billeted during placement – we didn't even have uniforms yet, just plain coveralls we wore during the day and our own clothes after hours. I went to my room and started packing, as I was shipping out early in the morning – packing to send stuff home, I mean; Weiss had cautioned me not to take along anything but family photographs and possibly a musical instrument if I played one (which I didn't). Carl had shipped out three days earlier, having gotten the R&D assignment he wanted. I was just as glad, as he would have been just too confounded understanding about the billet I had drawn. Little Carmen had shipped out, too, with the rank of cadet midshipman (probationary) – she was going to be a pilot, all right, if she could cut it . . . and I suspected that she could.

My temporary roomie came in while I was packing. 'Got your orders?' he asked.

'Yup.'

'What?'

'Mobile Infantry.'

'The *Infantry*? Oh, you poor stupid clown! I feel sorry for you, I really do.'

I straightened up and said angrily, 'Shut up! The Mobile Infantry is the best outfit in the Army – it *is* the Army! The rest of you jerks are just along to hand us the saw – *we* do the work.'

He laughed. 'You'll find out!'

'You want a mouthful of knuckles?'

Chapter 3

He shall rule them with a rod of iron.

– Revelations II:25

I did Basic at Camp Arthur Currie on the northern prairies, along with a couple of thousand other victims – and I do mean 'Camp,' as the only permanent buildings there were to shelter equipment. We slept and ate in tents; we lived outdoors – if you call that 'living,' which I didn't, at the time. I was used to a warm climate; it seemed to me that the North Pole was just five miles north of camp and getting closer. Ice Age returning, no doubt.

But exercise will keep you warm and they saw to it that we got plenty of that.

The first morning we were there they woke us up before daybreak. I had had trouble adjusting to the change in time zones and it seemed to me that I had just got to sleep; I couldn't believe that anyone seriously intended that I should get up in the middle of the night.

But they did mean it. A speaker somewhere was blaring out a military march, fit to wake the dead, and a hairy nuisance who had come charging down the company street yelling, '*Everybody out! Show a leg! On the bounce!*' came marauding back again just as I had pulled the covers over my head, tipped over my cot and dumped me on the cold hard ground.

It was an impersonal attention; he didn't even wait to see if I hit.

Ten minutes later, dressed in trousers, undershirt, and

shoes, I was lined up with the others in ragged ranks for setting-up exercises just as the sun looked over the eastern horizon. Facing us was a big broad-shouldered, mean-looking man, dressed just as we were – except that while I looked and felt like a poor job of embalming, his chin was shaved blue, his trousers were sharply creased, you could have used his shoes for mirrors, and his manner was alert, wide-awake, relaxed, and rested. You got the impression that he never needed to sleep – just ten-thousand-mile checkups and dust him off occasionally.

He bellowed, 'C'p*nee* At*ten* . . . *shut!* I am Career Ship's Sergeant Zim, your company commander. When you speak to me, you will salute and say, "Sir" – you will salute and "sir" anyone who carries an instructor's baton—' He was carrying a swagger cane and now made a quick reverse moulinet with it to show what he meant by an instructor's baton; I had noticed men carrying them when we had arrived the night before and had intended to get one myself – they looked smart. Now I changed my mind. '—because we don't have enough officers around here for you to practice on. You'll practice on us. Who sneezed?'

No answer –

'WHO SNEEZED?'

'I did,' a voice answered.

'"I did" *what*?'

'I sneezed.'

'"I sneezed," SIR!'

'I sneezed, sir. I'm cold, sir.'

'Oho!' Zim strode up to the man who had sneezed, shoved the ferrule of the swagger cane an inch under his nose and demanded, 'Name?'

'Jenkins . . . sir.'

'Jenkins . . .' Zim repeated as if the word were somehow distasteful, even shameful. 'I suppose some night on patrol you're going to sneeze just because you've got a runny nose. Eh?'

'I hope not, sir.'

'So do I. But you're cold. Hmm . . . we'll fix that.' He pointed with his stick. 'See that armory over there?' I looked and could see nothing but prairie except for one building that seemed to be almost on the skyline.

'Fall out. Run around it. *Run*, I said. Fast! Bronski! Pace him.'

'Right, Sarge.' One of the five or six other baton carriers took out after Jenkins, caught up with him easily, cracked him across the tight of his pants with the baton. Zim turned back to the rest of us, still shivering at attention. He walked up and down, looked us over, and seemed awfully unhappy. At last he stepped out in front of us, shook his head, and said, apparently to himself but he had a voice that carried: 'To think that this had to happen to *me*!'

He looked at us. 'You apes – No, not "apes"; you don't rate that much. You pitiful mob of sickly monkeys . . . you sunken-chested, slack-bellied, drooling refugees from apron strings. In my whole life I never saw such a disgraceful huddle of momma's spoiled little darlings in – you, there! Suck up the gut! Eyes front! I'm talking to *you!*'

I pulled in my belly, even though I was not sure he had addressed me. He went on and on and I began to forget my goose flesh in hearing him storm. He never once repeated himself and he never used either profanity or obscenity. (I learned later that he saved those for *very* special occasions, which this wasn't.) But he described our shortcomings, physical, mental, moral, and genetic, in great and insulting detail.

But somehow I was not insulted; I became greatly interested in studying his command of language. I wished that we had had him on our debate team.

At last he stopped and seemed about to cry. 'I can't *stand* it,' he said bitterly. 'I've just got to work some of it off – I had a better set of wooden soldiers when I was six. ALL RIGHT! Is there any one of you jungle lice who thinks he can whip me? Is there a *man* in the crowd? Speak up!'

There was a short silence to which I contributed. I didn't have any doubt at all that he could whip me; I was convinced.

I heard a voice far down the line, the tall end. 'Ah reckon ah can . . . suh.'

Zim looked happy. 'Good! Step out here where I can see you.' The recruit did so and he was impressive, at least three inches taller than Sergeant Zim and broader across the shoulders. 'What's your name, soldier?'

'Breckinridge, suh – and ah weigh two hundred and ten pounds an' theath ain't *any* of it "slack-bellied."'

'Any particular way you'd like to fight?'

'Suh, you jus' pick youah own method of dying. Ah'm not fussy.'

'Okay, no rules. Start whenever you like.' Zim tossed his baton aside.

It started – and it was over. The big recruit was sitting on the ground, holding his left wrist in his right hand. He didn't say anything.

Zim bent over him. 'Broken?'

'Reckon it might be . . . suh.'

'I'm sorry. You hurried me a little. Do you know where the dispensary is? Never mind – Jones! Take Breckinridge over to the dispensary.' As they left Zim slapped him on the right shoulder and said quietly, 'Let's try it again in a month or so. I'll show you what happened.' I think it was meant to be a private remark but they were standing about six feet in front of where I was slowly freezing solid.

Zim stepped back and called out, 'Okay, we've got one man in this company, at least. I feel better. Do we have another one? Do we have two more? Any *two* of you scrofulous toads think you can stand up to me?' He looked back and forth along our ranks. 'Chicken-livered, spineless – oh, oh! Yes? Step out.'

Two men who had been side by side in ranks stepped out together; I suppose they had arranged it in whispers right there, but they also were far down the tall end, so I didn't hear. Zim smiled at them. 'Names, for your next of kin, please.'

'Heinrich.'

'Heinrich *what*?'

'Heinrich, sir. Bitte.' He spoke rapidly to the other recruit and added politely, 'He doesn't speak much Standard English yet, sir.'

'Meyer, mein Herr,' the second man supplied.

'That's okay, lots of 'em don't speak much of it when they get here – I didn't myself. Tell Meyer not to worry, he'll pick it up. But he understands what we are going to do?'

'Jawohl,' agreed Meyer.

'Certainly, sir. He understands Standard, he just can't speak it fluently.'

'All right. Where did you two pick up those face scars? Heidelberg?'

'Nein – no, sir. Königsberg.'

'Same thing.' Zim had picked up his baton after fighting Breckinridge; he twirled it and asked, 'Perhaps you would each like to borrow one of these?'

'It would not be fair to you, sir,' Heinrich answered carefully. 'Bare hands, if you please.'

'Suit yourself. Though I might fool you. Königsberg, eh? Rules?'

'How can there be rules, sir, with three?'

'An interesting point. Well, let's agree that if eyes are gouged out they must be handed back when it's over. And tell your Korpsbruder that I'm ready now. Start when you like.' Zim tossed his baton away; someone caught it.

'You joke, sir. We will not gouge eyes.'

'No eye gouging, agreed. "Fire when ready, Gridley."'

'Please?'

'Come on and fight! Or get back into ranks!'

Now I'm not sure that I saw it happen this way; I may have learned part of it later, in training. But here is what I think happened: The two moved out on each side of our company commander until they had him completely flanked but well out of contact. From this position there is a choice of four basic moves for the man working alone, moves that take advantage of his own mobility and of the superior co-ordination of one man as compared with two – Sergeant Zim says (correctly) that any group is weaker than a man alone unless they are perfectly trained to work together. For example, Zim could have feinted at one of them, bounced fast to the other with a disabler, such as a broken kneecap – then finished off the first at his leisure.

Instead he let them attack. Meyer came at him fast, intending to body check and knock him to the ground, I think, while Heinrich would follow through from above, maybe with his boots. That's the way it appeared to start.

And here's what I think I saw. Meyer never reached him with that body check. Sergeant Zim whirled to face him, while kicking out and getting Heinrich in the belly – and then Meyer was sailing through the air, his lunge helped along with a hearty assist from Zim.

But all I am sure of is that the fight started and then there were two German boys sleeping peacefully, almost end to end, one face down and one face up, and Zim was standing over them, not even breathing hard. 'Jones,' he said. 'No, Jones left, didn't he? Mahmud! Let's have the water bucket, then stick them back into their sockets. Who's got my toothpick?'

A few moments later the two were conscious, wet, and back

in ranks. Zim looked at us and inquired gently, 'Anybody else? Or shall we get on with setting-up exercises?'

I didn't expect anybody else and I doubt if he did. But from down on the left flank, where the shorties hung out, a boy stepped out of ranks, came front and center. Zim looked down at him. 'Just you? Or do you want to pick a partner?'

'Just myself, sir.'

'As you say. Name?'

'Shujumi, sir.'

Zim's eyes widened. 'Any relation to Colonel Shujumi?'

'I have the honor to be his son, sir.'

'Ah so! Well! Black Belt?'

'No, sir. Not yet.'

'I'm glad you qualified that. Well, Shujumi, are we going to use contest rules, or shall I send for the ambulance?'

'As you wish, sir. But I think, if I may be permitted an opinion, that contest rules would be more prudent.'

'I don't know just how you mean that, but I agree.' Zim tossed his badge of authority aside, then, so help me, they backed off, faced each other, and bowed.

After that they circled around each other in a half crouch, making tentative passes with their hands, and looking like a couple of roosters.

Suddenly they touched – and the little chap was down on the ground and Sergeant Zim was flying through the air over his head. But he didn't land with the dull, breath-paralyzing thud that Meyer had; he lit rolling and was on his feet as fast as Shujumi was and facing him. 'Banzai!' Zim yelled and grinned.

'Arigato,' Shujumi answered and grinned back.

They touched again almost without a pause and I thought the Sergeant was going to fly again. He didn't; he slithered straight in, there was a confusion of arms and legs and when the motion slowed down you could see that Zim was tucking Shujumi's left foot in his right ear – a poor fit.

Shujumi slapped the ground with a free hand; Zim let him up at once. They again bowed to each other.

'Another fall, sir?'

'Sorry. We've got work to do. Some other time, eh? For fun . . . and honor. Perhaps I should have told you; your honorable father trained me.'

'So I had already surmised, sir. Another time it is.'

Zim slapped him hard on the shoulder. 'Back in ranks, soldier. *C'pnee!*'

Then, for twenty minutes, we went through calesthenics that left me as dripping hot as I had been shivering cold. Zim led it himself, doing it all with us and shouting the count. He hadn't been mussed that I could see; he wasn't breathing hard as we finished. He never led the exercises after that morning (we never saw him again before breakfast; rank hath its privileges), but he did that morning, and when it was over and we were all bushed, he led us at a trot to the mess tent, shouting at us the whole way to 'Step it up! On the bounce! You're dragging your tails!'

We *always* trotted *everywhere* at Camp Arthur Currie. I never did find out who Currie was, but he must have been a trackman.

Breckinridge was already in the mess tent, with a cast on his wrist but thumb and fingers showing. I heard him say, 'Naw, just a greenstick fractchuh – ah've played a whole quahtuh with wuss. But you wait – ah'll fix him.'

I had my doubts. Shujumi, maybe – but not that big ape. He simply didn't know when he was outclassed. I disliked Zim from the first moment I laid eyes on him. But he had style.

Breakfast was all right – all the meals were all right; there was none of that nonsense some boarding schools have of making your life miserable at the table. If you wanted to slump down and shovel it in with both hands, nobody bothered you – which was good, as meals were practically the only time somebody wasn't riding you. The menu for breakfast wasn't anything like what I had been used to at home and the civilians that waited on us slapped the food around in a fashion that would have made Mother grow pale and leave for her room – but it was hot and it was plentiful and the cooking was okay if plain. I ate about four times what I normally do and washed it down with mug after mug of coffee with cream and lots of sugar – I would have eaten a shark without stopping to skin him.

Jenkins showed up with Corporal Bronski behind him as I was starting on seconds. They stopped for a moment at a table where Zim was eating alone, then Jenkins slumped onto a vacant stool by mine. He looked mighty seedy – pale, exhausted, and his breath rasping. I said, 'Here, let me pour you some coffee.'

He shook his head.

'You better eat,' I insisted. 'Some scrambled eggs – they'll go down easily.'

'Can't eat. Oh, that dirty, dirty so-and-so.' He began cussing out Zim in a low, almost expressionless monotone. 'All I asked him was to let me go lie down and skip breakfast. Bronski wouldn't let me – said I had to see the company commander. So I did and I *told* him I was sick, I *told* him. He just felt my cheek and counted my pulse and told me sick call was nine o'clock. Wouldn't let me go back to my tent. Oh, that rat! I'll catch him on a dark night, I will.'

I spooned out some eggs for him anyway and poured coffee. Presently he began to eat. Sergeant Zim got up to leave while most of us were still eating, and stopped by our table. 'Jenkins.'

'Uh? Yes, sir.'

'At oh-nine-hundred muster for sick call and see the doctor.'

Jenkins' jaw muscles twitched. He answered slowly, 'I don't need any pills – sir I'll get by.'

‘Oh-nine-hundred. That’s an order.’ He left.

Jenkins started his monotonous chant again. Finally he slowed down, took a bite of eggs and said somewhat more loudly, ‘I can’t help wondering what kind of a mother produced *that.* I’d just like to have a look at her, that’s all. Did he ever *have* a mother?’

It was a rhetorical question but it got answered. At the head of our table, several stools away, was one of the instructor-corporals. He had finished eating and was smoking and picking his teeth, simultaneously; he had evidently been listening. ‘Jenkins—’

‘Uh – sir?’

‘Don’t you know about sergeants?’

‘Well . . . I’m learning.’

‘They don’t have mothers. Just ask any trained private.’ He blew smoke toward us. ‘They reproduce by fission . . . like all bacteria.’

Chapter 4

And the LORD said unto Gideon, The people that are with thee are too many . . . Now therefore go to, proclaim in the ears of the people, saying, Whosoever is fearful and afraid, let him return . . . And there returned of the people twenty and two thousand; and there remained ten thousand. And the LORD said unto Gideon, The people are yet too many; bring them down unto the water, and I will try them for thee there . . . so he brought down the people unto the water: and the LORD said unto Gideon, Every one that lappeth of the water with his tongue, as a dog lappeth, him shalt thou set by himself; likewise everyone that boweth down upon his knees to drink. And the number of them that drank, putting their hand to their mouth, were three hundred men . . .

And the LORD said unto Gideon, By the three hundred . . . will I save you . . . let all the other people go . . .

– Judges VII: 2–7

Two weeks after we got there they took our cots away from us. That is to say that we had the dubious pleasure of folding them, carrying them four miles, and stowing them in a warehouse. By then it didn't matter; the ground seemed much warmer and quite soft – especially when the alert sounded in the middle of the night and we had to scramble out and play soldier. Which it did about three times a week. But I could get back to sleep after one of those mock exercises at once; I had learned to sleep any place, any time – sitting up, standing up, even marching in ranks. Why, I could even sleep through evening parade standing at attention, enjoy the music without being waked by it – and wake instantly at the command to pass in review.

I made a very important discovery at Camp Currie. Happiness consists in getting enough sleep. Just that, nothing more. All the wealthy, unhappy people you've ever met take sleeping pills; Mobile Infantrymen don't need them. Give a cap trooper a bunk and time to sack out in it and he's as happy as a worm in an apple – asleep.

Theoretically you were given eight full hours of sack time every night and about an hour and a half after evening chow for your own use. But in fact your night sack time was subject to alerts, to night duty, to field marches, and to acts of God and the whims of those over you, and your evenings, if not ruined by awkward squad or extra duty for minor offenses, were likely to be taken up by shining shoes, doing laundry, swapping haircuts (some of us got pretty fair barbers but a clean sweep like a billiard ball was acceptable and anybody can do that) – not to mention a thousand other chores having to do with equipment, person, and the demands of sergeants. For example we learned to answer morning roll call with: 'Bathed!' meaning you had taken at least one bath since last reveille. A man might lie about it and get away with it (I did, a couple of times) but at least one in our company who pulled that dodge in the face of convincing evidence that he was not recently bathed got scrubbed with stiff brushes and floor soap by his squad mates while a corporal-instructor chaperoned and made helpful suggestions.

But if you didn't have more urgent things to do after supper, you could write a letter, loaf, gossip, discuss the myriad mental and moral shortcomings of sergeants and, dearest of all, talk about the female of the species (we became convinced that there were no such creatures, just mythology created by inflamed imaginations – one boy in our company claimed to have seen a girl, over at regimental headquarters; he was unanimously judged a liar and a braggart). Or you could play cards. I learned, the hard way, not to draw to an inside straight and I've never done it since. In fact I haven't played cards since.

Or, if you actually did have twenty minutes of your very own, you could sleep. This was a choice very highly thought of; we were always several weeks minus on sleep.

I may have given the impression that boot camp was made harder than necessary. This is not correct.

It was made *as hard as possible* and on purpose.

It was the firm opinion of every recruit that this was sheer meanness, calculated sadism, fiendish delight of witless morons in making other people suffer.

It was not. It was too scheduled, too intellectual, too efficiently and impersonally organized to be cruelty for the sick pleasure of cruelty; it was planned like surgery for purposes as unimpassioned as those of a surgeon. Oh, I admit that some of the instructors may have enjoyed it but I don't *know* that they did – and I *do* know (now) that the psych officers tried to weed out any bullies in selecting instructors. They looked for skilled and dedicated craftsmen to follow the art of making things as tough as possible for a recruit; a bully is too stupid, himself too emotionally involved, and too likely to grow tired of his fun and slack off, to be efficient.

Still, there may have been bullies among them. But I've heard that some surgeons (and not necessarily bad ones) enjoy the cutting and the blood which accompanies the humane art of surgery.

That's what it was: surgery. It's immediate purpose was to get rid of, run right out of the outfit, those recruits who were too soft or too babyish ever to make Mobile Infantrymen. It accomplished that, in droves. (They darn near ran *me* out.) Our company shrank to platoon size in the first six weeks.

Some of them were dropped without prejudice and allowed, if they wished, to sweat out their terms in the non-combatant services; others got Bad Conduct Discharges, or Unsatisfactory Performance Discharges, or Medical Discharges.

Usually you didn't know why a man left unless you saw him leave and he volunteered the information. But some of them got fed up, said so loudly, and resigned, forfeiting forever their chances of franchise. Some, especially the older men, simply couldn't stand the pace physically no matter how hard they tried. I remember one, a nice old geezer named Carruthers, must have been thirty-five; they carried him away in a stretcher while he was still shouting feebly that it wasn't fair! – and that he would be back.

It was sort of sad, because we liked Carruthers and he *did* try – so we looked the other way and figured we would never see him again, that he was a cinch for a medical discharge and civilian clothes. Only I *did* see him again, long after. He had refused discharge (you don't have to accept a medical) and wound up as third cook in a troop transport. He remembered me and wanted to talk old times, as proud of being an alumnus of Camp Currie as Father is of his Harvard accent – he felt that he was a little bit better than the ordinary Navy man. Well, maybe he was.

But, much more important than the purpose of carving away the fat quickly and saving the government the training costs of those who would never cut it, was the prime purpose of making as sure as was humanly possible that no cap trooper ever climbed into a capsule for a combat drop unless he was prepared for it – fit, resolute, disciplined, and skilled. If he is not, it's not fair to the Federation, it's certainly not fair to his teammates, and worst of all it's not fair to *him*.

But was boot camp more cruelly hard than was necessary?

All I can say to that is this: The next time I have to make a combat drop, I want the men on my flanks to be graduates of Camp Currie or its Siberian equivalent. Otherwise I'll refuse to enter the capsule.

But I certainly thought it was a bunch of crumby, vicious nonsense at the time. Little things – When we were there a week, we were issued undress maroons for parade to supplement the fatigues we had been wearing. (Dress and full-dress uniforms came much later.) I took my tunic back to the issue shed and complained to the supply sergeant. Since he was only a supply sergeant and rather fatherly in manner I thought of him as a semi-civilian – I didn't know how, as of then, to read the ribbons on his chest or I wouldn't have dared speak to him. 'Sergeant, this tunic is too large. My company commander says it fits like a tent.'

He looked at the garment, didn't touch it. 'Really?'

'Yeah. I want one that fits.'

He still didn't stir. 'Let me wise you up, sonny boy. There are just two sizes in this army – too large and too small.'

'But my company commander—'

'No doubt.'

'But what am I going to *do*?'

'Oh, it's *advice* you want! Well, I've got that in stock – new issue, just today. Mmm . . . tell you what I'll do. Here's a needle and I'll even give you a spool of thread. You won't need a pair of scissors; a razor blade is better. Now you tight 'em plenty across the hips but leave cloth to loose 'em again across the shoulders; you'll need it later.'

Sergeant Zim's only comment on my tailoring was: 'You can do better than that. Two hours extra duty.'

So I did better than that by next parade.

Those first six weeks were all hardening up and hazing, with lots of parade drill and lots of route march. Eventually, as files dropped out and went home or elsewhere, we reached the point where we could do fifty miles in ten hours on the level – which is good mileage for a good horse in case you've never used your legs. We rested, not by stopping, but by changing pace, slow march, quick march, and trot. Sometimes we went out the full distance, bivouacked and ate field rations, slept in sleeping bags and marched back the next day.

One day we started out on an ordinary day's march, no bed bags on our shoulders, no rations. When we didn't stop for lunch, I wasn't surprised, as I had already learned to sneak sugar and hard bread and such out of the mess tent and conceal it about my person, but when we kept on marching away from camp in the afternoon I began to wonder. But I had learned not to ask silly questions.

We halted shortly before dark, three companies, now somewhat abbreviated. We formed a battalion parade and marched through it, without music, guards were mounted, and we were dismissed. I immediately looked up Corporal-Instructor Bronski because he was a little easier to deal with than the others . . . and because I felt a certain amount of responsibility; I happened to be, at the time, a recruit-corporal myself. These boot chevrons didn't mean much – mostly the privilege of being chewed out for whatever your squad did as well as for what you did yourself – and they could vanish as quickly as they appeared. Zim had tried out all of the older men as temporary non-coms first and I had inherited a brassard with chevrons on it a couple of days before when our squad leader had folded up and gone to hospital.

I said, 'Corporal Bronski, what's the straight word? When is chow call?'

He grinned at me. 'I've got a couple of crackers on me. Want me to split 'em with you?'

'Huh? Oh, no, sir. Thank you.' (I had considerably more than a couple of crackers; I was learning.) 'No chow call?'

'They didn't tell me either, sonny. But I don't see any

copters approaching. Now if I was you, I'd round up my squad and figure things out. Maybe one of you can hit a jack rabbit with a rock.'

'Yes, sir. But – Well, are we staying here all night? We don't have our bedrolls.'

His eye brows shot up. 'No bedrolls? Well, I do declare!' He seemed to think it over. 'Mmm . . . ever see sheep huddle together in a snowstorm?'

'Uh, no, sir'

'Try it. They don't freeze, maybe you won't. Or, if you don't care for company, you might walk around all night. Nobody'll bother you, as long as you stay inside the posted guards. You won't freeze if you keep moving. Of course you may be a little tired tomorrow.' He grinned again.

I saluted and went back to my squad. We divvied up, share and share alike – and I came out with less food than I had started; some of those idiots either hadn't sneaked out anything to eat, or had eaten all they had while we marched. But a few crackers and a couple of prunes will do a lot to quiet your stomach's sounding alert.

The sheep trick works, too; our whole section, three squads, did it together. I don't recommend it as a way to sleep; you are either in the outer layer, frozen on one side and trying to worm your way inside, or you are inside, fairly warm but with everybody else trying to shove his elbows, feet, and halitosis on you. You migrate from one condition to the other all night long in a sort of Brownian movement, never quite waking up and never really sound asleep. All this makes a night about a hundred years long.

We turned out at dawn to the familiar shout of: 'Up you come! On the bounce!' encouraged by instructors' batons applied smartly on fundaments sticking out of the piles . . . and then we did setting-up exercises. I felt like a corpse and didn't see how I could touch my toes. But I did, though it hurt, and twenty minutes later when we hit the trail I merely felt elderly. Sergeant Zim wasn't even mussed and somehow the scoundrel had managed to shave.

The sun warmed our backs as we marched and Zim started us singing, oldies at first, like '*Le Regiment de Sambre et Meuse*' and '*Caissons*' and 'Halls of Montezuma' and then our own 'Cap Trooper's Polka' which moves you into quick-step and pulls you on into a trot. Sergeant Zim couldn't carry a tune in a sack; all he had was a loud voice. But Breckinridge had a sure, strong lead and could hold the rest of us in the teeth of Zim's terrible false notes. We all felt cocky and covered with spines.

But we didn't feel cocky fifty miles later. It had been a long night; it was an endless day – and Zim chewed us out for the way we looked on parade and several boots got gigged for failing to shave in the nine whole minutes between the time we fell out after the march and fell back in again for parade. Several recruits resigned that evening and I thought about it but didn't because I had those silly boot chevrons and hadn't been busted yet.

That night there was a two-hour alert.

But eventually I learned to appreciate the homey luxury of two or three dozen warm bodies to snuggle up to, because twelve weeks later they dumped me down raw naked in a primitive area of the Canadian Rockies and I had to make my way forty miles through mountains. I made it – and hated the Army every inch of the way.

I wasn't in too bad shape when I checked in, though. A couple of rabbits had failed to stay as alert as I was, so I didn't go entirely hungry . . . nor entirely naked; I had a nice warm thick coat of rabbit fat and dirt on my body and moccasins on my feet – the rabbits having no further use for their skins. It's amazing what you can do with a flake of rock if you have to – I guess our cave-man ancestors weren't such dummies as we usually think.

The others made it, too, those who were still around to try and didn't resign rather than take the test – all except two boys who died trying. Then we all went back into the mountains and spent thirteen days finding them, working with copters overhead to direct us and all the best communication gear to help us and our instructors in powered command suits to supervise and to check rumors – because the Mobile Infantry doesn't abandon its own while there is any thin shred of hope.

Then we buried them with full honors to the strains of 'This Land Is Ours' and with the posthumous rank of PFC, the first of our boot regiment to go that high – because a cap trooper isn't necessarily expected to stay alive (dying is part of his trade) . . . but they care a lot about *how* you die. It has to be heads up, on the bounce, and still trying.

Breckinridge was one of them; the other was an Aussie boy I didn't know. They weren't the first to die in training; they weren't the last.

Chapter 5

He's bound to be guilty 'r he
wouldn't *be* here!
Starboard gun . . . FIRE!
Shoot*ing's too* good *for 'im*, kick
the house out!
Port gun . . . FIRE!
Ancient chanty used to time saluting guns

But that was after we had left Camp Currie and a lot had happened in between. Combat training, mostly – combat drill and combat exercises and combat maneuvers, using everything from bare hands to simulated nuclear weapons. I hadn't known there were so many different ways to fight. Hands and feet to start with – and if you think those aren't weapons you haven't seen Sergeant Zim and Captain Frankel, our battalion commander, demonstrate *la savate*, or had little Shujumi work you over with his hands and a toothy grin – Zim made Shujumi an instructor for that purpose at once and required us to take his orders, although we didn't have to salute him and say 'sir.'

As our ranks thinned down Zim quit bothering with formations himself, except parade, and spent more and more time in personal instruction, supplementing the corporal-instructors. He was sudden death with anything but he loved knives, and made and balanced his own, instead of using the perfectly good general-issue ones. He mellowed quite a bit as a personal teacher, too, becoming merely unbearable instead of downright disgusting – he could be quite patient with silly questions.

Once, during one of the two-minute rest periods that were scattered sparsely through each day's work, one of the boys – a kid named Ted Hendrick – asked, 'Sergeant? I guess this knife throwing is fun . . . but why do we have to learn it? What possible use is it?'

'Well,' answered Zim, 'suppose all you have is a knife? Or maybe not even a knife? What do you do? Just say your prayers and die? Or wade in and make him buy it anyhow? Son, this is *real* – it's not a checker game you can concede if you find yourself too far behind.'

'But that's just what I mean, sir. Suppose you aren't armed at all? Or just one of these toadstickers, say? And the man you're up against has all sorts of dangerous weapons? There's nothing you can do about it; he's got you licked on showdown.'

Zim said almost gently, 'You've got it all wrong, son. There's no such thing as a "dangerous weapon."'

'Huh? Sir?'

'There are no dangerous weapons; there are only dangerous men. We're trying to teach you to be dangerous – to the enemy. Dangerous even without a knife. Deadly as long as you still have one hand or one foot and are still alive. If you don't know what I mean, go read "Horatius at the Bridge" or "The Death of the Bon Homme Richard"; they're both in the Camp library. But take the case you first mentioned; I'm you and all you have is a knife. That target behind me – the one you've been missing, number three – is a sentry, armed with everything but an H-bomb. You've got to get him . . . quietly, at once, and without letting him call for help.' Zim turned slightly – *thunk!* – a knife he hadn't even had in his hand was quivering in the center of target number three. 'You see? Best to carry two knives – but get him you must, even barehanded.'

'Uh—'

'Something still troubling you? Speak up. That's what I'm here for, to answer your questions.'

'Uh, yes, sir. You said the sentry didn't have any H-bomb. But he *does* have an H-bomb; that's just the point. Well, at least we have, if we're the sentry . . . and any sentry we're up against is likely to have them, too. I don't mean the sentry, I mean the side he's on.'

'I understood you.'

'Well . . . you see, sir? If we can use an H-bomb – and, as you said, it's no checker game; it's real, it's war and nobody is fooling around – isn't it sort of ridiculous to go crawling around in the weeds, throwing knives and maybe getting yourself killed . . . and even losing the war . . . when you've got a real weapon you can use to win? What's the point in a whole lot of men risking their lives with obsolete weapons when one professor type can do so much more just by pushing a button?'

Zim didn't answer at once, which wasn't like him at all. Then he said softly, 'Are you happy in the Infantry, Hendrick? You can resign, you know.'

Hendrick muttered something; Zim said, 'Speak up!'

'I'm not itching to resign, sir. I'm going to sweat out my term.'

'I see. Well, the question you asked is one that a sergeant isn't really qualified to answer . . . and one that you shouldn't ask me. You're supposed to *know* the answer before you join up. Or you should. Did your school have a course in History and Moral Philosophy?'

'What? Sure – yes, sir.'

'Then you've heard the answer. But I'll give you my own – unofficial – views on it. If you wanted to teach a baby a lesson, would you cut its head off?'

'Why . . . no, sir!'

'Of course not. You'd paddle it. There can be circumstances when it's just as foolish to hit an enemy city with an H-bomb as it would be to spank a baby with an ax. War is not violence and killing, pure and simple; war is *controlled* violence, for a purpose. The purpose of war is to support your government's decisions by force. The purpose is never to kill the enemy just to be killing him . . . but to make him do what *you* want him to do. Not killing . . . but controlled and purposeful violence. But it's not your business or mine to decide the purpose or the control. It's never a soldier's business to decide when or where or how – or *why* – he fights; that belongs to the statesmen and the generals. The statesmen decide why and how much; the generals take it from there and tell us where and when and how. *We* supply the violence; other people – "older and wiser heads?" as they say – supply the control. Which is as it should be. That's the best answer I can give you. If it doesn't satisfy you, I'll get you a chit to go talk to the regimental commander. If *he* can't convince you – then go home and be a civilian! Because in that case you will certainly never make a soldier.'

Zim bounced to his feet. 'I think you've kept me talking just to goldbrick. Up you come, soldiers! On the bounce! Man stations, on target – Hendrick, you first. This time I want you to throw that knife south of you. *South*, get it? Not north. That target is due south of you and I want that knife to go in a general southerly direction, at least. I know you won't hit the target but see if you can't scare it a little. Don't slice your ear off, don't let go of it and cut somebody behind you – just keep what tiny mind you have fixed on the idea of "south'! Ready – on target! *Let fly!*'

Hendrick missed it again.

We trained with sticks and we trained with wire (lots of nasty things you can improvise with a piece of wire) and we learned what can be done with really modern weapons and how to do it and how to service and maintain the equipment – simulated nuclear weapons and infantry rockets and various sorts of gas and poison and incendiary and demolition. As well as other things maybe best not discussed. But we learned a lot of 'obsolete' weapons, too. Bayonets on dummy guns for example, and guns that weren't dummies, too, but were almost identical with the infantry rifle of the XXth century – much like the sporting rifles used in hunting game, except that we fired nothing but solid slugs, alloy-jacketed lead bullets, both at targets on measured ranges and at surprise targets on boobytrapped skirmish runs. This was supposed to prepare us to learn to use any aimed weapon and to train us to be on the bounce, alert, ready for anything. Well, I suppose it did. I'm pretty sure it did.

We used these rifles in field exercises to simulate a lot of deadlier and nastier aimed weapons, too. We used a lot of simulation; we had to. An 'explosive' bomb or grenade, against material or personnel, would explode just enough to put out a lot of black smoke; another sort of gave off a gas that would make you sneeze and weep – that told you that you were dead or paralyzed . . . and that was nasty enough to make you careful about anti-gas precautions, to say nothing of the chewing out you got if you were caught by it.

We got still less sleep; more than half the exercises were held at night, with snoopers and radar and audio gear and such.

The rifles used to simulate aimed weapons were loaded with blanks except one in five hundred rounds at random, which was a real bullet. Dangerous? Yes and no. It's dangerous just to be alive . . . and a nonexplosive bullet probably won't kill you unless it hits you in the head or the heart and maybe not then. What that one-in-five-hundred 'for real' did was to give us a deep interest in taking cover, especially as we knew that some of the rifles were being fired by instructors who were crack shots and actually trying their best to hit you – if the round happened not to be a blank. They assured us that they would not intentionally shoot a man in the head . . . but accidents do happen.

This friendly assurance wasn't very reassuring. That 500th bullet turned tedious exercises into large-scale Russian roulette; you stop being bored the very first time you hear a slug go *wheet!* past your ear before you hear the crack of the rifle.

But we did slack down anyhow and word came down from the top that if we didn't get on the bounce, the incidence of real ones would be changed to one in a hundred . . . and if that didn't work, to one in fifty. I don't know whether a change was made or not – no way to tell – but I do know we tightened up again, because a boy in the next company got creased across his buttocks with a live one, producing an amazing scar and a lot of half-witty comments and a renewed interest by all hands in taking cover. We laughed at this kid for getting shot where he did . . . but we all knew it could have been his head – or our *own* heads.

The instructors who were not firing rifles did not take cover. They put on white shirts and walked around upright with their silly canes, apparently calmly certain that even a recruit would not intentionally shoot an instructor – which may have been overconfidence on the part of some of them. Still, the chances were five hundred to one that even a shot aimed with murderous intent would not be live and the safety factor increased still higher because the recruit probably couldn't shoot that well anyhow. A rifle is not an easy weapon; it's got no target-seeking qualities at all – I understand that even back in the days when wars were fought and decided with just such rifles it used to take several thousand fired shots to average killing one man. This seems impossible but the military histories agree that it is true – apparently most shots weren't really aimed but simply acted to force the enemy to keep his head down and interfere with *his* shooting.

In any case we had no instructors wounded or killed by rifle fire. No trainees were killed, either, by rifle bullets; the deaths were all from other weapons or things – some of which could turn around and bite you if you didn't do things by the book. Well, one boy did manage to break his neck taking cover too enthusiastically when they first started shooting at him – but no bullet touched him.

However, by a chain reaction, this matter of rifle bullets and taking cover brought me to my lowest ebb at Camp Currie. In the first place I had been busted out of my boot chevrons, not over what I did but over something one of my squad did when I wasn't even around . . . which I pointed out. Bronski told me to button my lip. So I went to see Zim about it. He told me coldly that I was responsible for what my men did, regardless . . . and tacked on six hours of extra duty besides busting me for having spoken to him about it without Bronski's permission. Then I got a letter that upset me a lot; my mother finally wrote to me. Then I sprained a shoulder in my first drill with powered armor (they've got those practice suits rigged so that the instructor can cause casualties in the suit at will, by radio control; I got dumped and hurt my shoulder) and this put me on light duty with too much time to think at a time when I had many reasons, it seemed to me, to feel sorry for myself.

Because of 'light duty' I was orderly that day in the battalion commander's office. I was eager at first, for I had never been there before and wanted to make a good impression. I discovered that Captain Frankel didn't want zeal; he wanted me to sit still, say nothing, and not bother him. This left me time to sympathize with myself, for I didn't dare go to sleep.

Then suddenly, shortly after lunch, I wasn't a bit sleepy; Sergeant Zim came in, followed by three men. Zim was smart and neat as usual but the expression on his face made him look like Death on a pale horse and he had a mark on his right eye that looked as if it might be shaping up into a shiner – which was impossible, of course. Of the other three, the one in the middle was Ted Hendrick. He was dirty – well, the company had been on a field exercise; they don't scrub those prairies and you spend a lot of your time snuggling up to the dirt. But his lip was split and there was blood on his chin and on his shirt and his cap was missing. He looked wild-eyed.

The men on each side of him were boots. They each had rifles; Hendrick did not. One of them was from my squad, a kid named Leivy. He seemed excited and pleased, and slipped me a wink when nobody was looking.

Captain Frankel looked surprised. 'What is this, Sergeant?'

Zim stood frozen straight and spoke as if he were reciting something by rote. 'Sir, H Company Commander reports to the Battalion Commander. Discipline. Article nine-one-oh-seven. Disregard of tactical command and doctrine, the team being in simulated combat. Article nine-one-two-oh. Disobedience of orders, same conditions.'

Captain Frankel looked puzzled. 'You are bringing this to *me*, Sergeant? Officially?'

I don't see how a man can manage to look as embarrassed as Zim looked and still have no expression of any sort in his face or voice. 'Sir. If the Captain pleases. The man refused administrative discipline. He insisted on seeing the Battalion Commander.'

'I see. A bedroll lawyer. Well, I still don't understand it, Sergeant, but technically that's his privilege. What was the tactical command and doctrine?'

'A "freeze," sir.' I glanced at Hendrick, thinking: Oh, oh,

he's going to catch it. In a "freeze" you hit dirt, taking any cover you can, fast, and then *freeze* – don't move at all, not even twitch an eyebrow, until released. Or you can freeze when you're already in cover. They tell stories about men who had been hit while in freeze . . . and had died slowly but without ever making a sound or a move.

Frankel's brows shot up. 'Second part?'

'Same thing, sir. After breaking freeze, failing to return to it on being so ordered.'

Captain Frankel looked grim. 'Name?'

Zim answered. 'Hendrick, T. C., sir. Recruit Private R-P-seven-nine-six-oh-nine-two-four.'

'Very well, Hendrick, you are deprived of all privileges for thirty days and restricted to your tent when not on duty or at meals, subject only to sanitary necessities. You will serve three hours extra duty each day under the Corporal of the Guard, one hour to be served just before taps, one hour just before reveille, one hour at the time of the noonday meal and in place of it. Your evening meal will be bread and water – as much bread as you can eat. You will serve ten hours extra duty each Sunday, the time to be adjusted to permit you to attend divine services if you so elect.'

(I thought: Oh my! He threw the book.)

Captain Frankel went on: 'Hendrick, the only reason you are getting off so lightly is that I am not permitted to give you any more than that without convening a court-martial . . . and I don't want to spoil your company's record. Dismissed.' He dropped his eyes back to the papers on his desk, the incident already forgotten –

– and Hendrick yelled, 'You didn't hear *my* side of it!'

The Captain looked up. 'Oh. Sorry. You have a side?'

'You darn right I do! Sergeant Zim's got it in for me! He's been riding me, riding me, riding me, all day long from the time I got here! He—'

'That's his job,' the Captain said coldly. 'Do you deny the two charges against you?'

'No, but – *He didn't tell you I was lying on an anthill!*'

Frankel looked disgusted. 'Oh. So you would get yourself killed and perhaps your teammates as well because of a few little ants?'

'Not "just a few" – there were hundreds of 'em. Stingers.'

'So? Young man, let me put you straight. Had it been a nest of rattlesnakes you would still have been expected – and required – to freeze.' Frankel paused. 'Have you anything at all to say in your own defense?'

Hendrick's mouth was open. 'I certainly do! He hit me! *He laid hands on me!* The whole bunch of 'em are always strutting around with those silly batons, whackin' you across the fanny, punchin' you between the shoulders and tellin' you to brace up – and I put up with it. But he hit me with his *hands* – he knocked me down to the ground and yelled, "*Freeze!* you stupid jackass!" How about *that?*'

Captain Frankel looked down at his hands, looked up again at Hendrick. 'Young man, you are under the misapprehension very common among civilians. You think that your superior officers are not permitted to "lay hands on you," as you put it. Under purely social conditions, that is true – say if we happened to run across each other in a theater or a shop, I would have no more right, as long as you treated me with the respect due my rank, to slap your face than you have to slap mine. But in line of duty the rule is entirely different—'

The Captain swung around in his chair and pointed at some loose-leaf books. 'There are the laws under which you live. You can search every article in those books, every court-martial case which has arisen under them, and you will not find *one word* which says, or implies, that your superior officer may not "lay hands on you" or strike you in any other manner in line of duty. Hendrick, I could break your jaw . . .

and I simply would be responsible to my own superior officers as to the appropriate necessity of the act. But I would not be responsible to *you*. I could do more than that. There are circumstances under which a superior officer, commissioned or not, is not only permitted but *required* to kill an officer or a man under him, without delay and perhaps without warning – and, far from being punished, be commended. To put a stop to pusillanimous conduct in the face of the enemy, for example.'

The Captain tapped on his desk. 'Now about those batons – They have two uses. First, they mark the men in authority. Second, we expect them to be used on you, to touch you up and keep you on the bounce. You can't possibly be hurt with one, not the way they are used; at most they sting a little. But they save thousands of words. Say you don't turn out on the bounce at reveille. No doubt the duty corporal could wheedle you, say "pretty please with sugar on it," inquire if you'd like breakfast in bed this morning – if we could spare one career corporal just to nursemaid you. We can't, so he gives your bedroll a whack and trots on down the line, applying the spur where needed. Of course, he could simply kick you, which would be just as legal and nearly as effective. But the general in charge of training and discipline thinks that it is more dignified, both for the duty corporal and for you, to snap a late sleeper out of his fog with the impersonal rod of authority. And so do I. Not that it matters what you and I think about it; this is the way we do it.'

Captain Frankel sighed. 'Hendrick, I have explained these matters to you because it is useless to punish a man unless he knows why he is being punished. You've been a bad boy – I say "boy" because you quite evidently aren't a man yet, although we'll keep trying – a surprisingly bad boy in view of the stage of your training. Nothing you have said is any defense, nor even any mitigation; you don't seem to know the score nor have any idea of your duty as a soldier. So tell me in your own words why you feel mistreated; I want to get you straightened out. There might even be something in your favor, though I confess that I cannot imagine what it could be.'

I had sneaked a look or two at Hendrick's face while the Captain was chewing him out – somehow his quiet, mild words were a worse chewing-out than any Zim had ever given us. Hendrick's expression had gone from indignation to blank astonishment to sullenness.

'Speak up!' Frankel added sharply.

'Uh . . . well, we were ordered to freeze and I hit the dirt and I found I was on this anthill. So I got to my knees, to move over a couple of feet, and I was hit from behind and knocked flat and he yelled at me – and I bounced up and popped him one and he—'

'STOP!' Captain Frankel was out of his chair and standing ten feet tall, though he's hardly taller than I am. He stared at Hendrick.

'You . . . *struck* . . . your . . . company commander?'

'Huh? I said so. But he hit me first. From behind, I didn't even see him. I don't take that off of anybody. I popped him and then he hit me again and then—'

'Silence!'

Hendrick stopped. Then he added, 'I just want out of this lousy outfit.'

'*I think* we can accommodate you,' Frankel said icily. 'And quickly, too.'

'Just gimme a piece of paper, I'm resigning.'

'One moment. Sergeant Zim.'

'Yes, sir.' Zim hadn't said a word for a long time. He just stood, eyes front and rigid as a statue, nothing moving but his twitching jaw muscles. I looked at him now and saw that it certainly was a shiner – a beaut. Hendrick must have caught him just right. But he hadn't said anything about it and Captain

Frankel hadn't asked – maybe he had just assumed Zim had run into a door and would explain it if he felt like it, later.

'Have the pertinent articles been published to your company, as required?'

'Yes, sir. Published and logged, every Sunday morning.'

'I know they have. I asked simply for the record.'

Just before church call every Sunday they lined us up and read aloud the disciplinary articles out of the Laws and Regulations of the Military Forces. They were posted on the bulletin board, too, outside the orderly tent. Nobody paid them much mind – it was just another drill; you could stand still and sleep through it. About the only thing we noticed, if we noticed anything, was what we called 'the thirty-one ways to crash land.' After all, the instructors see to it that you soak up all the regulations you need to know, through your skin. The 'crash landings' were a worn-out joke, like 'reveille oil' and 'tent jacks' . . . they were the thirty-one capital offenses. Now and then somebody boasted, or accused somebody else, of having found a thirty-second way – always something preposterous and usually obscene.

'Striking a Superior Officer – !'

It suddenly wasn't amusing any longer. Popping Zim? *Hang* a man for that? Why, almost everybody in the company had taken a swing at Sergeant Zim and some of us had even landed . . . when he was instructing us in hand-to-hand combat. He would take us on after the other instructors had worked us over and we were beginning to feel cocky and pretty good at it – then he would put the polish on. Why, shucks, I once saw Shujumi knock him unconscious. Bronski threw water on him and Zim got up and grinned and shook hands – and threw Shujumi right over the horizon.

Captain Frankel looked around, motioned at me. 'You. Flash regimental headquarters.'

I did it, all thumbs, stepped back when an officer's face

came on and let the Captain take the call. 'Adjutant,' the face said.

Frankel said crisply, 'Second Battalion Commander's respects to the Regimental Commander. I request and require an officer to sit as a court.'

The face said, 'When do you need him, Ian?'

'As quickly as you can get him here.'

'Right away. I'm pretty sure Jake is in his HQ. Article and name?'

Captain Frankel identified Hendrick and quoted an article number. The face in the screen whistled and looked grim. 'On the bounce, Ian. If I can't get Jake, I'll be over myself – just as soon as I tell the Old Man.'

Captain Frankel turned to Zim. 'This escort – are they witnesses?'

'Yes, sir.'

'Did his section leader see it?'

Zim barely hesitated. 'I think so, sir.'

'Get him. Anybody out that way in a powered suit?'

'Yes, sir.'

Zim used the phone while Frankel said to Hendrick, 'What witnesses do you wish to call in your defense?'

'Huh? I don't need any witnesses, he knows what he did! Just hand me a piece of paper – I'm getting out of here.'

'All in good time.'

In very fast time, it seemed to me. Less than five minutes later Corporal Jones came bouncing up in a command suit, carrying Corporal Mahmud in his arms. He dropped Mahmud and bounced away just as Lieutenant Spieksma came in. He said, 'Afternoon, Cap'n. Accused and witnesses here?'

'All set. Take it, Jake.'

'Recorder on?'

'It is now.'

'Very well. Hendrick, step forward.' Hendrick did so, looking puzzled and as if his nerve was beginning to crack. Lieutenant Spieksma said briskly: 'Field Court-Martial, convened by order of Major F. X. Malloy, commanding Third Training Regiment, Camp Arthur Currie, under General Order Number Four, issued by the Commanding General, Training and Discipline Command, pursuant to the Laws and Regulations of the Military Forces, Terran Federation. Remanding officer: Captain Ian Frankel, M.I., assigned to and commanding Second Battalion, Third Regiment. The Court: Lieutenant Jacques Spieksma, M.I., assigned to and commanding First Battalion, Third Regiment. Accused: Hendrick, Theodore C., Recruit Private RP7960924. Article 9080. Charge: Striking his superior officer, the Terran Federation then being in a state of emergency.'

The thing that got me was how *fast* it went. I found myself suddenly appointed an 'officer of the court' and directed to 'remove' the witnesses and have them ready. I didn't know how I would 'remove' Sergeant Zim if he didn't feel like it, but he gathered Mahmud and the two boots up by eye and they all went outside, out of earshot. Zim separated himself from the others and simply waited; Mahmud sat down on the ground and rolled a cigarette – which he had to put out; he was the first one called. In less than twenty minutes all three of them had testified, all telling much the same story Hendrick had. Zim wasn't called at all.

Lieutenant Spieksma said to Hendrick, 'Do you wish to cross-examine the witnesses? The Court will assist you, if you so wish.'

'No.'

'Stand at attention and say "sir" when you address the Court.'

'No, sir.' He added, 'I want a lawyer.'

'The Law does not permit counsel in field courts-martial.

Do you wish to testify in your own defense? You are not required to do so and, in view of the evidence thus far, the Court will take no judicial notice if you choose not to do so. But you are warned that any testimony that you give may be used against you and that you will be subject to cross-examination.'

Hendrick shrugged. 'I haven't anything to say. What good would it do me?'

'The Court repeats: Will you testify in your own defense?'

'Uh, no, sir.'

'The Court must demand of you one technical question. Was the article under which you are charged published to you *before* the time of the alleged offense of which you stand accused? You may answer yes, or no, or stand mute – but you are responsible for your answer under Article 9167 which relates to perjury.'

The accused stood mute.

'Very well. The Court will reread the article of the charge aloud to you and again ask you that question. "Article 9080: Any person in the Military Forces who strikes or assaults, or attempts to strike or assault – "'

'Oh, I suppose they did. They read a lot of that stuff, every Sunday morning – a whole long list of things you couldn't do.'

'Was or was not that particular article read to you?'

'Uh . . . yes, sir. It was.'

'Very well. Having declined to testify, do you have any statement to make in mitigation or extenuation?'

'Sir?'

'Do you want to tell the Court anything about it? Any circumstance which you think might possibly affect the evidence already given? Or anything which might lessen the alleged offense? Such things as being ill, or under drugs or medication. You are not under oath at this point; you may say anything at all which you think may help you. What the Court is trying to find out is this: Does anything about this matter strike you as being unfair? If so, why?'

'Huh! Of course it is! Everything about it is unfair! He hit me first! You heard 'em – *he hit me first!* '

'Anything more?'

'Huh? No, sir. Isn't that enough?'

'The trial is completed. Recruit Private Theodore C. Hendrick, stand forth!' Lieutenant Spieksma had been standing at attention the whole time; now Captain Frankel stood up. The place suddenly felt chilly.

'Private Hendrick, you are found guilty as charged.'

My stomach did a flip-flop. They were going to do it to him . . . they were going to do the 'Danny Deever' to Ted Hendrick. And I had eaten breakfast beside him just this morning.

'The Court sentences you,' he went on, while I felt sick, 'to ten lashes and Bad Conduct Discharge.'

Hendrick gulped, 'I want to resign!'

'The Court will not permit you to resign. The Court wishes to add that your punishment is light simply because this Court possesses no jurisdiction to assign greater punishment. The authority which remanded you specified a field court-martial – why it so chose, this Court will not speculate. But had you been remanded for general court-martial, it seems certain that the evidence before this Court would have caused a general court to sentence you to hang by the neck until dead. You are very lucky – and the remanding authority has been most merciful.' Lieutenant Spieksma paused, then went on, 'The sentence will be carried out at the earliest hour after the convening authority has reviewed and approved the record, if it does so approve. Court is adjourned. Remove and confine him.'

The last was addressed to me, but I didn't actually have to

do anything about it, other than phone the guard tent and then get a receipt for him when they took him away.

At afternoon sick call Captain Frankel took me off orderly and sent me to see the doctor, who sent me back to duty. I got back to my company just in time to dress and fall in for parade – and to get gigged by Zim for 'spots on uniform.' Well, he had a bigger spot over one eye but I didn't mention it.

Somebody had set up a big post in the parade ground just back of where the adjutant stood. When it came time to publish the orders, instead of 'routine order of the day' or other trivia, they published Hendrick's court-martial.

Then they marched him out, between two armed guards, with his hands cuffed together in front of him.

I had never seen a flogging. Back home, while they do it in public of course, they do it back of the Federal Building – and Father had given me strict orders to stay away from there. I tried disobeying him on it once . . . but it was postponed and I never tried to see one again.

Once is too many.

The guards lifted his arms and hooked the manacles over a big hook high up on the post. Then they took his shirt off and it turned out that it was fixed so that it could come off and he didn't have an undershirt. The adjutant said crisply, 'Carry out the sentence of the Court.'

A corporal-instructor from some other battalion stepped forward with the whip. The Sergeant of the Guard made the count.

It's a slow count, five seconds between each one and it seems *much* longer. Ted didn't let out a peep until the third, then he sobbed.

The next thing I knew I was staring up at Corporal Bronski. He was slapping me and looking intently at me. He stopped and asked, 'Okay now? All right, back in ranks. On the bounce; we're about to pass in review.' We did so and marched back to our company areas. I didn't eat much dinner but neither did a lot of them.

Nobody said a word to me about fainting. I found out later that I wasn't the only one – a couple of dozen of us had passed out.

Chapter 6

What we obtain too cheap, we esteem too lightly . . . it would be strange indeed if so celestial an article as FREEDOM *should not be highly rated.*

– Thomas Paine

It was the night after Hendrick was kicked out that I reached my lowest slump at Camp Currie. I couldn't sleep – and you have to have been through boot camp to understand just how far down a recruit has to sink before that can happen. But I hadn't had any real exercise all day so I wasn't physically tired, and my shoulder still hurt even though I had been marked 'duty,' and I had that letter from my mother preying on my mind, and every time I closed my eyes I would hear that *crack!* and see Ted slump against the whipping post.

I wasn't fretted about losing my boot chevrons. That no longer mattered at all because I was ready to resign, determined to. If it hadn't been the middle of the night and no pen and paper handy, I would have done so right then.

Ted had made a bad mistake, one that lasted all of half a second. And it really had been just a mistake, too, because, while he hated the outfit (who liked it?), he had been trying to sweat it out and win his franchise; he meant to go into politics – he talked a lot about how, when he got his citizenship, 'There will be some changes made – you wait and see.'

Well, he would never be in public office now; he had taken his finger off his number for a single instant and he was through.

If it could happen to him, it could happen to me. Suppose I slipped? Next day or next week? Not even allowed to resign . . . but drummed out with my back striped.

Time to admit that I was wrong and Father was right, time to put in that little piece of paper and slink home and tell Father that I was ready to go to Harvard and then go to work in the business – if he would still let me. Time to see Sergeant Zim, first thing in the morning, and tell him that I had had it. But not until morning, because you don't wake Sergeant Zim except for something you're certain that *he* will class as an emergency – believe me, you don't! Not Sergeant Zim.

Sergeant Zim –

He worried me as much as Ted's case did. After the court-martial was over and Ted had been taken away, he stayed behind and said to Captain Frankel, 'May I speak with the Battalion Commander, sir?'

'Certainly. I was intending to ask you to stay behind for a word. Sit down.'

Zim flicked his eyes my way and the Captain looked at me and I didn't have to be told to get out; I faded. There was nobody in the outer office, just a couple of civilian clerks. I didn't dare go outside because the Captain might want me; I found a chair back of a row of files and sat down.

I could hear them talking, through the partition I had my head against. BHQ was a building rather than a tent, since it housed permanent communication and recording equipment, but it was a 'minimum field building,' a shack; the inner partitions weren't much. I doubt if the civilians could hear as they each were wearing transcriber phones and were bent over typers – besides, they didn't matter. I didn't mean to eavesdrop. Uh, well, maybe I did.

Zim said: 'Sir, I request transfer to a combat team.'

Frankel answered: 'I can't hear you, Charlie. My tin ear is bothering me again.'

Zim: 'I'm quite serious, sir. This isn't my sort of duty.'

Frankel said testily, 'Quit bellyaching your troubles to me, Sergeant. At least wait until we've disposed of duty matters. What in the world happened?'

Zim said stiffly, 'Captain, that boy doesn't rate ten lashes.'

Frankel answered, 'Of course he doesn't. You know who goofed – and so do I.'

'Yes, sir, I know.'

'Well? You know even better than I do that these kids are wild animals at this stage. You know when it's safe to turn your back on them and when it isn't. You know the doctrine and the standing orders about article nine-oh-eight-oh – you must *never* give them a *chance* to violate it. Of course some of them are going to try it – if they weren't aggressive they wouldn't be material for the M.I. They're docile in ranks; it's safe enough to turn your back when they're eating, or sleeping, or sitting on their tails and being lectured. But get them out in the field in a combat exercise, or anything that gets them keyed up and full of adrenalin, and they're as explosive as a hatful of mercury fulminate. You know that, all you instructors know that; you're trained – trained to watch for it, trained to snuff it out before it happens. Explain to me how it was possible for an untrained recruit to hang a mouse on your eye? He should never have laid a hand on you; you should have knocked him cold when you saw what he was up to. So why weren't you on the bounce? Are you slowing down?'

'I don't know,' Zim answered slowly. 'I guess I must be.'

'Hmm! If true, a combat team is the last place for you. But it's not true. Or wasn't true the last time you and I worked out together, three days ago. So what slipped?'

Zim was slow in answering. 'I think, I had him tagged in my mind as one of the safe ones.'

'There are no such.'

'Yes, sir. But he was so earnest, so doggedly determined to

sweat it out – he didn't have any aptitude but he kept on trying – that I must have done that, subconsciously.' Zim was silent, then added, 'I guess it was because I liked him.'

Frankel snorted. 'An instructor can't afford to like a man.'

'I know it, sir. But I do. They're a nice bunch of kids. We've dumped all the real twerps by now – Hendrick's only shortcoming, aside from being clumsy, was that he thought he knew all the answers. I didn't mind that; I knew it all at that age myself. The twerps have gone home and those that are left are eager, anxious to please, and on the bounce – as cute as a litter of collie pups. A lot of them will make soldiers.'

'So *that* was the soft spot. You liked him . . . so you failed to clip him in time. So he winds up with a court and the whip and a B.C.D. Sweet.'

Zim said earnestly, 'I wish to heaven there were some way for me to take that flogging myself, sir.'

'You'd have to take your turn, I outrank you. What do you think I've been wishing the past hour? What do you think I was afraid of from the moment I saw you come in here sporting a shiner? I did my best to brush it off with administrative punishment and the young fool wouldn't let well enough alone. But I never thought he would be crazy enough to blurt out that he had hung one on you – he's *stupid;* you should have eased him out of the outfit weeks ago . . . instead of nursing him along until he got into trouble. But blurt it out he did, to me, in front of witnesses, forcing me to take official notice of it – and that licked us. No way to get it off the record, no way to avoid a court . . . just go through the whole dreary mess and take our medicine, and wind up with one more civilian who'll be against us the rest of his days. Because he *has* to be flogged; neither you nor I can take it for him, even though the fault was ours. Because the regiment has to see what happens when nine-oh-eight-oh is violated. Our fault . . . but his lumps.'

'*My* fault, Captain. That's why I want to be transferred. Uh, sir, I think it's best for the outfit.'

'You do, eh? But I decide what's best for my battalion, not you, Sergeant. Charlie, who do you think pulled your name out of the hat? And why? Think back twelve years. You were a corporal, remember? Where were you?'

'Here, as you know quite well, Captain. Right here on this same godforsaken prairie – and I wish I had never come back to it!'

'Don't we all. But it happens to be the most important and the most delicate work in the Army – turning unspanked young cubs into soldiers Who was the worst unspanked young cub in your section?'

'Mmm . . .' Zim answered slowly. 'I wouldn't go so far as to say you were the worst, Captain.'

'You wouldn't, eh? But you'd have to think hard to name another candidate. I hated your guts, "Corporal" Zim.'

Zim sounded surprised, and a little hurt. 'You did, Captain? I didn't hate you – I rather liked you.'

'So? Well, "hate" is the other luxury an instructor can never afford. We must not hate them, we must not like them; we must teach them. But if you like me then – mmm, it seemed to me that you had very strange ways of showing it. Do you still like me? Don't answer that; I don't care whether you do or not – or, rather, I don't want to know, whichever it is. Never mind; I despised you then and I used to dream about ways to get you. But you were always on the bounce and never gave me a chance to buy a nine-oh-eight-oh court of my own. So here I am, thanks to you. Now to handle your request: You used to have one order that you gave to me over and over again when I was a boot. I got so that I loathed it almost more than anything else you did or said. Do you remember it? *I* do and now I'll give it back to you: "Soldier, shut up and soldier!"'

'Yes, sir.'

'Don't go yet. This weary mess isn't all loss; any regiment of boots needs a stern lesson in the meaning of nine-oh-eight-oh, as we both know. They haven't yet learned to think, they won't read, and they rarely listen – but they can *see* . . . and young Hendrick's misfortune may save one of his mates, some day, from swinging by the neck until he's dead, dead, dead. But I'm sorry the object lesson had to come from my battalion and I certainly don't intend to let this battalion supply another one. You get your instructors together and warn them. For about twenty-four hours those kids will be in a state of shock. Then they'll turn sullen and the tension will build. Along about Thursday or Friday some boy who is about to flunk out anyhow will start thinking over the fact that Hendrick didn't get so very much, not even the number of lashes for drunken driving . . . and he's going to start brooding that it might be worth it, to take a swing at the instructor he hates worst. Sergeant – *that blow must never land!* Understand me?'

'Yes, sir.'

'I want them to be eight times as cautious as they have been. I want them to keep their distance, I want them to have eyes in the backs of their heads, want them to be as alert as a mouse at a cat show. Bronski – you have a special word with Bronski; he has a tendency to fraternize.'

'I'll straighten Bronski out, sir.'

'See that you do. Because when the next kid starts swinging, it's *got* to be stop-punched – not muffed, like today. The boy has got to be knocked cold and the instructor must do so without ever being touched himself – or I'll damned well break him for incompetence. Let them know that. They've got to teach those kids that it's not merely expensive but *impossible* to violate nine-oh-eight-oh . . . that even trying it wins a short nap, a bucket of water in the face, and a very sore jaw – and nothing else.'

'Yes, sir. It'll be done.'

'It had better be done. I will not only break the instructor who slips, I will personally take him 'way out on the prairie and give him lumps . . . because *I will not have another one of my boys strung up to that whipping post* through sloppiness on the part of his teachers. Dismissed.'

'Yes, sir. Good afternoon, Captain.'

'What's good about it? Charlie—'

'Yes, sir?'

'If you're not too busy this evening, why don't you bring your soft shoes and your pads over to officers' row and we'll go waltzing Matilda? Say about eight o'clock.'

'Yes, sir.'

'That's not an order, that's an invitation. If you really are slowing down, maybe I'll be able to kick your shoulder blades off.'

'Uh, would the Captain care to put a small bet on it?'

'Huh? With me sitting here at this desk getting swivel-chair spread? I will not! Not unless you agree to fight with one foot in a bucket of cement. Seriously, Charlie, we've had a miserable day and it's going to be worse before it gets better. If you and I work up a good sweat and swap a few bumps, maybe we'll be able to sleep tonight despite all of mother's little darlings.'

'I'll be there, Captain. Don't eat too much dinner – I need to work off a couple of matters myself.'

'I'm not going to dinner; I'm going to sit right here and sweat out this quarterly report . . . which the Regimental Commander is graciously pleased to see right after *his* dinner . . . and which somebody whose name I won't mention has put me two hours behind on. So I may be a few minutes late for our waltz. Go 'way now, Charlie, and don't bother me. See you later.'

Sergeant Zim left so abruptly that I barely had time to lean over and tie my shoe and thereby be out of sight behind the file cases as he passed through the outer office. Captain Frankel was already shouting. 'Orderly! *Orderly!* ORDERLY! – do I have to call you three times? What's your name? Put yourself down for an hour's extra duty, full kit. Find the company commanders of E, F, and G, my compliments and I'll be pleased to see them before parade. Then bounce over to my tent and fetch me a clean dress uniform, cap, side arms, shoes, ribbons – no medals. Lay it out for me here. Then make afternoon sick call – if you can scratch with that arm, as I've seen you doing, your shoulder can't be too sore. You've got thirteen minutes until sick call – on the bounce, soldier!'

I made it . . . by catching two of them in the senior instructors' showers (an orderly can go anywhere) and the third at his desk; the orders you get aren't impossible, they merely seem so because they nearly are. I was laying out Captain Frankel's uniform for parade as sick call sounded. Without looking up he growled, 'Belay that extra duty. Dismissed.' So I got home just in time to catch extra duty for 'Uniform, Untidy in, Two Particulars' and see the sickening end of Ted Hendrick's time in the M.I.

So I had plenty to think about as I lay awake that night. I had known that Sergeant Zim worked hard, but it had never occurred to me that he could possibly be other than completely and smugly self-satisfied with what he did. He *looked* so smug, so self-assured, so at peace with the world and with himself.

The idea that this invincible robot could feel that he had failed, could feel so deeply and personally disgraced that he wanted to run away, hide his face among strangers, and offer the excuse that his leaving would be 'best for the outfit,' shook me up as much, and in a way even more, than seeing Ted flogged.

To have Captain Frankel agree with him – as to the

seriousness of the failure, I mean – and then rub his nose in it, chew him out. Well! I mean really. Sergeants don't get chewed out; sergeants do the chewing. A law of nature.

But I had to admit that what Sergeant Zim had taken, and swallowed, was so completely humiliating and withering as to make the worst I had ever heard or overheard from a sergeant sound like a love song. And yet the Captain hadn't even raised his voice.

The whole incident was so preposterously unlikely that I was never even tempted to mention it to anyone else.

And Captain Frankel himself – Officers we didn't see very often. They showed up for evening parade, sauntering over at the last moment and doing nothing that would work up a sweat; they inspected once a week, making private comments to sergeants, comments that invariably meant grief for somebody else, not them; and they decided each week what company had won the honor of, guarding the regimental colors. Aside from that, they popped up occasionally on surprise inspections, creased, immaculate, remote, and smelling faintly of cologne – and went away again.

Oh, one or more of them did always accompany us on route marches and twice Captain Frankel had demonstrated his virtuosity at *la savate*. But officers didn't work, not real work, and they had no worries because sergeants were *under* them, not *over* them.

But it appeared that Captain Frankel worked so hard that he skipped meals, was kept so busy with something or other that he complained of lack of exercise and would waste his own free time just to work up a sweat.

As for worries, he had honestly seemed to be even more upset at what had happened to Hendrick than Zim had been. And yet he hadn't even known Hendrick by sight; he had been forced to ask his name.

I had an unsettling feeling that I had been completely

mistaken as to the very nature of the world I was in, as if every part of it was something wildly different from what it appeared to be – like discovering that your own mother isn't anyone you've ever seen before, but a stranger in a rubber mask.

But I was sure of one thing: I didn't want to find out what the M.I. really was. If it was so tough that even the gods-that-be – sergeants and officers – were made unhappy by it, it was certainly too tough for Johnnie! How could you keep from making mistakes in an outfit you didn't understand? *I* didn't want to swing by my neck till I was dead, dead, dead! I didn't even want to risk being flogged . . . even though the doctor stands by to make certain that it doesn't do any permanent injury. Nobody in our family had *ever* been flogged (except paddlings in school, of course, which isn't at all the same thing). There were no criminals in our family on either side, none who had ever been accused of crime. We were a proud family; the only thing we lacked was citizenship and Father regarded that as no real honor, a vain and useless thing. But if I were flogged – Well, he'd probably have a stroke.

And yet Hendrick hadn't done anything that I hadn't thought about doing a thousand times. Why hadn't I? Timid, I guess. I *knew* that those instructors, any one of them, could beat the tar out of me, so I had buttoned my lip and hadn't tried it. No guts, Johnnie. At least Ted Hendrick had had guts. I didn't have . . . and a man with no guts has no business in the Army in the first place.

Besides that, Captain Frankel hadn't even considered it to be Ted's fault. Even if I didn't buy a 9080, through lack of guts, what day would I do something other than a 9080 – something not my fault – and wind up slumped against the whipping post anyhow?

Time to get out, Johnnie, while you're still ahead.

My mother's letter simply confirmed my decision. I had been able to harden my heart to my parents as long as they were refusing me – but when they softened, I couldn't stand it. Or when Mother softened, at least. She had written:

– but I am afraid I must tell you that your father will still not permit your name to be mentioned. But, dearest, that is his way of grieving, since he cannot cry. You must understand, my darling baby, that he loves you more than life itself – more than he does me – and that you have hurt him very deeply. He tells the world that you are a grown man, capable of making your own decisions, and that he is proud of you. But that is his own pride speaking, the bitter hurt of a proud man who has been wounded deep in his heart by the one he loves best. You must understand, Juanito, that he does not speak of you and has not written to you because he cannot – not yet, not till his grief becomes bearable. When it has, I will know it, and then I will intercede for you – and we will all be together again.

Myself? How could anything her baby boy does anger his mother? You can hurt me, but you cannot make me love you the less. Wherever you are, whatever you choose to do, you are always my little boy who bangs his knee and comes running to my lap for comfort. My lap has shrunk, or perhaps you have grown (though I have never believed it), but nonetheless it will always be waiting, when you need it. Little boys never get over needing their mother's laps – do they, darling? I hope not. I hope that you will write and tell me so.

But I must add that, in view of the terribly long time that you have not written, it is probably best (until I let you know otherwise) for you to write to me care of your Aunt Eleanora. She will pass it on to me at once – and without causing any more upset. You understand?

A thousand kisses to my baby,

YOUR MOTHER

I understood, all right – and if Father could not cry, I could. I did.

And at last I got to sleep . . . and was awakened at once by an alert. We bounced out to the bombing range, the whole regiment, and ran through a simulated exercise, without ammo. We were wearing full unarmored kit otherwise, including ear-plug receivers, and we had no more than extended when the word came to freeze.

We held that freeze for at least an hour – and I mean we held it, barely breathing. A mouse tiptoeing past would have sounded noisy. Something did go past and ran right over me, a coyote I think. I never twitched. We got awfully cold holding that freeze, but I didn't care; I knew it was my last.

I didn't even hear reveille the next morning; for the first time in weeks I had to be whacked out of my sack and barely made formation for morning jerks. There was no point in trying to resign before breakfast anyhow, since I had to see Zim as the first step. But he wasn't at breakfast. I did ask Bronski's permission to see the C.C. and he said, 'Sure. Help yourself,' and didn't ask me why.

But you can't see a man who isn't there. We started a route march after breakfast and I still hadn't laid eyes on him. It was an out-and-back, with lunch fetched out to us by copter – an unexpected luxury, since failure to issue field rations before marching usually meant practice starvation except for whatever you had cached . . . and I hadn't; too much on my mind.

Sergeant Zim came out with the rations and he held mail call in the field – which was not an unexpected luxury. I'll say this for the M.I.; they might chop off your food, water, sleep, or anything else, without warning, but they never held up a person's mail a minute longer than circumstances required. That was yours, and they got it to you by the first transportation available and you could read it at your earliest break, even on maneuvers. This hadn't been too important for me, as (aside from a couple of letters from Carl) I hadn't had anything but junk mail until Mother wrote to me.

I didn't even gather around when Zim handed it out; I figured now on not speaking to him until we got in – no point in giving him reason to notice me until we were actually in reach of headquarters. So I was surprised when he called my name and held up a letter. I bounced over and took it.

And was surprised again – it was from Mr. Dubois, my high school instructor in History and Moral Philosophy. I would sooner have expected a letter from Santa Claus.

Then, when I read it, it still seemed like a mistake. I had to check the address and the return address to convince myself that he had written it and had meant it for me.

MY DEAR BOY,

I would have written to you much sooner to express my delight and my pride in learning that you had not only volunteered to serve but also had chosen my own service. But not to express surprise; it is what I expected of you – except, possibly, the additional and very personal bonus that you chose the M.I. This is the sort of consummation, which does not happen too often, that nevertheless makes all of a teacher's efforts worth while. We necessarily sift a great many pebbles, much sand, for each nugget – but the nuggets are the reward.

By now the reason I did not write at once is obvious to you. Many young men, not necessarily through any reprehensible fault, are dropped during recruit training. I have waited (I have kept in touch through my own connections) until you had 'sweated it out' past the hump (how well we all know that hump!) and were certain, barring accidents or illness, of completing your training and your term.

You are now going through the hardest part of your

service – not the hardest physically (though physical hardship will never trouble you again; you now have its measure), but the hardest spiritually . . . the deep, soul-turning readjustments and revaluations necessary to metamorphize a potential citizen into one in being. Or, rather, I should say: you have already gone through the hardest part, despite all the tribulations you still have ahead of you and all the hurdles, each higher than the last, which you still must clear. But it is that 'hump' that counts – and, knowing you, lad, I know that I have waited long enough to be sure that you are past your 'hump' – or you would be home now.

When you reached that spiritual mountaintop you felt something, a new something. Perhaps you haven't words for it (I know I didn't, when I was a boot). So perhaps you will permit an older comrade to lend you the words, since it often helps to have discrete words. Simply this: The noblest fate that a man can endure is to place his own mortal body between his loved home and the war's desolation. The words are not mine, of course, as you will recognize. Basic truths cannot change and once a man of insight expresses one of them it is never necessary, no matter how much the world changes, to reformulate them. This is an immutable, true everywhere, throughout all time, for all men and all nations.

Let me hear from you, please, if you can spare an old man some of your precious sack time to write an occasional letter. And if you should happen to run across any of my former mates, give them my warmest greetings.

Good luck, trooper! You've made me proud.

JEAN V. DUBOIS

Lt.-Col, M.I., rtd.

The signature was as amazing as the letter itself. Old Sour Mouth a short colonel? Why, our regimental commander was only a major. Mr. Dubois had never used any sort of rank around school. We had supposed (if we thought about it at all) that he must have been a corporal or some such who had been let out when he lost his hand and had been fixed up with a soft job teaching a course that didn't have to be passed, or even taught – just audited. Of course we had known that he was a veteran since History and Moral Philosophy must be taught by a citizen. But an M.I.? He didn't look it. Prissy, faintly scornful, a dancing-master type – not one of us apes.

But that was the way he had signed himself.

I spent the whole long hike back to camp thinking about that amazing letter. It didn't sound in the least like anything he had ever said in class. Oh, I don't mean it contradicted anything he had told us in class; it was entirely different in tone. Since when does a short colonel call a recruit private 'comrade'?

When he was plain 'Mr. Dubois' and I was one of the kids who had to take his course he hardly seemed to see me – except once when he got me sore by implying that I had too much money and not enough sense. (So my old man could have bought the school and given it to me for Christmas – is that a crime? It was none of his business.)

He had been droning along about 'value,' comparing the Marxist theory with the orthodox 'use' theory, Mr. Dubois had said, 'Of course, the Marxian definition of value is ridiculous. All the work one cares to add will not turn a mud pie into an apple tart; it remains a mud pie, value zero. By corollary, unskillful work can easily subtract value; an untalented cook can turn wholesome dough and fresh green apples, valuable already, into an inedible mess, value zero. Conversely, a great chef can fashion of those same materials a confection of greater value than a commonplace apple tart, with no more effort than an ordinary cook uses to prepare an ordinary sweet.

'These kitchen illustrations demolish the Marxian theory of value – the fallacy from which the entire magnificent fraud of communism derives – and to illustrate the truth of the common-sense definition as measured in terms of use.'

Dubois had waved his stump at us. 'Nevertheless – wake up, back there! – nevertheless this disheveled old mystic of *Das Kapital*, turgid, tortured, confused, and neurotic, unscientific, illogical, this pompous fraud Karl Marx, *nevertheless* had a glimmering of a very important truth. If he had possessed an analytical mind, he might have formulated the first adequate definition of value . . . and this planet might have been saved endless grief.

'Or might not,' he added. 'You!'

I had sat up with a jerk.

'If you can't listen, perhaps you can tell the class whether "value" is relative, or an absolute?'

I had been listening; I just didn't see any reason not to listen with eyes closed and spine relaxed. But his question caught me out; I hadn't read that day's assignment. 'An absolute,' I answered, guessing.

'Wrong,' he said coldly. '"Value" has no meaning other than in relation to living beings. The value of a thing is always relative to a particular person, is completely personal and different in quantity for each living human – "market value" is a fiction, merely a rough guess at the average personal values, all of which must be quantitively different or trade would be impossible.' (I had wondered what Father would have said if he had heard 'market value' called a 'fiction' – snort in disgust, probably.)

'This very personal relationship, "value," has two factors for a human being: first, what he can do with a thing, its *use* to him . . . and second, what he must do to get it, its *cost* to him. There is an old song which asserts that "the best things in life are free." Not true! Utterly false! This was the tragic fallacy which brought on the decadence and collapse of the democracies of the twentieth century; those noble experiments failed because the people had been led to believe that they could simply vote for whatever they wanted . . . and get it, without toil, without sweat, without tears.

'Nothing of value is free. Even the breath of life is purchased at birth only through gasping effort and pain.' He had been still looking at me and added, 'If you boys and girls had to sweat for your toys the way a newly born baby has to struggle to live you would be happier . . . and much richer. As it is, with some of you, I pity the poverty of your wealth. You! I've just awarded you the prize for the hundred-meter dash. Does it make you happy?'

'Uh, I suppose it would.'

'No dodging, please. You have the prize – here, I'll write it out: "Grand prize for the championship, one hundred-meter sprint."' He had actually come back to my seat and pinned it on my chest. 'There! Are you happy? You value it – or don't you?'

I was sore. First that dirty crack about rich kids – a typical sneer of those who haven't got it – and now this farce. I ripped it off and chucked it at him.

Mr. Dubois had looked surprised. 'It doesn't make you happy?'

'You know darn well I placed fourth!'

'*Exactly!* The prize for first place is worthless to you . . . because you haven't earned it. But you enjoy a modest satisfaction in placing fourth; you earned it. I trust that some of the somnambulists here understood this little morality play. I fancy that the poet who wrote that song meant to imply that the best things in life must be purchased other than with money – which is *true* – just as the literal meaning of his words is false. The best things in life are beyond money; their price is agony and sweat and devotion . . . and the price demanded for the most precious of all things in life is life itself – ultimate cost for perfect value.'

I mulled over things I had heard Mr. Dubois – *Colonel* Dubois – say, as well as his extraordinary letter, while we went swinging back toward camp. Then I stopped thinking because the band dropped back near our position in column and we sang for a while, a French group – '*Marseillaise*,' of course, and '*Madelon*' and 'Sons of Toil and Danger,' and then '*Légion Étrangère*' and 'Mademoiselle from Armentières.'

It's nice to have the band play; it picks you right up when your tail is dragging the prairie. We hadn't had anything but canned music at first and that only for parade and calls. But the powers-that-be had found out early who could play and who couldn't; instruments were provided and a regimental band was organized, all our own – even the director and the drum major were boots.

It didn't mean they got out of anything. Oh, no! It just meant they were allowed and encouraged to do it on their own time, practicing evenings and Sundays and such – and that they got to strut and countermarch and show off at parade instead of being in ranks with their platoons. A lot of things that we did were run that way. Our chaplain, for example, was a boot. He was older than most of us and had been ordained in some obscure little sect I had never heard of. But he put a lot of passion into his preaching whether his theology was orthodox or not (don't ask me) and he was certainly in a position to understand the problems of a recruit. And the singing was fun. Besides, there was nowhere else to go on Sunday morning between morning police and lunch.

The band suffered a lot of attrition but somehow they always kept it going. The camp owned four sets of pipes and some Scottish uniforms, donated by Lochiel of Cameron whose son had been killed there in training – and one of us boots turned out to be a piper; he had learned it in the Scottish Boy Scouts. Pretty soon we had four pipers, maybe not good but loud. Pipes seem very odd when you first hear them, and a tyro practicing can set your teeth on edge – it sounds and looks as if he had a cat under his arm, its tail in his mouth, and biting it.

But they grow on you. The first time our pipers kicked their heels out in front of the band, skirling away at 'Alamein Dead,' my hair stood up so straight it lifted my cap. It gets you – makes tears.

We couldn't take a parade band out on route march, of course, because no special allowances were made for the band. Tubas and bass drums had to stay behind because a boy in the band had to carry full kit, same as everybody, and could only manage an instrument small enough to add to his load. But the M.I. has band instruments which I don't believe anybody else has, such as a little box hardly bigger than a harmonica, an electronic gadget which does an amazing job of faking a big horn and is played the same way. Come band call when you are headed for the horizon, each bandsman sheds his kit without stopping, his squadmates split it up, and he trots to the column position of the color company and starts blasting.

It helps.

The band drifted aft, almost out of earshot, and we stopped singing because your own singing drowns out the beat when it's too far away.

I suddenly realized I felt good.

I tried to think why I did. Because we would be in after a couple of hours and could resign?

No. When I had decided to resign, it had indeed given me a measure of peace, quieted down my awful jitters and let me go to sleep. But this was something else – and no reason for it, that I could see.

Then I knew. *I had passed my hump!*

I was over the 'hump' that Colonel Dubois had written about. I actually walked over it and started down, swinging easily. The prairie through there was as flat as a griddle cake, but just the same I had been plodding wearily uphill all the way out and about halfway back. Then, at some point – I think it was while we were singing – I had passed the hump and it was all downhill. My kit felt lighter and I was no longer worried.

When we got in, I didn't speak to Sergeant Zim; I no longer needed to. Instead he spoke to me, motioned me to him as we fell out.

'Yes, sir?'

'This is a personal question . . . so don't answer it unless you feel like it.' He stopped, and I wondered if he suspected that I had overheard his chewing-out, and shivered.

'At mail call today,' he said, 'you got a letter. I noticed – purely by accident, none of my business – the name on the return address. It's a fairly common name, some places, but – this is the personal question you need not answer – by any chance does the person who wrote that letter have his left hand off at the wrist?'

I guess my chin dropped. 'How did you know? Sir?'

'I was nearby when it happened. It *is* Colonel Dubois? Right?'

'Yes, sir.' I added, 'He was my high school instructor in History and Moral Philosophy.'

I think that was the only time I ever impressed Sergeant Zim, even faintly. His eyebrows went up an eighth of an inch and his eyes widened slightly. 'So? You were extraordinarily fortunate.' He added, 'When you answer his letter – if you don't mind – you might say that Ship's Sergeant Zim sends his respects.'

'Yes, sir. Oh . . . I think maybe he sent you a message, sir.'

'What?'

'Uh, I'm not certain.' I took out the letter, read just: "' – if you should happen to run across any of my former mates, give them my warmest greetings." Is that for you, sir?'

Zim pondered it, his eyes looking through me, somewhere else. 'Eh? Yes, it is. For me among others. Thanks very much.' Then suddenly it was over and he said briskly, 'Nine minutes to parade. And you still have to shower and change. On the bounce, soldier.'

Chapter 7

The young recruit is silly – 'e
thinks o' suicide.
'E's lost 'is gutter-devil; 'e 'asn't
got 'is pride;
But day by day they kicks 'im,
which 'elps 'im on a bit,
Till 'e finds 'isself one mornin'
with a full an' proper kit.
Gettin' clear o' dirtiness, gettin'
done with mess,
Gettin' shut o' doin' things
rather-more-or-less.

– Rudyard Kipling

I'm not going to talk much more about my boot training. Mostly it was simply work, but I was squared away – enough said.

But I do want to mention a little about powered suits, partly because I was fascinated by them and also because that was what led me into trouble. No complaints – I rated what I got.

An M.I. lives by his suit the way a K-9 man lives by and with and on his doggie partner. Powered armor is one-half the reason we call ourselves 'mobile infantry' instead of just 'infantry.' (The other half are the spaceships that drop us and the capsules we drop in.) Our suits give us better eyes, better ears, stronger backs (to carry heavier weapons and more ammo), better legs, more intelligence ('intelligence' in the military meaning; a man in a suit can be just as stupid as anybody else – only he had better not be), more firepower, greater endurance, less vulnerability.

A suit isn't a space suit – although it can serve as one. It is not primarily armor – although the Knights of the Round Table were not armored as well as we are. It isn't a tank – but a single M.I. private could take on a squadron of those things and knock them off unassisted if anybody was silly enough to put tanks against M.I. A suit is not a ship but it can fly, a little – on the other hand neither spaceships nor atmosphere craft can fight against a man in a suit except by saturation bombing of the area he is in (like burning down a house to get one flea!). Contrariwise we can do many things that no ship – air, submersible, or space – can do.

There are a dozen different ways of delivering destruction in impersonal wholesale, via ships and missiles of one sort or another, catastrophes so widespread, so unelective, that the war is over because that nation or planet has ceased to exist. What we do is entirely different. We make war as personal as a punch in the nose. We can be selective, applying precisely the required amount of pressure at the specified point at a designated time – we've never been told to go down and kill or capture all left-handed redheads in a particular area, but if they tell us to, we can. We will.

We are the boys who go to a particular place, at H-hour, occupy a designated terrain, stand on it, dig the enemy out of their holes, force them then and there to surrender or die. We're the bloody infantry, the doughboy, the duckfoot, the foot soldier who goes where the enemy is and takes him on in person. We've been doing it, with changes in weapons but very little change in our trade, at least since the time five thousand years ago when the foot sloggers of Sargon the Great forced the Sumerians to cry 'Uncle!'

Maybe they'll be able to do without us someday. Maybe

some mad genius with myopia, a bulging forehead, and a cybernetic mind will devise a weapon that can go down a hole, pick out the opposition, and force it to surrender or die – without killing that gang of your own people they've got imprisoned down there. I wouldn't know; I'm not a genius I'm an M.I. In the meantime, until they build a machine to replace us, my mates can handle the job – and I might be some help on it, too.

Maybe someday they'll get everything nice and tidy and we'll have that thing we sing about, when 'we ain't a-gonna study war no more.' Maybe. Maybe the same day the leopard will take off his spots and get a job as a Jersey cow, too. But again, I wouldn't know; I am not a professor of cosmo-politics; I'm an M.I. When the government sends me, I go. In between, I catch a lot of sack time.

But, while they have not yet built a machine to replace us, they've surely thought up some honeys to help us. The suit, in particular.

No need to describe what it looks like, since it has been pictured so often. Suited up, you look like a big steel gorilla, armed with gorilla-sized weapons. (This may be why a sergeant generally opens his remarks with 'You apes—' However, it seems more likely that Caesar's sergeants used the same honorific.)

But the suits are considerably stronger than a gorilla. If an M.I. in a suit swapped hugs with a gorilla, the gorilla would be dead, crushed; the M.I. and the suit wouldn't be mussed.

The 'muscles,' the pseudo-muscalature, get all the publicity but it's the control of all that power which merits it. The real genius in the design is that you *don't* have to control the suit; you just wear it, like your clothes, like skin. Any sort of ship you have to learn to pilot; it takes a long time, a new full set of reflexes, a different and artificial way of thinking. Even riding a bicycle demands an acquired skill, very different from walking, whereas a spaceship – oh, brother! I won't live that long. Spaceships are for acrobats who are also mathematicians.

But a suit you just wear.

Two thousand pounds of it, maybe, in full kit – yet the very first time you are fitted into one you can immediately walk, run, jump, lie down, pick up an egg without breaking it (that takes a trifle of practice, but anything improves with practice), dance a jig (if you can dance a jig, that is, *without* a suit) – and jump right over the house next door and come down to a feather landing.

The secret lies in negative feedback and amplification.

Don't ask me to sketch the circuitry of a suit; I can't. But I understand that some very good concert violinists can't build a violin, either. I can do field maintenance and field repairs and check off the three hundred and forty-seven items from 'cold' to ready to wear, and that's all a dumb M.I. is expected to do. But if my suit gets really sick, I call the doctor – a doctor of science (electromechanical engineering) who is a staff Naval officer, usually a lieutenant (read 'captain' for our ranks), and is part of the ship's company of the troop transport – or who is reluctantly assigned to a regimental headquarters at Camp Currie, a fate-worse-than-death to a Navy man.

But if you really are interested in the prints and stereos and schematics of a suit's physiology, you can find most of it, the unclassified part, in any fairly large public library. For the small amount that is classified you must look up a reliable enemy agent – 'reliable' I say, because spies are a tricky lot; he's likely to sell you the parts you could get free from the public library.

But here is how it works, minus the diagrams. The inside of the suit is a mass of pressure receptors, hundreds of them. You push with the heel of your hand; the suit feels it, amplifies it, pushes with you to take the pressure off the receptors that gave the order to push. That's confusing, but negative feedback is always a confusing idea the first time, even though your body has been doing it ever since you quit kicking helplessly as a baby. Young children are still learning it; that's why they are clumsy. Adolescents and adults do it without knowing they ever learned it – and a man with Parkinson's disease has damaged his circuits for it.

The suit has feedback which causes it to match *any* motion you make, exactly – but with great force.

Controlled force . . . force controlled without your having to think about it. You jump, that heavy suit jumps, but higher than you can jump in your skin. Jump really hard and the suit's jets cut in, amplifying what the suit's leg 'muscles' did, giving you a three-jet shove, the axis of pressure of which passes through your center of mass. So you jump over that house next door. Which makes you come down as fast as you went up . . . which the suit notes through your proximity & closing gear (a sort of simple-minded radar resembling a proximity fuse) and therefore cuts in the jets again just the right amount to cushion your landing without your having to think about it.

And *that* is the beauty of a powered suit: you don't have to think about it. You don't have to drive it, fly it, conn it, operate it; you just wear it and it takes its orders directly from your muscles and does for you what your muscles are trying to do. This leaves you with your whole mind free to handle your weapons and notice what is going on around you . . . which is *supremely* important to an infantryman who wants to die in bed. If you load a mud foot down with a lot of gadgets that he has to watch, somebody a lot more simply equipped – say with a stone ax – will sneak up and bash his head in while he is trying to read a vernier.

Your 'eyes' and your 'ears' are rigged to help you without

cluttering up your attention, too. Say you have three audio circuits, common in a marauder suit. The frequency control to maintain tactical security is very complex, at least two frequencies for each circuit both of which are necessary for any signal at all and each of which wobbles under the control of a cesium clock timed to a micromicrosecond with the other end – but all this is no problem of yours. You want circuit A to your squad leader, you bite down once – for circuit B, bite down twice – and so on. The mike is taped to your throat, the plugs are in your ears and can't be jarred out; just talk. Besides that, outside mikes on each side of your helmet give you binaural hearing for your immediate surroundings just as if your head were bare – or you can suppress any noisy neighbors and not miss what your platoon leader is saying simply by turning your head.

Since your head is the one part of your body not involved in the pressure receptors controlling the suit's muscles, you use your head – your jaw muscles, your chin, your neck – to switch things for you and thereby leave your hands free to fight. A chin plate handles all visual displays the way the jaw switch handles the audios. All displays are thrown on a mirror in front of your forehead from where the work is actually going on above and back of your head. All this helmet gear makes you look like a hydrocephalic gorilla but, with luck, the enemy won't live long enough to be offended by your appearance, and it is a very convenient arrangement; you can flip through your several types of radar displays quicker than you can change channels to avoid a commercial – catch a range & bearing, locate your boss, check your flank men, whatever.

If you toss your head like a horse bothered by a fly, your infrared snoopers go up on your forehead – toss it again, they come down. If you let go of your rocket launcher, the suit snaps it back until you need it again. No point in discussing water nipples, air supply, gyros, etc. – the point to *all* the arrangements is the same: to leave you free to follow your trade, slaughter.

Of course these things do require practice and you do practice until picking the right circuit is as automatic as brushing your teeth, and so on. But simply wearing the suit, moving in it, requires almost no practice. You practice jumping because, while you do it with a completely natural motion, you jump higher, faster, farther, and stay up longer. The last alone calls for a new orientation; those seconds in the air can be used – seconds are jewels beyond price in combat. While off the ground in a jump, you can get a range & bearing, pick a target, talk & receive, fire a weapon, reload, decide to jump again without landing and override your automatics to cut in the jets again. You can do *all* of these things on one bounce, with practice.

But, in general, powered armor doesn't require practice; it simply does it for you, just the way you were doing it, only better. All but one thing – you *can't* scratch where it itches. If I ever find a suit that will let me scratch between my shoulder blades, I'll marry it.

There are three main types of M.I. armor: marauder, command, and scout. Scout suits are very fast and very long-range, but lightly armed. Command suits are heavy on go juice and jump juice, are fast and can jump high; they have three times as much comm & radar gear as other suits, and a dead-reckoning tracker, inertial. Marauders are for those guys in ranks with the sleepy look – the executioners.

As I may have said, I fell in love with powered armor, even though my first crack at it gave me a strained shoulder. Any day thereafter that my section was allowed to practice in suits was a big day for me. The day I goofed I had simulated sergeant's chevrons as a simulated section leader and was armed with simulated A-bomb rockets to use in simulated darkness against a simulated enemy. That was the trouble; everything was simulated – but you are required to behave as if it is all real.

We were retreating – 'advancing toward the rear,' I mean – and one of the instructors cut the power on one of my men, by radio control, making him a helpless casualty. Per M.I. doctrine, I ordered the pickup, felt rather cocky that I had managed to get the order out before my number two cut out to do it anyhow, turned to do the next thing I had to do, which was to lay down a simulated atomic ruckus to discourage the simulated enemy overtaking us.

Our flank was swinging; I was supposed to fire it sort of diagonally but with the required spacing to protect my own men from blast while still putting it in close enough to trouble the bandits. On the bounce, of course. The movement over the terrain and the problem itself had been discussed ahead of time; we were still green – the only variations supposed to be left in were casualties.

Doctrine required me to locate *exactly*, by radar beacon, my own men who could be affected by the blast. But this all had to be done fast and I wasn't too sharp at reading those little radar displays anyhow. I cheated just a touch – flipped my snoopers up and looked, bare eyes in broad daylight. I left plenty of room. Shucks, I could *see* the only man affected, half a mile away, and all I had was just a little bitty H.E. rocket, intended to make a lot of smoke and not much else. So I picked a spot by eye, took the rocket launcher and let fly.

Then I bounced away, feeling smug – no seconds lost.

And had my power cut in the air. This doesn't hurt you; it's a delayed action, executed by your landing. I grounded and there I stuck, squatting, held upright by gyros but unable to move. You do not repeat *not* move when surrounded by a ton of metal with your power dead.

Instead I cussed to myself – I hadn't thought that they

would make me a casualty when I was supposed to be leading the problem. Shucks and other comments.

I should have known that Sergeant Zim would be monitoring the section leader.

He bounced over to me, spoke to me privately on the face-to-face. He suggested that I might be able to get a job sweeping floors since I was too stupid, clumsy, and careless to handle dirty dishes. He discussed my past and probable future and several other things that I did not want to hear about. He ended by saying tonelessly, 'How would you like to have Colonel Dubois see what you've done?'

Then he left me. I waited there, crouched over, for two hours until the drill was over. The suit, which had been feather-light, real seven-league boots, felt like an Iron Maiden. At last he returned for me, restored power, and we bounced together at top speed to BHQ.

Captain Frankel said less but it cut more.

Then he paused and added in that flat voice officers use when quoting regulations: 'You may demand trial by court-martial if such be your choice. How say you?'

I gulped and said, 'No, sir!' Until that moment I hadn't fully realized just how *much* trouble I was in.

Captain Frankel seemed to relax slightly. 'Then we'll see what the Regimental Commander has to say. Sergeant, escort the prisoner.' We walked rapidly over to RHQ and for the first time I met the Regimental Commander face to face – and by then I was sure I was going to catch a court no matter what. But I remembered sharply how Ted Hendrick had talked himself into one; I said nothing.

Major Malloy said a total of five words to me. After hearing Sergeant Zim, he said three of them: 'Is that correct?'

I said, 'Yes, sir,' which ended my part of it.

Major Malloy said, to Captain Frankel: 'Is there any possibility of salvaging this man?'

Captain Frankel said, 'I believe so, sir.'

Major Malloy said, 'Then we'll try administrative punishment,' turned to me and said:

'Five lashes.'

Well, they certainly didn't keep me dangling. Fifteen minutes later the doctor had completed checking my heart and the Sergeant of the Guard was outfitting me with that special shirt which comes off without having to be pulled over the hands – zippered from the neck down the arms. Assembly for parade had just sounded. I was feeling detached, unreal . . . which I have learned is one way of being scared right out of your senses. The nightmare hallucination –

Zim came into the guard tent just as the call ended. He glanced at the Sergeant of the Guard – Corporal Jones – and Jones went out. Zim stepped up to me, slipped something into my hand. 'Bite on that,' he said quietly. 'It helps. I know.'

It was a rubber mouthpiece such as we used to avoid broken teeth in hand-to-hand combat drill. Zim left. I put it in my mouth. Then they handcuffed me and marched me out.

The order read: '—in simulated combat, gross negligence which would in action have caused the death of a teammate.' Then they peeled off my shirt and strung me up.

Now here is a very odd thing: A flogging isn't as hard to *take* as it is to *watch*. I don't mean it's a picnic. It hurts worse than anything else I've had happen to me, and the waits between strokes are worse than the strokes themselves. But the mouthpiece did help and the only yelp I let out never got past it.

Here's the second odd thing: Nobody mentioned it to me, not even other boots. So far as I could see, Zim and the instructors treated me exactly the same afterwards as they had before. From the instant the doctor painted the marks and told me to go back to duty it was all done with, completely. I even managed to eat a little at dinner that night and pretend to take part in the jawing at the table.

Another thing about administrative punishment: There is no permanent black mark. Those records are destroyed at the end of boot training and you start clean. The only record is one where it counts most.

You *don't* forget it.

Chapter 8

Train up a child in the way he should go; and when he is old he will not depart from it.

– Proverbs XXII: 6

There were other floggings but darn few. Hendrick was the only man in our regiment to be flogged by sentence of court-martial; the others were administrative punishment, like mine, and for lashes it was necessary to go all the way to the Regimental Commander – which a subordinate commander finds distasteful, to put it faintly. Even then, Major Malloy was much more likely to kick the man out, 'Undesirable Discharge,' than to have the whipping post erected. In a way, an administrative flogging is the mildest sort of a compliment; it means that your superiors think that there is a faint possibility that you just might have the character eventually to make a soldier and a citizen, unlikely as it seems at the moment.

I was the only one to get the maximum administrative punishment; none of the others got more than three lashes. Nobody else came as close as I did to putting on civilian clothes but still squeaked by. This is a social distinction of sorts. I don't recommend it.

But we had another case, much worse than mine or Ted Hendrick's – a really sick-making one. Once they erected gallows.

Now, look, get this straight. The case didn't really have anything to do with the Army. The crime didn't take place at

Camp Currie and the placement officer who accepted this boy for M.I. should turn in his suit.

He deserted, only two days after we arrived at Currie. Ridiculous, of course, but nothing about the case made sense – why didn't he resign? Desertion, naturally, is one of the 'thirty-one crash landings' but the Army doesn't invoke the death penalty for it unless there are special circumstances, such as 'in the face of the enemy' or something else that turns it from a highly informal way of resigning into something that can't be ignored.

The Army makes no effort to find deserters and bring them back. This makes the hardest kind of sense. We're all volunteers; we're M.I. because we want to be, we're proud to be M.I. and the M.I. is proud of us. If a man doesn't feel that way about it, from his callused feet to his hairy ears, I don't want him on my flank when trouble starts. If I buy a piece of it, I want men around me who will pick me up because they're M.I. and I'm M.I. and my skin means as much to them as their own. I don't want any ersatz soldiers, dragging their tails and ducking out when the party gets rough. It's a whole lot safer to have a blank file on your flank than to have an alleged soldier who is nursing the 'conscript' syndrome. So if they run, let 'em run; it's a waste of time and money to fetch them back.

Of course most of them do come back, though it may take them years – in which case the Army tiredly lets them have their fifty lashes instead of hanging them, and turns them loose. I suppose it must wear on a man's nerves to be a fugitive when everybody else is either a citizen or a legal resident, even when the police aren't trying to find him. 'The wicked flee when no man pursueth.' The temptation to turn yourself in, take your lumps, and breathe easily again must get to be overpowering.

But this boy didn't turn himself in. He was gone four

months and I doubt if his own company remembered him, since he had been with them only a couple of days; he was probably just a name without a face, the 'Dillinger, N. L.' who had to be reported, day after day, as absent without leave on the morning muster.

Then he killed a baby girl.

He was tried and convicted by a local tribunal but identity check showed that he was an undischarged soldier; the Department had to be notified and our commanding general at once intervened. He was returned to us, since military law and jurisdiction take precedence over civil code.

Why did the general bother? Why didn't he let the local sheriff do the job?

In order to 'teach us a lesson'?

Not at all. I'm quite sure that our general did not think that any of his boys needed to be nauseated in order not to kill any baby girls. By now I believe that he would have spared us the sight – had it been possible.

We did learn a lesson, though nobody mentioned it at the time and it is one that takes a long time to sink in until it becomes second nature.

The M.I. take care of their own – no matter what.

Dillinger belonged to us, he was still on our rolls. Even though we didn't want him, even though we should never have had him, even though we would have been happy to disclaim him, he was a member of our regiment. We couldn't brush him off and let a sheriff a thousand miles away handle it. If it had to be done, a man – a real man – shoots his own dog himself; he doesn't hire a proxy who may bungle it.

The regimental records said that Dillinger was ours, so taking care of him was our duty.

That evening we marched to the parade ground at slow march, sixty beats to the minute (hard to keep step, when you're used to a hundred and forty), while the band played

'Dirge for the Unmourned.' Then Dillinger was marched out, dressed in M.I. full dress just as we were, and the band played 'Danny Deever' while they stripped off every trace of insignia, even buttons and cap, leaving him in a maroon and light blue suit that was no longer a uniform. The drums held a sustained roll and it was all over.

We passed in review and on home at a fast trot. I don't think anybody fainted and I don't think anybody quite got sick, even though most of us didn't eat much dinner that night and I've never heard the mess tent so quiet. But, grisly as it was (it was the first time I had seen death, first time for most of us), it was not the shock that Ted Hendrick's flogging was – I mean, you couldn't put yourself in Dillinger's place; you didn't have any feeling of: 'It could have been *me*.' Not counting the technical matter of desertion, Dillinger had committed at least four capital crimes; if his victim had lived, he still would have danced Danny Deever for any one of the other other three – kidnapping, demand of ransom, criminal neglect, etc.

I had no sympathy for him and still haven't. That old saw about 'To understand all is to forgive all' is a lot of tripe. Some things, the more you understand the more you loathe them. My sympathy is reserved for Barbara Anne Enthwaite whom I had never seen, and for her parents, who would never again see their little girl.

As the band put away their instruments that night we started thirty days of mourning for Barbara and of disgrace for us, with our colors draped in black, no music at parade, no singing on route march. Only once did I hear anybody complain and another boot promptly asked him how he would like a full set of lumps? Certainly it hadn't been our fault – but our business was to guard little girls, not kill them. Our regiment had been dishonored; we had to clean it. We were disgraced and we *felt* disgraced.

That night I tried to figure out how such things could be kept from happening. Of course, they hardly ever do nowadays – but even once is 'way too many. I never did reach an answer that satisfied me. This Dillinger – he looked like anybody else, and his behavior and record couldn't have been too odd or he would never have reached Camp Currie in the first place. I suppose he was one of those pathological personalities you read about – no way to spot them.

Well, if there was no way to keep it from happening once, there was only one sure way to keep it from happening twice. Which we had used.

If Dillinger had understood what he was doing (which seemed incredible) then he got what was coming to him . . . except that it seemed a shame that he hadn't suffered as much as had little Barbara Anne – he practically hadn't suffered at all.

But suppose, as seemed more likely, that he was so crazy that he had never been aware that he was doing anything wrong? What then?

Well, we shoot mad dogs, don't we?

Yes, but being crazy that way is a sickness –

I couldn't see but two possibilities. Either he couldn't be made well – in which case he was better dead for his own sake and for the safety of others – or he could be treated and made sane. In which case (it seemed to me) if he ever became sane enough for civilized society . . . and thought over what he had done while he was 'sick' – what could be left for him but suicide? How could he *live* with himself?

And suppose he escaped *before* he was cured and did the same thing again? And maybe *again*? How do you explain *that* to bereaved parents? In view of his record?

I couldn't see but one answer.

I found myself mulling over a discussion in our class in History and Moral Philosophy. Mr. Dubois was talking about the disorders that preceded the breakup of the North American republic, back in the XXth century. According to him, there was a time just before they went down the drain when such crimes as Dillinger's were as common as dogfights. The Terror had not been just in North America – Russia and the British Isles had it, too, as well as other places. But it reached its peak in North America shortly before things went to pieces.

'Law-abiding people,' Dubois had told us, 'hardly dared go into a public park at night. To do so was to risk attack by wolf packs of children, armed with chains, knives, home-made guns, bludgeons . . . to be hurt at least, robbed most certainly, injured for life probably – or even killed. This went on for years, right up to the war between the Russo-Anglo-American Alliance and the Chinese Hegemony. Murder, drug addiction, larceny, assault, and vandalism were commonplace. Nor were parks the only places – these things happened also on the streets in daylight, on school grounds, even inside school buildings. But parks were so notoriously unsafe that honest people stayed clear of them after dark.'

I had tried to imagine such things happening in our schools. I simply couldn't. Nor in our parks. A park was a place for fun, not for getting hurt. As for getting killed in one – 'Mr. Dubois, didn't they have police? Or courts?'

'They had many more police than we have. And more courts. All overworked.'

'I guess I don't get it.' If a boy in our city had done anything half that bad . . . well, he and his father would have been flogged side by side. But such things just didn't happen.

Mr Dubois then demanded of me, 'Define a "juvenile delinquent."'

'Uh, one of those kids – the ones who used to beat up people.'

'Wrong.'

'Huh? But the book said—'

'My apologies. Your textbook does so state. But calling a tail a leg does not make the name fit. "Juvenile delinquent" is a contradiction in terms, one which gives a clue to their problem and their failure to solve it. Have you ever raised a puppy?'

'Yes, sir.'

'Did you housebreak him?'

'Err . . . yes, sir. Eventually.' It was my slowness in this that caused my mother to rule that dogs must stay out of the house.

'Ah, yes. When your puppy made mistakes, were you angry?'

'What? Why, he didn't know any better; he was just a puppy.'

'What did you do?'

'Why, I scolded him and rubbed his nose in it and paddled him.'

'Surely he could not understand your words?'

'No, but he could tell I was sore at him!'

'But you just said that you were not angry.'

Mr. Dubois had an infuriating way of getting a person mixed up. 'No, but I had to make him *think* I was. He had to learn, didn't he?'

'Conceded. But, having made it clear to him that you disapproved, how could you be so cruel as to spank him as well? You said the poor beastie didn't know that he was doing wrong. Yet you inflicted pain. Justify yourself! Or are you a sadist?'

I didn't then know what a sadist was – but I knew pups. 'Mr. Dubois, you *have* to! You scold him so that he knows he's in trouble, you rub his nose in it so that he will know what trouble you mean, you paddle him so that he darn well won't do it again – and you have to do it right away! It doesn't do a bit of good to punish him later; you'll just confuse him. Even so, he won't learn from one lesson, so you watch and catch him again and paddle him still harder. Pretty soon he learns. But it's a waste of breath just to scold him.' Then I added, 'I guess you've never raised pups.'

'Many. I'm raising a dachshund now – by your methods. Let's get back to those juvenile criminals. The most vicious averaged somewhat younger than you here in this class . . . and they often started their lawless careers much younger. Let us never forget that puppy. These children were often caught; police arrested batches every day. Were they scolded? Yes, often scathingly. Were their noses rubbed in it? Rarely. News organs and officials usually kept their names secret – in many places the law so required for criminals under eighteen. Were they spanked? Indeed not! Many had never been spanked even as small children; there was a widespread belief that spanking, or any punishment involving pain, did a child permanent psychic damage.'

(I had reflected that my father must never have heard of that theory.)

'Corporal punishment in schools was forbidden by law,' he had gone on. 'Flogging was lawful as sentence of court only in one small province, Delaware, and there only for a few crimes and was rarely invoked; it was regarded as "cruel and unusual punishment."' Dubois had mused aloud, 'I do not understand objections to "cruel and unusual" punishment. While a judge should be benevolent in purpose, his awards should cause the criminal to suffer, else there is no punishment – and pain is the basic mechanism built into us by millions of years of evolution which safeguards us by warning when something threatens our survival. Why should society refuse to use such a highly perfected survival mechanism? However, that period was loaded with pre-scientific pseudo-psychological nonsense.

'As for "unusual," punishment *must* be unusual or it serves no purpose.' He then pointed his stump at another boy. 'What would happen if a puppy were spanked every hour?'

'Uh . . . probably drive him crazy!'

'Probably. It certainly will not teach him anything. How long has it been since the principal of this school last had to switch a pupil?'

'Uh, I'm not sure. About two years. The kid that swiped—'

'Never mind. Long enough. It means that such punishment is so unusual as to be significant, to deter, to instruct. Back to these young crimnals – They probably were not spanked as babies; they certainly were not flogged for their crimes. The usual sequence was: for a first offence, a warning – a scolding, often without trial. After several offenses a sentence of confinement but with sentence suspended and the youngster placed on probation. A boy might be arrested many times and convicted several times before he was punished – and then it would be merely confinement, with others like him from whom he learned still more criminal habits. If he kept out of major trouble while confined, he could usually evade most of even that mild punishment, be given probation – "paroled" in the jargon of the times.

'This incredible sequence could go on for years while his crimes increased in frequency and viciousness, with no punishment whatever save rare dull-but-comfortable confinements. Then suddenly, usually by law on his eighteenth birthday, this so-called "juvenile delinquent" becomes an adult criminal – and sometimes wound up in only weeks or months in a death cell awaiting execution for murder. *You*—'

He had singled me out again. 'Suppose you merely scolded your puppy, never punished him, let him go on making messes in the house . . . and occasionally locked him up in an outbuilding but soon let him back into the house with a warning not to do it again. Then one day you notice that he is now a grown dog and *still* not housebroken – whereupon you whip out a gun and shoot him dead. Comment, please?'

'Why . . . that's the craziest way to raise a dog I ever heard of!'

'I agree. Or a child. Whose fault would it be?'

'Uh . . . why, mine, I guess.'

'Again I agree. But I'm not guessing.'

'Mr. Dubois,' a girl blurted out, 'but *why*? Why didn't they spank little kids when they needed it and use a good dose of the strap on any older ones who deserved it – the sort of lesson they wouldn't forget! I mean ones who did things really *bad*. Why not?'

'I don't know,' he had answered grimly, 'except that the time-tested method of instilling social virtue and respect for law in the minds of the young did not appeal to a pre-scientific pseudo-professional class who called themselves "social workers" or sometimes "child psychologists." It was too simple for them, apparently, since anybody could do it, using only the patience and firmness needed in training a puppy. I have sometimes wondered if they cherished a vested interest in disorder – but that is unlikely; adults almost always act from conscious "highest motives" no matter what their behavior.'

'But – good heavens!' the girl answered. 'I didn't like being spanked any more than any kid does, but when I needed it, my mama delivered. The only time I ever got a switching in school I got another one when I got home – and that was years and years ago. I don't ever expect to be hauled up in front of a judge and sentenced to a flogging; you behave yourself and such things don't happen. I don't see anything wrong with our system; it's a lot better than not being able to walk outdoors for fear of your life – why, that's *horrible!*'

'I agree. Young lady, the tragic wrongness of what those well-meaning people did, contrasted with what they *thought* they were doing, goes very deep. They had no scientific theory of morals. They did have a theory of morals and they tried to live by it (I should not have sneered at their motives), but their theory was *wrong* – half of it fuzzy-headed wishful thinking, half of it rationalized charlatanry. The more earnest they were, the farther it led them astray. You see, they assumed that Man has a moral instinct.'

'Sir? But I thought – but he does! *I* have.'

'No, my dear, you have a cultivated conscience, a most carefully trained one. Man has *no moral instinct.* He is not born with a moral sense. You were not born with it, I was not – and a puppy has none. We *acquire* moral sense, when we do, through training, experience, and hard sweat of the mind. These unfortunate juvenile criminals were born with none, even as you and I, and they had no chance to acquire any; their experiences did not permit it. What *is* "moral sense'? It is an elaboration of the instinct to survive. The instinct to survive is human nature itself, and every aspect of our personalities derives from it. Anything that conflicts with the survival instinct acts sooner or later to eliminate the individual and thereby fails to shows up in future generations. This truth is mathematically demonstrable, everywhere verifiable; it is the single eternal imperative controlling everything we do.

'But the instinct to survive,' he had gone on, 'can be cultivated into motivations more subtle and much more complex than the blind, brute urge of the individual to stay alive. Young lady, what you called your "moral instinct" was the instilling in you by your elders of the truth that survival can have stronger imperatives than that of your own personal survival. Survival of your family, for example. Of your children, when you have them. Of your nation, if you struggle that high up the scale. And so on up. A scientifically verifiable theory of morals must be rooted in the individual's instinct to survive – *and nowhere else!* – and must correctly describe the hierarchy of survival, note the motivations at each level, and resolve all conflicts.

'We have such a theory now; we can solve any moral problem, on any level. Self-interest, love of family, duty to country, responsibility toward the human race – we are even developing an exact ethic for extra-human relations. But all moral problems can be illustrated by one misquotation: "Greater love hath no man than a mother cat dying to defend her kittens." Once you understand the problem facing that cat and how she solved it, you will then be ready to examine yourself and learn how high up the moral ladder you are capable of climbing.

'These juvenile criminals hit a low level. Born with only the instinct for survival, the highest morality they achieved was a shaky loyalty to a peer group, a street gang. But the do-gooders attempted to "appeal to their better natures," to "reach them," to "spark their moral sense." *Tosh!* They *had* no "better natures"; experience taught them that what they were doing was the way to survive. The puppy never got his spanking; therefore what he did with pleasure and success must be "moral."

'The basis of all morality is duty, a concept with the same relation to group that self-interest has to individual. Nobody preached duty to these kids in a way they could understand – that is, with a spanking. But the society they were in told them endlessly about their "rights."

'The results should have been predictable, since a human being has *no natural rights of any nature*.'

Mr. Dubois had paused. Somebody took the bait. 'Sir? How about "life, liberty, and the pursuit of happiness"?'

'Ah, yes, the "unalienable rights." Each year someone quotes that magnificent poetry. Life? What "right" to life has a man who is drowning in the Pacific? The ocean will not hearken to his cries. What "right" to life has a man who must die if he is to save his children? If he chooses to save his own life, does he do so as a matter of "right'? If two men are starving and cannibalism is the only alternative to death, which man's right is "unalienable'? And is it "right'? As to liberty, the heroes who signed that great document pledged themselves to *buy* liberty with their lives. Liberty is *never* unalienable; it must be redeemed regularly with the blood of patriots or it *always* vanishes. Of all the so-called "natural human rights" that have ever been invented, liberty is least likely to be cheap and is *never* free of cost.

'The third "right'? – the "pursuit of happiness'? It is indeed unalienable but it is not a right; it is simply a universal condition which tyrants cannot take away nor patriots restore. Cast me into a dungeon, burn me at a stake, crown me king of kings, I can "pursue happiness" as long as my brain lives – but neither gods nor saints, wise men nor subtle drugs, can insure that I will catch it.'

Mr. Dubois then turned to me. 'I told you that "juvenile delinquent" is a contradiction in terms. "Delinquent" means "failing in duty." But *duty* is an *adult* virtue – indeed a juvenile becomes an adult when, and only when, he acquires a knowledge of duty and embraces it as dearer than the self-love he was born with. There never was, there cannot *be*, a "juvenile delinquent." But for every juvenile criminal there are always one or more adult delinquents – people of mature years who either do not know their duty, or who, knowing it, fail.

'And *that* was the soft spot which destroyed what was in many ways an admirable culture. The junior hoodlums who roamed their streets were symptoms of a greater sickness; their citizens (all of them counted as such) glorified their mythology of "rights" . . . and lost track of their duties. No nation, so constituted, can endure.'

I wondered how Colonel Dubois would have classified Dillinger. Was he a juvenile criminal who merited pity even though you had to get rid of him? Or was he an adult delinquent who deserved nothing but contempt?

I didn't know, I would never know. The one thing I was sure of was that he would never again kill any little girls.

That suited me. I went to sleep.

Chapter 9

We've got no place in this outfit for good losers. We want tough hombres who will go in there and win!

– Admiral Jonas Ingram, 1926

When we had done all that a mud foot can do in flat country, we moved into some rough mountains to do still rougher things – the Canadian Rockies between Good Hope Mountain and Mount Waddington. Camp Sergeant Spooky Smith was much like Camp Currie (aside from its rugged setting) but it was much smaller. Well, the Third Regiment was much smaller now, too – less than four hundred whereas we had started out with more than two thousand. H Company was now organized as a single platoon and the battalion paraded as if it were a company. But we were still called 'H Company' and Zim was 'Company Commander,' not platoon leader.

What the sweat-down meant, really, was much more personal instruction; we had more corporal-instructors than we had squads and Sergeant Zim, with only fifty men on his mind instead of the two hundred and sixty he had started with, kept his Argus eyes on each one of us all the time – even when he wasn't there. At least, if you goofed, it turned out he was standing right behind you.

However, the chewing-out you got had almost a friendly quality, in a horrid sort of way, because we had changed, too, as well as the regiment – the one-in-five who was left was almost a soldier and Zim seemed to be trying to make him into one, instead of running him over the hill.

We saw a lot more of Captain Frankel, too; he now spent most of his time teaching us, instead of behind a desk, and he knew all of us by name and face and seemed to have a card file in his mind of exactly what progress each man had made on every weapon, every piece of equipment – not to mention your extra-duty status, medical record, and whether you had had a letter from home lately.

He wasn't as severe with us as Zim was; his words were milder and it took a really stupid stunt to take that friendly grin off his face – but don't let that fool you; there was beryl armor under the grin. I never did figure out which one was the better soldier, Zim or Captain Frankel – I mean, if you took away the insignia and thought of them as privates. Unquestionably they were both better soldiers than any of the other instructors – but which was best? Zim did everything with precision and style, as if he were on parade; Captain Frankel did the same thing with dash and gusto, as if it were a game. The results were about the same – and it never turned out to be as easy as Captain Frankel made it look.

We needed the abundance of instructors. Jumping a suit (as I have said) was easy on flat ground. Well, the suit jumps just as high and just as easily in the mountains – but it makes a lot of difference when you have to jump up a vertical granite wall, between two close-set fir trees, and override your jet control at the last instant. We had three major casualties in suit practice in broken country, two dead and one medical retirement.

But that rock wall is even tougher without a suit, tackled with lines and pitons. I didn't really see what use alpine drill was to a cap trooper but I had learned to keep my mouth shut and try to learn what they shoved at us. I learned it and it wasn't too hard. If anybody had told me, a year earlier, that I could go up a solid chunk of rock, as flat and as perpendicular as a blank wall of a building, using only a hammer, some silly little steel pins, and a chunk of clothesline, I would have laughed in his face; I'm a sea-level type. Correction: I *was* a sea-level type. There had been some changes made.

Just how much I had changed I began to find out. At Camp Sergeant Spooky Smith we had liberty – to go to town, I mean. Oh, we had 'liberty' after the first month at Camp Currie, too. This meant that, on a Sunday afternoon, if you weren't in the duty platoon, you could check out at the orderly tent and walk just as far away from camp as you wished, bearing in mind that you had to be back for evening muster. But there was nothing within walking distance, if you don't count jack rabbits – no girls, no theaters, no dance halls, et cetera.

Nevertheless, liberty, even at Camp Currie, was no mean privilege; sometimes it can be very important indeed to be able to go so far away that you can't see a tent, a sergeant, nor even the ugly faces of your best friends among the boots . . . not to have to be on the bounce about anything, have time to take out your soul and look at it. You could lose that privilege in several degrees; you could be restricted to camp . . . or you could be restricted to your own company street, which meant that you couldn't go to the library nor to what was misleadingly called the 'recreation' tent (mostly some parcheesi sets and similar wild excitements) . . . or you could be under close restriction, required to stay in your tent when your presence was not required elsewhere.

This last sort didn't mean much in itself since it was usually added to extra duty so demanding that you didn't have any time in your tent other than for sleep anyhow; it was a decoration added like a cherry on top of a dish of ice cream to notify you and the world that you had pulled not some everyday goof-off but something unbecoming of a member of the M.I. and were thereby unfit to associate with other troopers until you had washed away the stain.

But at Camp Spooky we could go into town – duty status, conduct status, etc., permitting. Shuttles ran to Vancouver every Sunday morning, right after divine services (which were moved up to thirty minutes after breakfast) and came back again just before supper and again just before taps. The instructors could even spend Saturday night in town, or cop a three-day pass, duty permitting.

I had no more than stepped out of the shuttle, my first pass, than I realized in part that I had changed. Johnnie didn't fit in any longer. Civilian life, I mean. It all seemed amazingly complex and unbelievably untidy.

I'm not running down Vancouver. It's a beautiful city in a lovely setting; the people are charming and they are used to having the M.I. in town and they make a trooper welcome. There is a social center for us downtown, where they have dances for us every week and see to it that junior hostesses are on hand to dance with, and senior hostesses to make sure that a shy boy (*me*, to my amazement – but you try a few months with nothing female around but lady jack rabbits) gets introduced and has a partner's feet to step on.

But I didn't go to the social center that first pass. Mostly I stood around and gawked – at beautiful buildings, at display windows filled with all manner of unnecessary things (and not a weapon among them), at all those people running around, or even strolling, doing exactly as they pleased and no two of them dressed alike – and at girls.

Especially at girls. I hadn't realized just how wonderful they were. Look, I've approved of girls from the time I first noticed that the difference was more than just that they dress differently. So far as I remember I never did go through that period boys are supposed to go through when they know that girls are different but dislike them; I've *always* liked girls.

But that day I realized that I had long been taking them for granted.

Girls are simply wonderful. Just to stand on a corner and watch them going past is delightful. They don't *walk*. At least not what we do when we walk. I don't know how to describe it, but it's much more complex and utterly delightful. They don't move just their feet; everything moves and in different directions . . . and all of it graceful.

I might have been standing there yet if a policeman hadn't come by. He sized us up and said, 'Howdy, boys. Enjoying yourselves?'

I quickly read the ribbons on his chest and was impressed. 'Yes, *sir!*'

'You don't have to say "sir" to me. Not much to do here. Why don't you go to the hospitality center?' He gave us the address, pointed the direction and we started that way – Pat Leivy, 'Kitten' Smith, and myself. He called after us, 'Have a good time, boys . . . and stay out of trouble.' Which was exactly what Sergeant Zim had said to us as we climbed into the shuttle.

But we didn't go there. Pat Leivy had lived in Seattle when he was a small boy and wanted to take a look at his old home town. He had money and offered to pay our shuttle fares if we would go with him. I didn't mind and it was all right; shuttles ran every twenty minutes and our passes were not restricted to Vancouver. Smith decided to go along, too.

Seattle wasn't so very different from Vancouver and the girls were just as plentiful; I enjoyed it. But Seattle wasn't quite as used to having M.I. around in droves and we picked a poor spot to eat dinner, one where we weren't quite so welcome – a bar-restaurant, down by the docks.

Now, look, we weren't drinking. Well, Kitten Smith had had one repeat *one* beer with his dinner but he was never anything but friendly and nice. That is how he got his name; the first time we had hand-to-hand combat drill Corporal Jones had said to him disgustedly: 'A kitten would have hit me harder than *that!*' The nickname stuck.

We were the only uniforms in the place; most of the other customers were merchant marine sailors – Seattle handles an awful lot of surface tonnage. I hadn't known it at the time but merchant sailors don't like us. Part of it has to do with the fact that their guilds have tried and tried to get their trade classed as equivalent to Federal Service, without success – but I understand that some of it goes way back in history, centuries.

There were some young fellows there, too, about our age – the right age to serve a term, only they weren't – long-haired and sloppy and kind of dirty-looking. Well, say about the way I looked, I suppose, before I joined up.

Presently we started noticing that at the table behind us, two of these young twerps and two merchant sailors (to judge by clothes) were passing remarks that were intended for us to overhear. I won't try to repeat them.

We didn't say anything. Presently, when the remarks were even more personal and she laughs louder and everybody else in the place was keeping quiet and listening, Kitten whispered to me, 'Let's get out of here.'

I caught Pat Leivy's eye; he nodded. We had no score to settle; it was one of those pay-as-you-get-it places. We got up and left.

They followed us out.

Pat whispered to me, 'Watch it.' We kept on walking, didn't look back.

They charged us.

I gave my man a side-neck chop as I pivoted and let him fall past me, swung to help my mates. But it was over. Four in, four down. Kitten had handled two of them and Pat had sort of wrapped the other one around a lamppost from throwing him a little too hard.

Somebody, the proprietor I guess, must have called the police as soon as we stood up to leave, since they arrived almost at once while we were still standing around wondering what to do with the meat – two policemen; it was that sort of a neighborhood.

The senior of them wanted us to prefer charges, but none of us was willing – Zim had told us to 'stay out of trouble.' Kitten looked blank and about fifteen years old and said, 'I guess they stumbled.'

'So I see,' agreed the police officer and toed a knife away from the outflung hand of my man, put it against the curb and broke the blade. 'Well, you boys had better run along . . . farther uptown.'

We left. I was glad that neither Pat nor Kitten wanted to make anything of it. It's a mighty serious thing, a civilian assaulting a member of the Armed Forces, but what the deuce? – the books balanced. They jumped us, they got their lumps. All even.

But it's a good thing we *never* go on a pass armed . . . and have been trained to disable without killing. Because every bit of it happened by reflex. I didn't believe that they would jump us until they already had, and I didn't do any thinking at all until it was over.

But that's how I learned for the first time just how much I had changed.

We walked back to the station and caught a shuttle to Vancouver.

We started practice drops as soon as we moved to Camp Spooky – a platoon at a time, in rotation (a full platoon, that is – a company), would shuttle down to the field north of Walla Walla, go aboard, space, make a drop, go through an exercise, and home on a beacon. A day's work. With eight companies that gave us not quite a drop each week, and then it gave us a little more than a drop each week as attrition continued, whereupon the drops got tougher – over mountains, into the arctic ice, into the Australian desert, and, before we graduated, onto the face of the Moon, where your capsule is placed only a hundred feet up and explodes as it ejects – and you have to look sharp and land with only your suit (no air, no parachute) and a bad landing can spill your air and kill you.

Some of the attrition was from casualties, deaths or injuries, and some of it was just from refusing to enter the capsule – which some did, and that was that; they weren't even chewed out; they were just motioned aside and that night they were paid off. Even a man who had made several drops might get the panic and refuse . . . and the instructors were just gentle with him, treated him the way you do a friend who is ill and won't get well.

I never quite refused to enter the capsule – but I certainly learned about the shakes. I always got them, I was scared silly every time. I still am.

But you're not a cap trooper unless you drop.

They tell a story, probably not true, about a cap trooper who was sight-seeing in Paris. He visited Les Invalides, looked down at Napoleon's coffin and said to a French guard there: 'Who's he?'

The Frenchman was properly scandalized. 'Monsieur does not *know?* This is the tomb of *Napoleon!* Napoleon Bonaparte – the greatest soldier who ever lived!'

The cap trooper thought about it. Then he asked, 'So? Where were his drops?'

It is almost certainly not true, because there is a big sign outside there that tells you exactly who Napoleon was. But that is how cap troopers feel about it.

Eventually we graduated.

I can see that I've left out almost everything. Not a word about most of our weapons, nothing about the time we dropped everything and fought a forest fire for three days, no mention of the practice alert that was a real one, only we didn't know it until it was over, nor about the day the cook tent blew away – in fact not any mention of weather and, believe me, weather is important to a doughboy, rain and mud especially. But though weather is important while it happens it seems to me to be pretty dull to look back on. You can take descriptions of most any sort of weather out of an almanac and stick them in just anywhere; they'll probably fit.

The regiment had started with 2009 men; we graduated 187 – of the others, fourteen were dead (one executed and his name struck) and the rest resigned, dropped, transferred, medical discharge, etc. Major Malloy made a short speech, we each got a certificate, we passed in review for the last time, and the regiment was disbanded, its colors to be cased until they would be needed (three weeks later) to tell another couple of thousand civilians that they were an outfit, not a mob.

I was a 'trained soldier,' entitled to put 'TP' in front of my serial number instead of 'RP.' Big day.

The biggest I ever had.

Chapter 10

The Tree of liberty must be refreshed from time to time with the blood of patriots . . .

Thomas Jefferson, 1787

That is, I thought I was a 'trained soldier' until I reported to my ship. Any law against having a wrong opinion?

I see that I didn't make any mention of how the Terran Federation moved from 'peace' to a 'state of emergency' and then on into 'war.' I didn't notice it too closely myself. When I enrolled, it was 'peace,' the normal condition, at least so people think (who ever expects anything else?). Then, while I was at Currie, it became a 'state of emergency' but I still didn't notice it, as what Corporal Bronski thought about my haircut, uniform, combat drill, and kit was much more important – and what Sergeant Zim thought about such matters was overwhelmingly important. In any case, 'emergency' is still 'peace.'

'Peace' is a condition in which no civilian pays any attention to military casualties which do not achieve page-one, lead-story prominence – unless that civilian is a close relative of one of the casualties. But, if there ever was a time in history when 'peace' meant that there was no fighting going on, I have been unable to find out about it. When I reported to my first outfit, 'Willie's Wildcats,' sometimes known as Company K, Third Regiment, First M.I. Division, and shipped with them in the *Valley Forge* (with that misleading certificate in my kit) the fighting had already been going on for several years.

The historians can't seem to settle whether to call this one 'The Third Space War' (or the 'Fourth'), or whether 'The First Interstellar War' fits it better. We just call it 'The Bug War' if we call it anything, which we usually don't, and in any case the historians date the beginning of 'war' after the time I joined my first outfit and ship. Everything up to then and still later were 'incidents,' 'patrols,' or 'police actions.' However, you are just as dead if you buy a farm in an 'incident' as you are if you buy it in a declared war.

But, to tell the truth, a soldier doesn't notice a war much more than a civilian does, except his own tiny piece of it and that just on the days it is happening. The rest of the time he is much more concerned with sack time, the vagaries of sergeants, and the chances of wheedling the cook between meals. However, when Kitten Smith and Al Jenkins and I joined them at Luna Base, each of Willie's Wildcats had made more than one combat drop; they were soldiers and we were not. We weren't hazed for it – at least I was not – and the sergeants and corporals were amazingly easy to deal with after the calculated frightfulness of instructors.

It took a little while to discover that this comparatively gentle treatment simply meant that we were nobody, hardly worth chewing out, until we had proved in a drop – a real drop – that we might possibly replace real Wildcats who had fought and bought it and whose bunks we now occupied.

Let me tell you how green I was. While the *Valley Forge* was still at Luna Base, I happened to come across my section leader just as he was about to hit dirt, all slicked up in dress uniform. He was wearing in his left ear lobe a rather small earring, a tiny gold skull beautifully made and under it, instead of the conventional crossed bones of the ancient Jolly Roger design, was a whole bundle of little gold bones, almost too small to see.

Back home, I had always worn earrings and other jewelry

when I went out on a date – I had some beautiful ear clips, rubies as big as the end of my little finger which had belonged to my mother's grandfather. I like jewelry and had rather resented being required to leave it all behind when I went to Basic . . . but here was a type of jewelry which was apparently okay to wear with uniform. My ears weren't pierced – my mother didn't approve of it, for boys – but I could have the jeweler mount it on a clip . . . and I still had some money left from pay call at graduation and was anxious to spend it before it mildewed. 'Unh, Sergeant? Where do you get earrings like that one? Pretty neat.'

He didn't look scornful, he didn't even smile. He just said, 'You like it?'

'*I* certainly do!' The plain raw gold pointed up the gold braid and piping of the uniform even better than gems would have done. I was thinking that a pair would be still handsomer, with just crossbones instead of all the confusion at the bottom. 'Does the base PX carry them?'

'No, the PX here never sells them.' He added, 'At least, I don't think you'll ever be able to buy one here – I hope. But I tell you what – when we reach a place where you can buy one of your own, I'll see to it you know about it. That's a promise.'

'Uh, thanks!'

'Don't mention it.'

I saw several of the tiny skulls thereafter, some with more 'bones,' some with fewer; my guess had been correct, this was jewelry permitted with uniform, when on pass at least. Then I got my own chance to 'buy' one almost immediately thereafter and discovered that the prices were unreasonably high, for such plain ornaments.

It was Operation Bughouse, the First Battle of Klendathu in the history books, soon after Buenos Aires was smeared. It took the loss of B.A. to make the groundhogs realize that anything was going on, because people who haven't been out don't really believe in other planets, not down deep where it counts. I know I hadn't and I had been space-happy since I was a pup.

But B.A. really stirred up the civilians and inspired loud screams to bring all our forces home, from everywhere – orbit them around the planet practically shoulder to shoulder and interdict the space Terra occupies. This is silly, of course; you don't win a war by defense but by attack – no 'Department of Defense' ever won a war; see the histories. But it seems to be a standard civilian reaction to scream for defensive tactics as soon as they do notice a war. They then want to run the war – like a passenger trying to grab the controls away from the pilot in an emergency.

However, nobody asked my opinion at the time; I was told. Quite aside from the impossibility of dragging the troops home in view of our treaty obligations and what it would do to the colony planets in the Federation and to our allies, we were awfully busy doing something else, to wit: carrying the war to the Bugs. I suppose I noticed the destruction of B.A. much less than most civilians did. We were already a couple of parsecs away under the Cherenkov drive and the news didn't reach us until we got it from another ship after we came out of drive.

I remember thinking, 'Gosh, that's terrible!' and feeling sorry for the one Portefio in the ship. But B.A. wasn't my home and Terra was a long way off and I was very busy, as the attack on Klendathu, the Bugs' home planet, was mounted immediately after that and we spent the time to rendezvous strapped in our bunks, doped and unconscious, with the internal-gravity field of the *Valley Forge* off, to save power and give greater speed.

The loss of Buenos Aires did mean a great deal to me; it changed my life enormously, but this I did not know until many months later.

When it came time to drop onto Klendathu, I was assigned to PFC Dutch Bamburger as a supernumerary. He managed to conceal his pleasure at the news and as soon as the platoon sergeant was out of earshot, he said, 'Listen, boot, you stick close behind me and stay out of my way. You go slowing me down, I break your silly neck.'

I just nodded. I was beginning to realize that this was not a practice drop.

Then I had the shakes for a while and then we were down –

Operation Bughouse should have been called 'Operation Madhouse.' Everything went wrong. It had been planned as an all-out move to bring the enemy to their knees, occupy their capital and the key points of their home planet, and end the war. Instead it darn near lost the war.

I am not criticizing General Diennes. I don't know whether it's true that he demanded more troops and more support and allowed himself to be overruled by the Sky Marshal-in-Chief – or not. Nor was it any of my business. Furthermore I doubt if some of the smart second-guessers know all the facts.

What I do know is that the General dropped with us and commanded us on the ground and, when the situation became impossible, he personally led the diversionary attack that allowed quite a few of us (including me) to be retrieved – and, in so doing, bought his farm. He's radioactive debris on Klendathu and it's much too late to court-martial him, so why talk about it?

I do have one comment to make to any armchair strategist who has never made a drop. Yes, I agree that the Bugs' planet possibly could have been plastered with H-bombs until it was surfaced with radioactive glass. But would that have won the war? The Bugs are not like us. The Pseudo-Arachnids aren't even like spiders. They are arthropods who happen to look like a madman's conception of a giant, intelligent spider, but their organization, psychological and economic, is more like that of ants or termites; they are communal entities, the ultimate dictatorship of the hive. Blasting the surface of their planet would have killed soldiers and workers; it would not have killed the brain caste and queens – I doubt if anybody can be certain that even a direct hit with a burrowing H-rocket would kill a queen; we don't know how far down they are. Nor am I anxious to find out; none of the boys who went down those holes came up again.

So suppose we did ruin the productive surface of Klendathu? They still would have ships and colonies and other planets, same as we have, and their HQ is still intact – so unless they surrender, the war isn't over. We didn't have nova bombs at that time; we couldn't crack Klendathu open. If they absorbed the punishment and didn't surrender, the war was still on.

If they *can* surrender –

Their soldiers can't. Their workers can't fight (and you can waste a lot of time and ammo shooting up workers who wouldn't say *boo!*) and their soldier caste can't surrender. But don't make the mistake of thinking that the Bugs are just stupid insects because they look the way they do and don't know how to surrender. Their warriors are smart, skilled, and aggressive – smarter than you are, by the only universal rule, if the Bug shoots first. You can burn off one leg, two legs, three legs, and he just keeps on coming; burn off four on one side and he topples over – but keeps on shooting. You have to spot the nerve case and get it . . . whereupon he will trot right on past you, shooting at nothing, until he crashes into a wall or something.

The drop was a shambles from the start. Fifty ships were in our piece of it and they were supposed to come out of Cherenkov drive and into reaction drive so perfectly coordinated that they could hit orbit and drop us, in formation and where we were supposed to hit, without even making one planet circuit to dress up their own formation. I suppose this is difficult. Shucks, I *know* it is. But when it slips, it leaves the M.I. holding the sack.

We were lucky at that, because the *Valley Forge* and every Navy file in her bought it before we ever hit the ground. In that tight, fast formation (4.7 miles/sec. orbital speed is not a stroll) she collided with the *Ypres* and both ships were destroyed. We were lucky to get out of her tubes – those of us who did get out, for she was still firing capsules as she was rammed. But I wasn't aware of it; I was inside my cocoon, headed for the ground. I suppose our company commander knew that the ship had been lost (and half his Wildcats with it) since he was out first and would know when he suddenly lost touch, over the command circuit, with the ship's captain.

But there is no way to ask him, because he wasn't retrieved. All I ever had was a gradually dawning realization that things were in a mess.

The next eighteen hours were nightmare. I shan't tell much about it because I don't remember much, just snatches, stop-motion scenes of horror. I have never liked spiders, poisonous or otherwise; a common house spider in my bed can give me the creeps. Tarantulas are simply unthinkable, and I can't eat lobster, crab, or anything of that sort. When I got my first ever sight of a Bug, my mind jumped right out of my skull and started to yammer. It was seconds later that I realized that I had killed it and could stop shooting. I suppose it was a worker; I doubt if I was in any shape to tackle a warrior and win.

But, at that, I was in better shape than was the K-9 Corps. They were to be dropped (if the drop had gone perfectly) on the periphery of our entire target and the neodogs were supposed to range outward and provide tactical intelligence to interdiction squads whose business it was to secure the periphery. Those Calebs aren't armed, of course, other than their teeth. A neodog is supposed to hear, see, and smell and tell his partner what he finds by radio; all he carries is a radio and a destruction bomb with which he (or his partner) can blow the dog up in case of bad wounds or capture.

Those poor dogs didn't wait to be captured; apparently most of them suicided as soon as they made contact. They felt the way I do about the Bugs, only worse. They have neodogs now that are indoctrinated from puppyhood to observe and evade without blowing their tops at the mere sight or smell of a Bug. But these weren't.

But that wasn't all that went wrong. Just name it, it was fouled up. I didn't know what was going on, of course; I just stuck close behind Dutch, trying to shoot or flame anything that moved, dropping a grenade down a hole whenever I saw one. Presently I got so that I could kill a Bug without wasting ammo or juice, although I did not learn to distinguish between those that were harmless and those that were not. Only about one in fifty is a warrior – but he makes up for the other forty-nine. Their personal weapons aren't as heavy as ours but they are lethal just the same – they've got a beam that will penetrate armor and slice flesh like cutting a hard-boiled egg, and they co-operate even better than we do . . . because the brain that is doing the heavy thinking for a 'squad' isn't where you can reach it; it's down one of the holes.

Dutch and I stayed lucky for quite a long time, milling around over an area about a mile square, corking up holes with bombs, killing what we found above surface, saving our jets as much as possible for emergencies. The idea was to secure the entire target and allow the reinforcements and the heavy stuff to come down without important opposition; this was not a raid, this was a battle to establish a beachhead, stand on it, hold it, and enable fresh troops and heavies to capture or pacify the entire planet.

Only we didn't.

Our own section was doing all right. It was in the wrong pew and out of touch with the other section – the platoon leader and sergeant were dead and we never re-formed. But we had staked out a claim, our special-weapons squad had set up a strong point, and we were ready to turn our real estate over to fresh troops as soon as they showed up.

Only they didn't. They dropped in where we should have dropped, found unfriendly natives and had their own troubles. We never saw them. So we stayed where we were, soaking up casualties from time to time and passing them out ourselves as opportunity offered – while we ran low on ammo and jump juice and even power to keep the suits moving. This seemed to go on for a couple of thousand years.

Dutch and I were zipping along close to a wall, headed for our special-weapons squad in answer to a yell for help, when the ground suddenly opened in front of Dutch, a Bug popped out, and Dutch went down.

I flamed the Bug and tossed a grenade and the hole closed up, then turned to see what had happened to Dutch. He was down but he didn't look hurt. A platoon sergeant can monitor the physicals on every man in his platoon, sort out the dead from those who merely can't make it unassisted and must be picked up. But you can do the same thing manually from switches right on the belt of a man's suit.

Dutch didn't answer when I called to him. His body temperature read ninety-nine degrees, his respiration, heartbeat, and brain wave read zero – which looked bad but maybe his suit was dead rather than he himself. Or so I told myself, forgetting that the temperature indicator would give no reading if it were the suit rather than the man. Anyhow, I grabbed the can-opener wrench from my own belt and started to take him out of his suit while trying to watch all around me.

Then I heard an all-hands call in my helmet that I never

want to hear again. '*Sauve qui peut!* Home! Home! Pickup and *home!* Any beacon you can hear. Six minutes! All hands, save yourselves, pick up your mates. Home on any beacon! *Sauve qui—*'

I hurried.

His head came off as I tried to drag him out of his suit, so I dropped him and got out of there. On a later drop I would have had sense enough to salvage his ammo, but I was far too sluggy to think; I simply bounced away from there and tried to rendezvous with the strong point we had been heading for.

It was already evacuated and I felt lost . . . lost and deserted. Then I heard recall, not the recall it should have been: 'Yankee Doodle' (if it had been a boat from the *Valley Forge*) – but 'Sugar Bush,' a tune I didn't know. No matter, it was a beacon; I headed for it, using the last of my jump juice lavishly – got aboard just as they were about to button up and shortly thereafter was in the *Voortrek*, in such a state of shock that I couldn't remember my serial number.

I've heard it called a 'strategic victory' – but I was there and I claim we took a terrible licking.

Six weeks later (and feeling about sixty years older) at Fleet Base on Sanctuary I boarded another ground boat and reported for duty to Ship's Sergeant Jelal in the *Rodger Young*. I was wearing, in my pierced left ear lobe, a broken skull with one bone. Al Jenkins was with me and was wearing one exactly like it (Kitten never made it out of the tube). The few surviving Wildcats were distributed elsewhere around the Fleet; we had lost half our strength, about, in the collision between the *Valley Forge* and the *Ypres:* that disastrous mess on the ground had run our casualties up over 80 per cent and the powers-that-be decided that it was impossible to put the outfit back together with the survivors – close it out, put the records in the archives, and wait until the scars had healed before reactivating Company K (Wildcats) with new faces but old traditions.

Besides, there were a lot of empty files to fill in other outfits.

Sergeant Jelal welcomed us warmly, told us that we were joining a smart outfit, 'best in the Fleet,' in a taut ship, and didn't seem to notice our ear skulls. Later that day he took us forward to meet the Lieutenant, who smiled rather shyly and gave us a fatherly little talk. I noticed that Al Jenkins wasn't wearing his gold skull. Neither was I – because I had already noticed that nobody in Rasczak's Roughnecks wore the skulls.

They didn't wear them because, in Rasczak's Roughnecks, it didn't matter in the least how many combat drops you had made, nor which ones; you were either a Roughneck or you weren't – and if you were not, they didn't care who you were. Since we had come to them not as recruits but as combat veterans, they gave us all possible benefit of doubt and made us welcome with no more than that unavoidable trace of formality anybody necessarily shows to a house guest who is not a member of the family.

But, less than a week later when we had made one combat drop with them, we were full-fledged Roughnecks, members of the family, called by our first names, chewed out on occasion without any feeling on either side that we were less than blood brothers thereby, borrowed from and lent to, included in bull sessions and privileged to express our own silly opinions with complete freedom – and have them slapped down just as freely. We even called non-coms by their first names on any but strictly duty occasions. Sergeant Jelal was always on duty, of course, unless you ran across him dirtside, in which case he was 'Jelly' and went out of his way to behave as if his lordly rank meant nothing between Roughnecks.

But the Lieutenant was always 'The Lieutenant' – never 'Mr. Rasczak,' nor even 'Lieutenant Rasczak.' Simply 'The

Lieutenant,' spoken to and of in the third person. There was no god but the Lieutenant and Sergeant Jelal was his prophet. Jelly could say 'No' in his own person and it might be subject to further argument, at least from junior sergeants, but if he said, 'The Lieutenant wouldn't like it,' he was speaking *ex cathedra* and the matter was dropped permanently. Nobody ever tried to check up on whether or not the Lieutenant would or would not like it; the Word had been spoken.

The Lieutenant was father to us and loved us and spoiled us and was nevertheless rather remote from us aboard ship – and even dirtside . . . unless we reached dirt via a drop. But in a drop – well, you wouldn't think that an officer could worry about every man of a platoon spread over a hundred square miles of terrain. But he can. He can worry himself sick over each one of them. How he could keep track of us all I can't describe, but in the midst of a ruckus his voice would sing out over the command circuit: 'Johnson! Check squad six! Smitty's in trouble,' and it was better than even money that the Lieutenant had noticed it before Smith's squad leader.

Besides that, you knew with utter and absolute certainty that, as long as you were still alive, the Lieutenant would not get into the retrieval boat without you. There have been prisoners taken in the Bug War, but none from Rasczak's Roughnecks.

Jelly was mother to us and was close to us and took care of us and didn't spoil us at all. But he didn't report us to the Lieutenant – there was never a court-martial among the Roughnecks and no man was *ever* flogged. Jelly didn't even pass out extra duty very often; he had other ways of paddling us. He could look you up and down at daily inspection and simply say, 'In the Navy you might look good. Why don't you transfer?' – and get results, it being an article of faith among us that the Navy crew members slept in their uniforms and never washed below their collar lines.

But Jelly didn't have to maintain discipline among privates because he maintained discipline among his non-coms and expected them to do likewise. My squad leader, when I first joined, was 'Red' Greene. After a couple of drops, when I knew how *good* it was to be a Roughneck, I got to feeling gay and a bit too big for my clothes – and talked back to Red. He didn't report me to Jelly; he just took me back to the washroom and gave me a medium set of lumps, and we got to be pretty good friends. In fact, he recommended me for lance, later on.

Actually we didn't know whether the crew members slept in thier clothes or not; we kept to our part of the ship and the Navy men kept to theirs, because they were made to feel unwelcome if they showed up in our country other than on duty – after all, one has social standards one must maintain, mustn't one? The Lieutetant had his stateroom in male officers' country, a Navy part of the ship, but we never went there, either, except on duty and rarely. We did go forward for guard duty, because the *Rodger Young* was a mixed ship, female captain and pilot officers, some female Navy ratings; forward of bulkhead thirty was ladies' country – and two armed M.I. day and night stood guard at the one door cutting it. (At battle stations that door, like all other gastight doors, was secured; nobody missed a drop.)

Officers were privileged to go forward of bulkhead thirty on duty and all officers, including the Lieutenant, ate in a mixed mess just beyond it. But they didn't tarry there; they ate and got out. Maybe other corvette transports were run differently, but that was the way the *Rodger Young* was run – both the Lieutenant and Captain Deladrier wanted a taut ship and got it.

Nevertheless guard duty was a privilege. It was a rest to stand beside that door, arms folded, feet spread, doping off and thinking about nothing . . . but always warmly aware that any moment you might see a feminine creature even though you were not privileged to speak to her other than on duty. Once I was called all the way into the Skipper's office and she spoke to me – she looked right at me and said, 'Take this to the Chief Engineer, please.'

My daily shipside job, aside from cleaning, was servicing electronic equipment under the close supervision of 'Padre' Migliaccio, the section leader of the first section, exactly as I used to work under Carl's eye. Drops didn't happen too often and everybody worked every day. If a man didn't have any other talent he could always scrub bulkheads; nothing was ever quite clean enough to suit Sergeant Jelal. We followed the M.I. rule; everybody fights, everybody works. Our first cook was Johnson, the second section's sergeant, a big friendly boy from Georgia (the one in the western hemisphere, not the other one) and a very talented chef. He wheedled pretty well, too; he liked to eat between meals himself and saw no reason why other people shouldn't.

With the Padre leading one section and the cook leading the other, we were well taken care of, body and soul – but suppose one of them bought it? Which one would you pick? A nice point that we never tried to settle but could always discuss.

The *Rodger Young* kept busy and we made a number of drops, all different. Every drop has to be different so that they never can figure out a pattern on you. But no more pitched battles; we operated alone, patrolling, harrying, and raiding. The truth was that the Terran Federation was not then able to mount a large battle; the foul-up with Operation Bughouse had cost too many ships, 'way too many trained men. It was necessary to take time to heal up, train more men.

In the meantime, small fast ships, among them the *Rodger Young* and other corvette transports, tried to be everywhere at once, keeping the enemy off balance, hurting him and running. We suffered casualties and filled our holes when we returned to Sanctuary for more capsules. I still got the shakes every drop, but actual drops didn't happen too often nor were we ever down long – and between times there were days and days of shipboard life among the Roughnecks.

It was the happiest period of my life although I was never quite consciously aware of it – I did my full share of beefing just as everybody else did, and enjoyed that, too.

We weren't *really* hurt until the Lieutenant bought it.

I guess that was the worst time in all my life. I was already in bad shape for a personal reason: My mother had been in Buenos Aires when the Bugs smeared it.

I found out about it one time when we put in at Sanctuary for more capsules and some mail caught up with us – a note from my Aunt Eleanora, one that had not been coded and sent fast because she had failed to mark for that; the letter itself came. It was about three bitter lines. Somehow she seemed to blame me for my mother's death. Whether it was my fault because I was in the Armed Forces and should have therefore prevented the raid, or whether she felt that my mother had made a trip to Buenos Aires because I wasn't home where I should have been, was not clear; she managed to imply both in the same sentence.

I tore it up and tried to walk away from it. I thought that both my parents were dead – since Father would never send Mother on a trip that long by herself. Aunt Eleanora had not said so, but she wouldn't have mentioned Father in any case; her devotion was entirely to her sister. I was almost correct – eventually I learned that Father had planned to go with her but something had come up and he stayed over to settle it, intending to come along the next day. But Aunt Eleanora did not tell me this.

A couple of hours later the Lieutenant sent for me and

asked me very gently if I would like to take leave at Sanctuary while the ship went out on her next patrol – he pointed out that I had plenty of accumulated R&R and might as well use some of it. I don't know how he knew that I had lost a member of my family, but he obviously did. I said no, thank you, sir; I preferred to wait until the outfit all took R&R together.

I'm glad I did it that way, because if I hadn't, I wouldn't have been along when the Lieutenant bought it . . . and that would have been just too much to be borne. It happened very fast and just before retrieval. A man in the third squad was wounded, not badly but he was down; the assistant section leader moved in to pick up – and bought a small piece of it himself. The Lieutenant, as usual, was watching everything at once – no doubt he had checked physicals on each of them by remote, but we'll never know. What he did was to make sure that the assistant section leader was still alive; then made pick-up on both of them himself, one in each arm of his suit.

He threw them the last twenty feet and they were passed into the retrieval boat – and with everybody else in, the shield gone and no interdiction, was hit and died instantly.

I haven't mentioned the names of the private and of the assistant section leader on purpose. The Lieutenant was making pick-up on *all* of us, with his last breath. Maybe I was the private. It doesn't matter who he was. What did matter was that our family had had its head chopped off. The head of the family from which we took our name, the father who made us what we were.

After the Lieutenant had to leave us Captain Deladrier invited Sergeant Jelal to eat forward, with the other heads of departments. But he begged to be excused. Have you ever seen a widow with stern character keep her family together by behaving as if the head of the family had simply stepped out and would return at any moment? That's what Jelly did.

He was just a touch more strict with us than ever and if he ever had to say: 'The Lieutenant wouldn't like that,' it was almost more than a man could take. Jelly didn't say it very often.

He left our combat team organization almost unchanged; instead of shifting everybody around, he moved the assistant section leader of the second section over into the (nominal) platoon sergeant spot, leaving his section leaders where they were needed – with their sections – and he moved me from lance and assistant squad leader into acting corporal as a largely ornamental assistant section leader. Then he himself behaved as if the Lieutenant were merely out of sight and that he was just passing on the Lieutenant's orders, as usual.

It saved us.

Chapter 11

I have nothing to offer but blood, toil, tears, and sweat.
– W. Churchill, XXth century soldier-statesman

As we came back into the ship after the raid on the Skinnies – the raid in which Dizzy Flores bought it, Sergeant Jelal's first drop as platoon leader – a ship's gunner who was tending the boat lock spoke to me:

'How'd it go?'

'Routine,' I answered briefly. I suppose his remark was friendly but I was feeling very mixed up and in no mood to talk – sad over Dizzy, glad that we had made pickup anyhow, mad that the pickup had been useless, and all of it tangled up with that washed-out but happy feeling of being back in the ship again, able to muster arms and legs and note that they are all present. Besides, how can you talk about a drop to a man who has never made one?

'So?' he answered. 'You guys have got it soft. Loaf thirty days, work thirty minutes. Me, I stand a watch in three *and* turn to.'

'Yeah, I guess so,' I agreed and turned away. 'Some of us are born lucky.'

'Soldier, you ain't peddlin' vacuum,' he said to my back.

And yet there was much truth in what the Navy gunner had said. We cap troopers are like aviators of the earlier mechanized wars; a long and busy military career could contain only a few hours of actual combat facing the enemy, the rest being: train, get ready, go out – then come back, clean up the mess, get ready for another one, and practice, practice, practice, in between. We didn't make another drop for almost three weeks and that on a different planet around another star – a Bug colony. Even with Cherenkov drive, stars are far apart.

In the meantime I got my corporal's stripes, nominated by Jelly and confirmed by Captain Deladrier in the absence of a commissioned officer of our own. Theoretically the rank would not be permanent until approved against vacancy by the Fleet M.I. repple-depple, but that meant nothing, as the casualty rate was such that there were always more vacancies in the T.O. than there were warm bodies to fill them. I was a corporal when Jelly said I was a corporal; the rest was red tape.

But the gunner was not quite correct about 'loafing'; there were fifty-three suits of powered armor to check, service, and repair between each drop, not to mention weapons and special equipment. Sometimes Migliaccio would downcheck a suit, Jelly would confirm it, and the ship's weapon engineer, Lieutenant Farley, would decide that he couldn't cure it short of base facilities – whereupon a new suit would have to be broken out of stores and brought from 'cold' to 'hot,' an exacting process requiring twenty-six man-hours not counting the time of the man to whom it was being fitted.

We kept busy.

But we had fun, too. There were always several competitions going on, from acey-deucy to Honor Squad, and we had the best jazz band in several cubic light-years (well, the only one, maybe), with Sergeant Johnson on the trumpet leading them mellow and sweet for hymns or tearing the steel right off the bulkheads, as the occasion required. After that masterful (or should it be 'mistressful') retrieval rendezvous without a programmed ballistic, the platoon's metalsmith, PFC Archie Campbell, made a model of the *Rodger Young* for the Skipper and we all signed and Archie engraved our signatures on a base plate: *To Hot Pilot Yvette Deladrier, with thanks from Rasczak's Roughnecks*, and we invited her aft to eat with us and the Roughneck Downbeat Combo played during dinner and then the junior private presented it to her. She got tears and kissed him – and kissed Jelly as well and he blushed purple.

After I got my chevrons I simply had to get things straight with Ace, because Jelly kept me on as assistant section leader. This is not good. A man ought to fill each spot on his way up; I should have had a turn as squad leader instead of being bumped from lance and assistant squad leader to corporal and assistant section leader. Jelly knew this, of course, but I know perfectly well that he was trying to keep the outfit as much as possible the way it had been when the Lieutenant was alive – which meant that he left his squad leaders and section leaders unchanged.

But it left me with a ticklish problem; all three of the corporals under me as squad leaders were actually senior to me – but if Sergeant Johnson bought it on the next drop, it would not only lose us a mighty fine cook, it would leave me leading the section. There mustn't be any shadow of doubt when you give an order, not in combat; I had to clear up any possible shadow before we dropped again.

Ace was the problem. He was not only senior of the three, he was a career corporal as well and older than I was. If Ace accepted me, I wouldn't have any trouble with the other two squads.

I hadn't really had any trouble with him aboard. After we made pickup on Flores together he had been civil enough. On the other hand we hadn't had anything to have trouble over; our shipside jobs didn't put us together, except at daily muster and guard mount, which is all cut and dried. But you can feel it. He was not treating me as somebody he took orders from.

So I looked him up during off hours. He was lying in his bunk, reading a book, *Space Rangers against the Galaxy* – a pretty good yarn, except that I doubt if a military outfit ever had so many adventures and so few goof-offs. The ship had a good library.

'Ace. Got to see you.'

He glanced up. 'So? I just left the ship, I'm off duty.'

'I've got to see you now. Put your book down.'

'What's so aching urgent? I've got to finish this chapter.'

'Oh, come off it, Ace. If you can't wait, I'll tell you how it comes out.'

'You do and I'll clobber you.' But he put the book down, sat up, and listened.

I said, 'Ace, about this matter of the section organization – you're senior to me, you ought to be assistant section leader.'

'Oh, so it's *that* again!'

'Yep. I think you and I ought to go see Johnson and get him to fix it up with Jelly.'

'You do, eh?'

'Yes, I do. That's how it's got to be.'

'So? Look, Shortie, let me put you straight. I got nothing against you at all. Matter of fact, you were on the bounce that day we had to pick up Dizzy; I'll hand you that. But if you want a squad, you go dig up one of your own. Don't go eying mine. Why, my boys wouldn't even peel potatoes for you.'

'That's your final word?'

'That's my first, last, and only word.'

I sighed. 'I thought it would be. But I had to make sure. Well, that settles that. But I've got one other thing on my mind. I happened to notice that the washroom needs cleaning . . . and I think maybe you and I ought to attend to it. So put your book aside . . . as Jelly says, non-coms are always on duty.'

He didn't stir at once. He said quietly, 'You really think it's necessary, Shortie? As I said, I got nothing against you.'

'Looks like.'

'Think you can do it?'

'I can sure try.'

'Okay. Let's take care of it.'

We went aft to the washroom, chased out a private who was about to take a shower he didn't really need, and locked the door. Ace said, 'You got any restrictions in mind, Shortie?'

'Well . . . I hadn't planned to kill you.'

'Check. And no broken bones, nothing that would keep either one of us out of the next drop – except maybe by accident, of course. That suit you?'

'Suits,' I agreed. 'Uh, I think maybe I'll take my shirt off.'

'Wouldn't want to get blood on your shirt.' He relaxed.

I started to peel it off and he let go a kick for my kneecap. No wind up. Flat-footed and not tense.

Only my kneecap wasn't there – I had learned.

A real fight ordinarily can last only a second or two, because that is all the time it takes to kill a man, or knock him out, or disable him to the point where he can't fight. But we had agreed to avoid inflicting permanent damage; this changes things. We were both young, in top condition, highly trained, and used to absorbing punishment. Ace was bigger, I was maybe a touch faster. Under such conditions the miserable business simply has to go on until one or the other is too beaten down to continue – unless a fluke settles it sooner. But neither one of us was allowing any flukes; we were professionals and wary.

So it did go on, for a long, tedious, painful time. Details would be trivial and pointless; besides, I had no time to take notes.

A long time later I was lying on my back and Ace was flipping water in my face. He looked at me, then hauled me to my feet, shoved me against a bulkhead, steadied me. 'Hit me!'

'Huh?' I was dazed and seeing double.

'Johnnie . . . hit me.'

His face was floating in the air in front of me; I zeroed in on it and slugged it with all the force in my body, hard enough to mash any mosquito in poor health. His eyes closed and he slumped to the deck and I had to grab at a stanchion to keep from following him.

He got slowly up. 'Okay, Johnnie,' he said, shaking his head, 'I've had my lesson. You won't have any more lip out of me . . . nor out of anybody in the section. Okay?'

I nodded and my head hurt.

'Shake?' he asked.

We shook on it, and that hurt, too.

Almost anybody else knew more about how the war was going than we did, even though we were in it. This was the period, of course, after the Bugs had located our home planet, through the Skinnies, and had raided it, destroying Buenos Aires and turning 'contact troubles' into all-out war, but *before* we had built up our forces and before the Skinnies had changed sides and become our co-belligerents and de facto allies. Partly effective interdiction for Terra had been set up from Luna (we didn't know it), but speaking broadly, the Terran Federation was losing the war.

We didn't know that, either. Nor did we know that strenuous efforts were being made to subvert the alliance against us and bring the Skinnies over to our side; the nearest we came to being told about that was when we got instructions, before the raid in which Flores was killed, to go easy on the Skinnies, destroy as much property as possible but to kill inhabitants only when unavoidable.

What a man doesn't know he can't spill if he is captured; neither drugs, nor torture, nor brainwash, nor endless lack of sleep can squeeze out a secret he doesn't possess. So we were told only what we had to know for tactical purposes. In the past, armies have been known to fold up and quit because the men didn't know what they were fighting for, or why, and therefore lacked the will to fight. But the M.I. does not have that weakness. Each one of us was a volunteer to begin with, each for some reason or other – some good, some bad. But now we fought because we were M.I. We were professionals, with *esprit de corps*. We were Rasczak's Roughnecks, the best unprintable outfit in the whole expurgated M.I.; we climbed into our capsules because Jelly told us it was time to do so and we fought when we got down there because that is what Rasczak's Roughnecks do.

We certainly didn't know that we were losing.

Those Bugs lay eggs. They not only lay them, they hold them in reserve, hatch them as needed. If we killed a warrior – or a thousand, or ten thousand – his or their replacements were hatched and on duty almost before we could get back to base. You can imagine, if you like, some Bug supervisor of population flashing a phone to somewhere down inside and saying, 'Joe, warm up ten thousand warriors and have 'em ready by Wednesday . . . and tell engineering to activate reserve incubators N, O, P, Q, and R; the demand is picking up.'

I don't say they did exactly that, but those were the results. But don't make the mistake of thinking that they acted purely from instinct, like termites or ants; their actions were as intelligent as ours (stupid races don't build spaceships!) and were much better co-ordinated. It takes a minimum of a year to train a private to fight and to mesh his fighting in with his mates; a Bug warrior is *hatched* able to do this.

Every time we killed a thousand Bugs at a cost of one M.I. it was a net victory for the Bugs. We were learning, expensively, just how efficient a total communism can be when used by a people actually adapted to it by evolution; the Bug commissars didn't care any more about expending soldiers than we cared about expending ammo. Perhaps we could have figured this out about the Bugs by noting the grief the Chinese Hegemony gave the Russo-Anglo-American Alliance; however the trouble with 'lessons from history' is that we usually read them best after falling flat on our chins.

But we were learning. Technical instructions and tactical doctrine orders resulted from every brush with them, spread through the Fleet. We learned to tell the workers from the warriors – if you had time, you could tell from the shape of the carapace, but the quick rule of thumb was: If he comes at you, he's a warrior; if he runs, you can turn your back on him. We learned not to waste ammo even on warriors except in self-protection; instead we went after theirs. Find a hole, drop down it first a gas bomb which explodes gently a few seconds later, releasing an oily liquid which evaporates as a nerve gas tailored to Bugs (it is harmless to us) and which is heavier than air and keeps on going down – then you use a second grenade of H.E. to seal the hole.

We still didn't know whether we were getting deep enough to kill the queens – but we did know that the Bugs didn't like these tactics; our intelligence through the Skinnies and on back into the Bugs themselves was definite on this point. Besides, we cleaned their colony of Sheol completely this way. Maybe they managed to evacuate the queens and the brains . . . but at least we were learning to hurt them.

But so far as the Roughnecks were concerned, these gas bombings were simply another drill, to be done according to orders, by the numbers, and on the bounce.

Eventually we had to go back to Sanctuary for more capsules. Capsules are expendable (well, so were we) and when they are gone, you must return to base, even if the Cherenkov generators could still take you twice around the Galaxy. Shortly before this a dispatch came through breveting Jelly to lieutenant, vice Rasczak. Jelly tried to keep it quiet but Captain

Deladrier published it and then required him to eat forward with the other officers. He still spent all the rest of his time aft.

But we had taken several drops by then with him as platoon leader and the outfit had gotten used to getting along without the Lieutenant – it still hurt but it was routine now. After Jelal was commissioned the word was slowly passed around among us and chewed over that it was time for us to name ourselves for our boss, as with other outfits.

Johnson was senior and took the word to Jelly; he picked me to go along with him as moral support. 'Yeah?' growled Jelly.

'Uh, Sarge – I mean Lieutenant, we've been thinking—'

'With what?'

'Well, the boys have been sort of talking it over and they think – well, they say the outfit ought to call itself: "Jelly's Jaguars."'

'They do, eh? How many of 'em favor that name?'

'Its unanimous,' Johnson said simply.

'So? Fifty-two ayes . . . and one no. The noes have it.' Nobody ever brought up the subject again.

Shortly after that we orbited at Sanctuary. I was glad to be there, as the ship's internal pseudo-gravity field had been off for most of two days before that, while the Chief Engineer tinkered with it, leaving us in free fall – which I hate. I'll never be a real spaceman. Dirt underfoot felt good. The entire platoon went on ten days' rest & recreation and transferred to accommodation barracks at the Base.

I never had learned the co-ordinates of Sanctuary, nor the name or catalogue number of the star it orbits – because what you don't know, you can't spill; the location is ultra-top-secret, known only to ships' captains, piloting officers, and such . . . and, I understand, with each of them under orders and hypnotic compulsion to suicide if necessary to avoid capture. So I don't want to know. With the possibility that Luna Base might be taken and Terra herself occupied, the Federation kept as much of its beef as possible at Sanctuary, so that a disaster back home would not necessarily mean capitulation.

But I can tell you what sort of a planet it is. Like Earth, but retarded.

Literally retarded, like a kid who takes ten years to learn to wave bye-bye and never does manage to master patty-cake. It is a planet as near like Earth as two planets can be, same age according to the planetologists and its star is the same age as the Sun and the same type, so say the astrophysicists. It has plenty of flora and fauna, the same atmosphere as Earth, near enough, and much the same weather; it even has a good-sized moon and Earth's exceptional tides.

With all these advantages it barely got away from the starting gate. You see, it's short on mutations; it does not enjoy Earth's high level of natural radiation.

Its typical and most highly developed plant life is a very primitive giant fern; its top animal life is a proto-insect which hasn't even developed colonies. I am not speaking of transplanted flora and fauna – *our* stuff moves in and brushes the native stuff aside.

With its evolutionary progress held down almost to zero by lack of radiation and a consequent most unhealthily low mutation rate, native life forms on Sanctuary just haven't had a decent chance to evolve and aren't fit to compete. Their gene patterns remain fixed for a relatively long time: they aren't adaptable – like being forced to play the same bridge hand over and over again, for eons, with no hope of getting a better one.

As long as they just competed with each other, this didn't matter too much – morons among morons, so to speak. But when types that had evolved on a planet enjoying high radiation and fierce competition were introduced, the native stuff was outclassed.

Now all the above is perfectly obvious from high school biology . . . but the high forehead from the research station there who was telling me about this brought up a point I would never have thought of.

What about the human beings who have colonized Sanctuary?

Not transients like me, but the colonists who live there, many of whom were born there, and whose descendants will live there, even unto the umpteenth generation – what about those descendants? It doesn't do a person any harm not to be radiated; in fact it's a bit safer – leukemia and some types of cancer are almost unknown there. Besides that, the economic situation is at present all in their favor; when they plant a field of (Terran) wheat, they don't even have to clear out the weeds. Terran wheat displaces anything native.

But the descendants of those colonists won't evolve. Not much, anyhow. This chap told me that they could improve a little through mutation from other causes, from new blood added by immigration, and from natural selection among the gene patterns they already own – but that is all very minor compared with the evolutionary rate on Terra and on any usual planet. So what happens? Do they stay frozen at their present level while the rest of the human race moves on past them, until they are living fossils, as out of place as a pithecanthropus in a spaceship?

Or will they worry about the fate of their descendants and dose themselves regularly with X-rays or maybe set off lots of dirty-type nuclear explosions each year to build up a fall-out reservoir in their atmosphere? (Accepting, of course, the immediate dangers of radiation to themselves in order to provide a proper genetic heritage of mutation for the benefit of their descendants.)

This bloke predicted that they will not do anything. He claims that the human race is too individualistic, too self-centered, to worry that much about future generations. He says that the genetic impoverishment of distant generations through lack of radiation is something most people are simply incapable of worrying about. And of course it is a far-distant threat; evolution works so slowly, even on Terra, that the development of a new species is a matter of many, many thousands of years.

I don't know. Shucks, I don't know what I myself will do more than half the time; how can I predict what a colony of strangers will do? But I'm sure of this: Sanctuary is going to be fully settled, either by us or by the Bugs. Or by somebody. It is a potential utopia, and, with desirable real estate so scarce in this end of the Galaxy, it will not be left in the possession of primitive life forms that failed to make the grade.

Already it is a delightful place, better in many ways for a few days R&R than is most of Terra. In the second place, while it has an awful lot of civilians, more than a million, as civilians go they aren't bad. They know there is a war on. Fully half of them are employed either at the Base or in war industry; the rest raise food and sell it to the Fleet. You might say they have a vested interest in war, but, whatever their reasons, they respect the uniform and don't resent the wearers thereof. Quite the contrary. If an M.I. walks into a shop there, the proprietor calls him 'Sir,' and really seems to mean it, even while he's trying to sell something worthless at too high a price.

But in the *first* place, half of those civilians are female.

You have to have been out on a long patrol to appreciate this properly. You need to have looked forward to your day of guard duty, for the privilege of standing two hours out of each six with your spine against bulkhead thirty and your ears cocked for just the *sound* of a female voice. I suppose it's actually easier in the all-stag ships . . . but I'll take the *Rodger*

Young. It's good to know that the ultimate reason you are fighting actually exists and that they are not just a figment of the imagination.

Besides the civilian wonderful 50 per cent, about 40 per cent of the Federal Service people on Sanctuary are female. Add it all up and you've got the most beautiful scenery in the explored universe.

Besides these unsurpassed natural advantages, a great deal has been done artificially to keep R&R from being wasted. Most of the civilians seem to hold two jobs; they've got circles under their eyes from staying up all night to make a service man's leave pleasant. Churchill Road from the Base to the city is lined both sides with enterprises intended to separate painlessly a man from money he really hasn't any use for anyhow, to the pleasant accompaniment of refreshment, entertainment, and music.

If you are able to get past these traps, through having already been bled of all valuta, there are still other places in the city almost as satisfactory (I mean there are girls there, too) which are provided free by a grateful populace – much like the social center in Vancouver, these are, but even more welcome.

Sanctuary, and especially Espiritu Santo, the city, struck me as such an ideal place that I toyed with the notion of asking for my discharge there when my term was up – after all, I didn't really care whether my descendants (if any) twenty-five thousand years hence had long green tendrils like everybody else, or just the equipment I had been forced to get by with. That professor type from the Research Station couldn't frighten me with that no radiation scare talk; it seemed to me (from what I could see around me) that the human race had reached its ultimate peak anyhow.

No doubt a gentleman wart hog feels the same way about a lady wart hog – but, if so, both of us are very sincere.

There are other opportunities for recreation there, too. I remember with particular pleasure one evening when a table of Roughnecks got into a friendly discussion with a group of Navy men (not from the *Rodger Young*) seated at the next table. The debate was spirited, a bit noisy, and some Base police came in and broke it up with stun guns just as we were warming to our rebuttal. Nothing came of it, except that we had to pay for the furniture – the Base Commandant takes the position that a man on R&R should be allowed a little freedom as long as he doesn't pick one of the 'thirty-one crash landings.'

The accommodation barracks are all right, too – not fancy, but comfortable and the chow line works twenty-five hours a day with civilians doing all the work. No reveille, no taps, you're actually on leave and you don't have to go to the barracks at all. I did, however, as it seemed downright preposterous to spend money on hotels when there was a clean, soft sack free and so many better ways to spend accumulated pay. That extra hour in each day was nice, too, as it meant nine hours solid and the day still untouched – I caught up sack time clear back to Operation Bughouse.

It might as well have been a hotel; Ace and I had a room all to ourselves in visiting non-com quarters. One morning, when R&R was regrettably drawing to a close, I was just turning over about local noon when Ace shook my bed. 'On the bounce, soldier! The Bugs are attacking.'

I told him what to do with the Bugs.

'Let's hit dirt,' he persisted.

'No dinero.' I had had a date the night before with a chemist (female, of course, and charmingly so) from the Research Station. She had known Carl on Pluto and Carl had written to me to look her up if I ever got to Sanctuary. She was a slender redhead, with expensive tastes. Apparently Carl had intimated to her that I had more money than was good for me, for she decided that the night before was just the time for her to get acquainted with the local champagne. I didn't let Carl down by admitting that all I had was a trooper's honorarium; I bought it for her while I drank what they said was (but wasn't) fresh pineapple squash. The result was that I had to walk home, afterwards – the cabs aren't free. Still, it had been worth it. After all, what is money? – I'm speaking of Bug money, of course.

'No ache,' Ace answered. 'I can juice you – I got lucky last night. Ran into a Navy file who didn't know percentages.'

So I got up and shaved and showered and we hit the chow line for half a dozen shell eggs and sundries such as potatoes and ham and hot cakes and so forth and then we hit dirt to get something to eat. The walk up Churchill Road was hot and Ace decided to stop in a cantina. I went along to see if their pineapple squash was real. It wasn't, but it was cold. You can't have everything.

We talked about this and that and Ace ordered another round. I tried their strawberry squash – same deal. Ace stared into his glass, then said, 'Ever thought about greasing for officer?'

I said, '*Huh?* Are you crazy?'

'Nope. Look, Johnnie, this war may run on quite a piece. No matter what propaganda they put out for the folks at home, you and I know that the Bugs aren't ready to quit. So why don't you plan ahead? As the man says, if you've got to play in the band, it's better to wave the stick than to carry the big drum.'

I was startled by the turn the talk had taken, especially from Ace. 'How about you? Are you planning to buck for a commission?'

'Me?' he answered. 'Check your circuits, son – you're getting wrong answers. I've got no education and I'm ten years older than you are. But you've got enough education to hit the selection exams for O.C.S. *and* you've got the I.Q. they like, I guarantee that if you go career, you'll make sergeant before I do . . . and get picked for O.C.S. the day after.'

'Now I know you're crazy!'

'You listen to your pop. I hate to tell you this, but you are just stupid and eager and sincere enough to make the kind of officer men love to follow into some silly predicament. But me – well, I'm a natural non-com, with the proper pessimistic attitude to offset the enthusiasm of the likes of you. Someday I'll make sergeant . . . and presently I'll have my twenty years in and retire and get one of the reserved jobs – cop, maybe – and marry a nice fat wife with the same low tastes I have, and I'll follow the sports and fish and go pleasantly to pieces.'

Ace stopped to wet his whistle. 'But *you*,' he went on. 'You'll stay in and probably make high rank and die gloriously and I'll read about it and say proudly, "I knew him when. Why, I used to lend him money – we were corporals together." Well?'

'I've never thought about it,' I said slowly. 'I just meant to serve my term.'

He grinned sourly. 'Do you see any term enrollees being paid off today? You expect to make it on two years?'

He had a point. As long as the war continued, a 'term' didn't end – at least not for cap troopers. It was mostly a difference in attitude, at least for the present. Those of us on 'term' could at least feel like short-timers; we could talk about: 'When this flea-bitten war is over.' A career man didn't say that; he wasn't going anywhere, short of retirement – or buying it.

On the other hand, neither were we. But if you went 'career' and then didn't finish twenty . . . well, they could be pretty sticky about your franchise even though they wouldn't keep a man who didn't want to stay.

'Maybe not a two-year term,' I admitted. 'But the war won't last forever.'

'It won't?'

'How can it?'

'Blessed if I know. They don't tell me these things. But I know that's not what is troubling you, Johnnie. You got a girl waiting?'

'No. Well, I had,' I answered slowly, 'but she "Dear-Johned" me.' As a lie, this was no more than a mild decoration, which I tucked in because Ace seemed to expect it. Carmen wasn't my girl and she never waited for anybody – but she *did* address letters with 'Dear Johnnie' on the infrequent occasions when she wrote to me.

Ace nodded wisely. 'They'll do it every time. They'd rather marry civilians and have somebody around to chew out when they feel like it. Never you mind, son – you'll find plenty of them more than willing to marry when you're retired . . . and you'll be better able to handle one at that age. Marriage is a young man's disaster and an old man's comfort.' He looked at my glass. 'It nauseates me to see you drinking that slop.'

'I feel the same way about the stuff you drink,' I told him.

He shrugged. 'As you say, it takes all kinds. You think it over.'

'I will.'

Ace got into a card game shortly after, and lent me some money and I went for a walk; I needed to think.

Go career? Quite aside from that noise about a commission, did I want to go career? Why, I had gone through all this to get my franchise, hadn't I? – and if I went career, I was just as far away from the privilege of voting as if I had never enrolled . . . because as long as you were still in uniform you weren't entitled to vote. Which was the way it should be, of course – why, if they let the Roughnecks vote, the idiots might vote not to make a drop. Can't have that.

Nevertheless I had signed up in order to win a vote.

Or had I?

Had I ever cared about voting? No, it was the prestige, the pride, the status . . . of being a citizen.

Or was it?

I couldn't to save my life remember *why* I had signed up.

Anyhow, it wasn't the process of voting that made a citizen – the Lieutenant had been a citizen in the truest sense of the word, even though he had not lived long enough ever to cast a ballot. He had 'voted' every time he made a drop.

And so had I!

I could hear Colonel Dubois in my mind: 'Citizenship is an attitude, a state of mind, an emotional conviction that the whole is greater than the part . . . and that the part should be humbly proud to sacrifice itself that the whole may live.'

I still didn't know whether I yearned to place my one-and-only body 'between my loved home and the war's desolation' – I still got the shakes every drop and that 'desolation' could be pretty desolate. But nevertheless I knew at last what Colonel Dubois had been talking about. The M.I. was mine and I was theirs. If that was what the M.I. did to break the monotony, then that was what I did. Patriotism was a bit esoteric for me, too large-scale to see. But the M.I. was my gang, I belonged. They were all the family I had left; they were the brothers I had never had, closer than Carl had ever been. If I left them, I'd be lost.

So why shouldn't I go career?

All right, all right – but how about this nonsense of greasing for a commission? That was something else again. I could see myself putting in twenty years and then taking it easy, the way Ace had described, with ribbons on my chest and carpet slippers on my feet . . . or evenings down at the Veterans Hall, rehashing old times with others who belonged. But O.C.S.? I could hear Al Jenkins, in one of the bull sessions we had about such things: 'I'm a private! I'm going to stay a private! When you're a private they don't expect anything of you. Who wants to be an officer? Or even a sergeant? You're breathing the same air, aren't you? Eating the same food? Going the same places, making the same drops. But no worries.'

Al had a point. What had chevrons ever gotten me? – aside from lumps.

Nevertheless I knew I would take sergeant if it was ever offered to me. You don't refuse, a cap trooper doesn't refuse anything; he steps up and takes a swing at it. Commission, too, I supposed.

Not that it would happen. Who was I to think that I could ever be what Lieutenant Rasczak had been?

My walk had taken me close to the candidates' school, though I don't believe I intended to come that way. A company of cadets were out on their parade ground, drilling at trot, looking for all the world like boots in Basic. The sun was hot and it looked not nearly as comfortable as a bull session in the drop room of the *Rodger Young* – why, I hadn't marched farther than bulkhead thirty since I had finished Basic; that breaking-in nonsense was past.

I watched them a bit, sweating through their uniforms; I heard them being chewed out – by sergeants, too. Old Home Week. I shook my head and walked away from there –

– went back to the accommodation barracks, over to the B.O.Q. wing, found Jelly's room.

He was in it, his feet up on a table and reading a magazine. I knocked on the frame of the door. He looked up and growled, 'Yeah?'

'Sarge – I mean, Lieutenant—'

'Spit it out!'

'Sir, I want to go career.'

He dropped his feet to the desk. 'Put up your right hand.'

He swore me, reached into the drawer of the table and pulled out papers.

He had my papers already made out, waiting for me, ready to sign. And I hadn't even told Ace. How about that?

Chapter 12

It is by no means enough that an officer should be capable.... He should be as well a gentleman of liberal education, refined manners, punctilious courtesy, and the nicest sense of personal honor.... No meritorious act of a subordinate should escape his attention, even if the reward be only one word of approval. Conversely, he should not be blind to a single fault in any subordinate.

True as may be the political principles for which we are now contending ... the ships themselves must be ruled under a system of absolute despotism.

I trust that I have now made clear to you the tremendous responsibilities ... We must do the best we can with what we have.

– John Paul Jones, September 14, 1775;
excerpts from a letter to the naval committee
of the N.A. insurrectionists.

The *Rodger Young* was again returning to Base for replacements, both capsules and men. Al Jenkins had bought his farm, covering a pickup – and that one had cost us the Padre, too. And besides that, I had to be replaced. I was wearing brand-new sergeant's chevrons (vice Migliaccio) but I had a hunch that Ace would be wearing them as soon as I was out of the ship – they were mostly honorary, I knew; the promotion was Jelly's way of giving me a good send-off as I was detached for O.C.S.

But it didn't keep me from being proud of them. At the Fleet landing field I went through the exit gate with my nose in the air and strode up to the quarantine desk to have my orders stamped. As this was being done I heard a polite, respectful voice behind me: 'Excuse me, Sergeant, but that boat that just came down – is it from the *Rodger*—'

I turned to see the speaker, flicked my eyes over his sleeves, saw that it was a small, slightly stoop-shouldered corporal, no doubt one of our –

'Father!'

Then the corporal had his arms around me. 'Juan! Juan! Oh, my little Johnnie!'

I kissed him and hugged him and started to cry. Maybe that civilian clerk at the quarantine desk had never seen two non-coms kiss each other before. Well, if I had noticed him so much as lifting an eyebrow, I would have pasted him. But I didn't notice him; I was busy. He had to remind me to take my orders with me.

By then we had blown our noses and quit making an open spectacle of ourselves. I said, 'Father, let's find a corner somewhere and sit down and talk. I want to know . . . well, *everything*!' I took a deep breath. 'I thought you were dead.'

'No. Came close to buying it once or twice, maybe. But, Son . . . Sergeant – I really do have to find out about that landing boat. You see—'

'Oh, that. It's from the *Rodger Young*. I just—'

He looked terribly disappointed. 'Then I've got to bounce, right now. I've got to report in.' Then he added eagerly, 'But you'll be back aboard soon, won't you, Juanito? Or are you going on R&R?'

'Uh, no.' I thought fast. Of all the ways to have things roll! 'Look, Father, I know the boat schedule. You can't go aboard for at least an hour and a bit. That boat is not on a fast retrieve; she'll make a minimum-fuel rendezvous when the *Rog* completes this pass – if the pilot doesn't have to wait over the next pass after that; they've got to load first.'

He said dubiously, 'My orders read to report at once to the pilot of the first available ship's boat.'

'Father, Father! Do you have to be so confounded regulation? The girl who's pushing that heap won't care whether you board the boat now, or just as they button up. Anyhow they'll play the ship's recall over the speakers in here ten minutes before boost and announce it. You *can't* miss it.'

He let me lead him over to an empty corner. As we sat down he added, 'Will you be going up in the same boat, Juan? Or later?'

'Uh—' I showed him my orders; it seemed the simplest way to break the news. Ships that pass in the night, like the Evangeline story – cripes, what a way for things to break!

He read them and got tears in his eyes and I said hastily, 'Look, Father, I'm going to try to come back – I wouldn't want any other outfit than the Roughnecks. And with you in them . . . oh, I know it's disappointing but—'

'It's not disappointment, Juan.'

'Huh?'

'It's pride. My boy is going to be an officer. My little Johnnie – Oh, it's disappointment, too; I had waited for this day. But I can wait a while longer.' He smiled through his tears. 'You've grown, lad. And filled out, too.'

'Uh, I guess so. But, Father, I'm not an officer yet and I might only be out of the *Rog* a few days. I mean, they sometimes bust 'em out pretty fast and—'

'Enough of that, young man!'

'Huh?'

'You'll make it. Let's have no more talk of "busting out."' Suddenly he smiled. 'That's the first time I've been able to tell a sergeant to shut up.'

'Well . . . I'll certainly try, Father. And if I do make it, I'll certainly put in for the old *Rog*. But—' I trailed off.

'Yes, I know. Your request won't mean anything unless

there's a billet for you. Never mind. If this hour is all we have, we'll make the most of it – and I'm so proud of you I'm splitting my seams. How have you been, Johnnie?'

'Oh, fine, just fine.' I was thinking that it wasn't all bad. He would be better off in the Roughnecks than in any other outfit. All my friends . . . they'd take care of him, keep him alive. I'd have to send a gram to Ace – Father like as not wouldn't even let them know he was related. 'Father, how long have you been in?'

'A little over a year.'

'And corporal already!'

Father smiled grimly. 'They're making them fast these days.'

I didn't have to ask what he meant. Casualties. There were always vacancies in the T.O.; you couldn't get enough trained soldiers to fill them. Instead I said, 'Uh . . . but, Father, you're – Well, I mean, aren't you sort of old to be soldiering? I mean the Navy, or Logistics, or—'

'I wanted the M.I. and I got it!' he said emphatically. 'And I'm no older than many sergeants – not as old, in fact. Son, the mere fact that I'm twenty-two years older than you are doesn't put me in a wheel chair. And age has its advantages, too.'

Well, there was something in that. I recalled how Sergeant Zim had always tried the older men first, when he was dealing out boot chevrons. And Father would never have goofed in Basic the way I had – no lashes for him. He was probably spotted as non-com material before he ever finished Basic. The Army needs a lot of really grown-up men in the middle grades; it's a paternalistic organization.

I didn't have to ask him why he had wanted M.I., nor why or how he had wound up in my ship – I just felt warm about it, more flattered by it than any praise he had ever given me in words. And I didn't want to ask him *why* he had joined up;

I felt that I knew. Mother. Neither of us had mentioned her – too painful.

So I changed the subject abruptly. 'Bring me up to date. Tell me where you've been and what you've done.'

'Well, I trained at Camp San Martín—'

'Huh? Not Currie?'

'New one. But the same old lumps, I understand. Only they rush you through two months faster, you don't get Sundays off. Then I requested the *Rodger Young* – and didn't get it – and wound up in McSlattery's Volunteers. A good outfit.'

'Yes, I know.' They had had a reputation for being rough, tough, and nasty – almost as good as the Roughnecks.

'I should say that it *was* a good outfit. I made several drops with them and some of the boys bought it and after a while I got these.' He glanced at his chevrons. 'I was a corporal when we dropped on Sheol—'

'You were *there?* So was I!' With a sudden warm flood of emotion I felt closer to my father than I ever had before in my life.

'I know. At least I knew your outfit was there. I was around fifty miles north of you, near as I can guess. We soaked up that counterattack when they came boiling up out of the ground like bats out of a cave.' Father shrugged. 'So when it was over I was a corporal without an outfit, not enough of us left to make a healthy cadre. So they sent me here. I could have gone with King's Kodiak Bears, but I had a word with the placement sergeant – and, sure as sunrise, the *Rodger Young* came back with a billet for a corporal. So here I am.'

'And when did you join up?' I realized that it was the wrong remark as soon as I had made it – but I had to get the subject away from McSlattery's Volunteers; an orphan from a dead outfit wants to forget it.

Father said quietly, 'Shortly after Buenos Aires.'

'Oh. I see.'

Father didn't say anything for several seconds. Then he said softly, 'I'm not sure that you do see, Son.'

'Sir?'

'Mmm . . . it will not be easy to explain. Certainly, losing your mother had a great deal to do with it. But I didn't enroll to avenge her – even though I had that in mind, too. You had more to do with it—'

'Me?'

'Yes, you. Son, I always understood what you were doing better than your mother did – don't blame her; she never had a chance to know, any more than a bird can understand swimming. And perhaps I knew *why* you did it, even though I beg to doubt that you knew yourself, at the time. At least half of my anger at you was sheer resentment . . . that you had actually done something that I knew, buried deep in my heart, I should have done. But you weren't the cause of my joining up, either . . . you merely helped trigger it and you did control the service I chose.'

He paused. 'I wasn't in good shape at the time you enrolled. I was seeing my hypnotherapist pretty regularly – you never suspected that, did you? – but we had gotten no farther than a clear recognition that I was enormously dissatisfied. After you left, I took it out on you – but it was not you, and I knew it and my therapist knew it. I suppose I knew that there was real trouble brewing earlier than most; we were invited to bid on military components fully a month before the state of emergency was announced. We had converted almost entirely to war production while you were still in training.

'I felt better during that period, worked to death and too busy to see my therapist. Then I became more troubled than ever.' He smiled. 'Son, do you know about civilians?'

'Well . . . we don't talk the same language. I know that.'

'Clearly enough put. Do you remember Madame Ruitman?

I was on a few days leave after I finished Basic and I went home. I saw some of our friends, said good-by – she among them. She chattered away and said, "So you're really going out? Well, if you reach Faraway, you really must look up my dear friends the Regatos."

'I told her, as gently as I could, that it seemed unlikely, since the Arachnids had occupied Faraway.

'It didn't faze her in the least. She said, "Oh, that's all right – they're civilians!"' Father smiled cynically.

'Yes, I know.'

'But I'm getting ahead of my story. I told you that I was getting still more upset. Your mother's death released me for what I had to do . . . even though she and I were closer than most, nevertheless it set me free to do it. I turned the business over to Morales—'

'Old man Morales? Can *he* handle it?'

'Yes. Because he has to. A lot of us are doing things we didn't know we could. I gave him a nice chunk of stock – you know the old saying about the kine that tread the grain – and the rest I split two ways, in a trust: half to the Daughters of Charity, half to you whenever you want to go back and take it. If you do. Never mind. I had at last found out what was wrong with me.' He stopped, then said very softly, 'I had to perform an act of faith. I had to prove to myself that I was a man. Not just a producing-consuming economic animal . . . but a *man*.'

At that moment, before I could answer anything, the wall speakers around us sang: '*—shines the name, shines the name of Rodger Young!*' and a girl's voice added, 'Personnel for F.C.T. *Rodger Young*, stand to boat. Berth H. Nine minutes.'

Father bounced to his feet, grabbed his kit roll. 'That's mine! Take care of yourself, Son – and hit those exams. Or you'll find you're still not too big to paddle.'

'I will, Father.'

He embraced me hastily. 'See you when we get back!' And he was gone, on the bounce.

In the Commandant's outer office I reported to a fleet sergeant who looked remarkably like Sergeant Ho, even to lacking an arm. However, he lacked Sergeant Ho's smile as well. I said, 'Career Sergeant Juan Rico, to report to the Commandant pursuant to orders.'

He glanced at the clock. 'Your boat was down seventy-three minutes ago. Well?'

So I told him. He pulled his lip and looked at me meditatively. 'I've heard every excuse in the book. But you've just added a new page. Your father, your own father, really was reporting to your old ship just as you were detached?'

'The bare truth, Sergeant. You can check it – Corporal Emilio Rico.'

'We don't check the statements of the "young gentlemen" around here. We simply cashier them if it ever turns out that they have not told the truth. Okay, a boy who wouldn't be late in order to see his old man off wouldn't be worth much in any case. Forget it.'

'Thanks, Sergeant. Do I report to the Commandant now?'

'You've reported to him.' He made a check mark on a list. 'Maybe a month from now he'll send for you along with a couple of dozen others. Here's your assignment, here's a check-off list you start with – and you can start by cutting off those chevrons. But save them; you may need them later. But as of this moment you are "Mister," not "Sergeant."'

'Yes, sir.'

'Don't call me "sir." *I* call *you* "sir." But you won't like it.'

I am not going to describe Officer Candidates School. It's like Basic, but squared and cubed with books added. In the mornings we behaved like privates, doing the same old things we had done in Basic and in combat and being chewed out for the way we did them – by sergeants. In the afternoons we were cadets and 'gentlemen,' and recited on and were lectured concerning an endless list of subjects: math, science, galactography, xenology, hypnopedia, logistics, strategy and tactics, communications, military law, terrain reading, special weapons, psychology of leadership, anything from the care and feeding of privates to why Xerxes lost the big one. Most especially how to be a one-man catastrophe yourself while keeping track of fifty other men, nursing them, loving them, leading them, saving them – but *never* babying them.

We had beds, which we used all too little; we had rooms and showers and inside plumbing; and each four candidates had a civilian servant, to make our beds and clean our rooms and shine our shoes and lay out our uniforms and run errands. This service was not intended as a luxury and was not; its purpose was to give the student more time to accomplish the plainly impossible by relieving him of things any graduate of Basic can already do perfectly.

Six days shalt thou work and do all thou art able,
The seventh the same and pound on the cable.

Or the Army version ends: – *and clean out the stable*, which shows how many centuries this sort of thing has been going on. I wish I could catch just one of those civilians who think we loaf and put them through one month of O.C.S.

In the evenings and all day Sundays we studied until our eyes burned and our ears ached – then slept (if we slept) with a hypnopedic speaker droning away under the pillow.

Our marching songs were appropriately downbeat: 'No Army for mine, no Army for mine! I'd rather be behind the plow any old time!' and 'Don't wanta study war no more,' and 'Don't make my boy a soldier, the weeping mother cried,' and

– favorite of all – the old classic 'Gentlemen Rankers' with its chorus about the Little Lost Sheep: '—God ha' pity on such as we. Baa! Yah! Bah!'

Yet somehow I don't remember being unhappy. Too busy, I guess. There was never that psychological 'hump' to get over, the one everybody hits in Basic; there was simply the ever-present fear of flunking out. My poor preparation in math bothered me especially. My roommate, a colonial from Hesperus with the oddly appropriate name of 'Angel,' sat up night after night, tutoring me.

Most of the instructors, especially the officers, were disabled. The only ones I can remember who had a full complement of arms, legs, eyesight, hearing, etc, were some of the non-commissioned combat instructors – and not all of those. Our coach in dirty fighting sat in a powered chair, wearing a plastic collar, and was completely paralyzed from the neck down. But his tongue wasn't paralyzed, his eye was photographic, and the savage way in which he could analyze and criticize what he had seen made up for his minor impediment.

At first I wondered why these obvious candidates for physical retirement and full-pay pension didn't take it and go home. Then I quit wondering.

I guess the high point in my whole cadet course was a visit from Ensign Ibañez, she of the dark eyes, junior watch officer and pilot-under-instruction of the Corvette Transport *Mannerheim*. Carmencita showed up, looking incredibly pert in Navy dress whites and about the size of a paperweight, while my class was lined up for evening meal muster – walked down the line and you could hear eyeballs click as she passed – walked straight up to the duty officer and asked for me by name in a clear, penetrating voice.

The duty officer, Captain Chandar, was widely believed never to have smiled at his own mother, but he smiled down at little Carmen, straining his face out of shape, and admitted my existence . . . whereupon she waved her long black lashes at him, explained that her ship was about to boost and could she *please* take me out to dinner?

And I found myself in possession of a highly irregular and totally unprecedented three-hour pass. It may be that the Navy has developed hypnosis techniques that they have not yet gotten around to passing on to the Army. Or her secret weapon may be older than that and not usable by M.I. In any case I not only had a wonderful time but my prestige with my classmates, none too high until then, climbed to amazing heights.

It was a glorious evening and well worth flunking two classes the next day. It was somewhat dimmed by the fact that we had each heard about Carl – killed when the Bugs smashed our research station on Pluto – but only somewhat, as we had each learned to live with such things.

One thing did startle me. Carmen relaxed and took off her hat while we were eating, and her blue-black hair was all gone. I knew that a lot of the Navy girls shaved their heads – after all, it's not practical to take care of long hair in a war ship and, most especially, a pilot can't risk having her hair floating around, getting in the way, in any free-fall maneuvers. Shucks, I shaved my own scalp, just for convenience and cleanliness. But my mental picture of little Carmen included this mane of thick, wavy hair.

But, do you know, once you get used to it, it's rather cute. I mean, if a girl looks all right to start with, she still looks all right with her head smooth. And it does serve to set a Navy girl apart from civilian chicks – sort of lodge pin, like the gold skulls for combat drops. It made Carmen look distinguished, gave her dignity, and for the first time I fully realized that she really was an officer and a fighting man – as well as a very pretty girl.

I got back to barracks with stars in my eyes and whiffing slightly of perfume. Carmen had kissed me good-by.

The only O.C.S. classroom course the content of which I'm even going to mention was: History and Moral Philosophy.

I was surprised to find it in the curriculum. H. & M.P. has nothing to do with combat and how to lead a platoon; its connection with war (where it is connected) is in *why* to fight – a matter already settled for any candidate long before he reaches O.C.S. An M.I. fights because he is M.I.

I decided that the course must be a repeat for the benefit of those of us (maybe a third) who had never had it in school. Over 20 per cent of my cadet class were not from Terra (a much higher percentage of colonials sign up to serve than do people born on Earth – sometimes it makes you wonder) and of the three-quarters or so from Terra, some were from associated territories and other places where H. & M. P. might not be taught. So I figured it for a cinch course which would give me a little rest from tough courses, the ones with decimal points.

Wrong again. Unlike my high school course, you had to pass it. Not by examination, however. The course included examinations and prepared papers and quizzes and such – but no marks. What you had to have was the instructor's opinion that you were worthy of commission.

If he gave you a downcheck, a board sat on you, questioning not merely whether you could be an officer but whether you belonged in the Army at *any* rank, no matter how fast you might be with weapons – deciding whether to give you extra instruction . . . or just kick you out and let you be a civilian.

History and Moral Philosophy works like a delayed-action bomb. You wake up in the middle of the night and think: Now what did he mean by *that*? That had been true even with my high school course; I simply hadn't known what Colonel Dubois was talking about. When I was a kid I thought it was silly for the course to be in the science department. It was nothing like physics or chemistry; why wasn't it over in the fuzzy studies where it belonged? The only reason I paid attention was because there were such lovely arguments.

I had no idea that 'Mr.' Dubois was trying to teach me *why* to fight until long after I had decided to fight anyhow.

Well, why *should* I fight? Wasn't it preposterous to expose my tender skin to the violence of unfriendly strangers? Especially as the pay at any rank was barely spending money, the hours terrible, and the working conditions worse? When I could be sitting at home while such matters were handled by thick-skulled characters who *enjoyed* such games? Particularly when the strangers against whom I fought never had done anything to me personally until I showed up and started kicking over their tea wagon – what sort of nonsense *is* this?

Fight because I'm an M.I.? Brother, you're drooling like Dr. Pavlov's dogs. Cut it out and start thinking.

Major Reid, our instructor, was a blind man with a disconcerting habit of looking straight at you and calling you by name. We were reviewing events after the war between the Russo-Anglo-American Alliance and the Chinese Hegemony, 1987 and following. But this was the day that we heard the news of the destruction of San Francisco and the San Joaquin Valley; I thought he would give us a pep talk. After all, even a civilian ought to be able to figure it out now – the Bugs or us. Fight or die.

Major Reid didn't mention San Francisco. He had one of us apes summarize the negotiated treaty of New Delhi, discuss how it ignored prisoners of war . . . and, by implication, dropped the subject forever; the armistice became a stalemate and prisoners stayed where they were – on one side; on the other side they were turned loose and, during the Disorders, made their way home – or not if they didn't want to.

Major Reid's victim summed up the unreleased prisoners: survivors of two divisions of British paratroopers, some thousands of civilians, captured mostly in Japan, the Philippines, and Russia and sentenced for 'political' crimes.

'Besides that, there were many other military prisoners,' Major Reid's victim went on, 'captured during and before the war – there were rumors that some had been captured in an earlier war and never released. The total of unreleased prisoners was never known. The best estimates place the number around sixty-five thousand.'

'Why the "best"?'

'Uh, that's the estimate in the textbook, sir.'

'Please be precise in your language. Was the number greater or less than one hundred thousand?'

'Uh, I don't know, sir.'

'And nobody else knows. Was it greater than one thousand?'

'Probably, sir. Almost certainly.'

'Utterly certain – because more than that eventually escaped, found their ways home, were tallied by name. I see you did not read your lesson carefully. *Mr. Rico!*'

Now I was the victim. 'Yes, sir.'

'Are a thousand unreleased prisoners sufficient reason to start or resume a war? Bear in mind that millions of innocent people may die, almost certainly *will* die, if war is started or resumed.'

I didn't hesitate. 'Yes, *sir!* More than enough reason.'

'"More than enough." Very well, is *one* prisoner, unreleased by the enemy, enough reason to start or resume a war?'

I hesitated. I knew the M.I. answer – but I didn't think that was the one he wanted. He said sharply, 'Come, come, Mister! We have an upper limit of one thousand; I invited you to consider a lower limit of one. But you can't pay a promissory note which reads "somewhere between one and one thousand pounds' – and starting a war is *much* more serious than paying a trifle of money. Wouldn't it be criminal to endanger a country – two countries in fact – to save one man? Especially as he may not deserve it? Or may die in the meantime? Thousands of people get killed every day in accidents . . . so why hesitate over one man? Answer! Answer yes, or answer no – you're holding up the class.'

He got my goat. I gave him the cap trooper's answer. 'Yes, sir!'

'"Yes" what?'

'It doesn't matter whether it's a thousand – or just one, sir. You fight.'

'Aha! The number of prisoners is irrelevant. Good. Now prove your answer.'

I was stuck. I *knew* it was the right answer. But I didn't know why. He kept hounding me. 'Speak up, Mr. Rico. This is an exact science You have made a mathematical statement; you must give proof. Someone may claim that you have asserted, by analogy, that one potato is worth the same price, no more, no less, as one thousand potatoes. No?'

'No, sir!'

'Why not? Prove it.'

'Men are not potatoes.'

'Good, good, Mr. Rico! I think we have strained your tired brain enough for one day. Bring to class tomorrow a written proof, in symbolic logic, of your answer to my original question. I'll give you a hint. See reference seven in today's chapter. Mr. Salomon! How did the present political organization evolve out of the Disorders? And what is its moral justification?'

Sally stumbled through the first part. However, nobody can describe accurately how the Federation came about; it just grew. With national governments in collapse at the end of the XXth century, something had to fill the vacuum, and in many cases it was returned veterans. They had lost a war, most of them had no jobs, many were sore as could be over the terms of the Treaty of New Delhi, especially the P.O.W. foul-up – and they knew how to fight. But it wasn't revolution; it was more like what happened in Russia in 1917 – the system collapsed; somebody else moved in.

The first known case, in Aberdeen, Scotland, was typical. Some veterans got together as vigilantes to stop rioting and looting, hanged a few people (including two veterans) and decided not to let anyone but veterans on their committee. Just arbitrary at first – they trusted each other a bit, they didn't trust anyone else. What started as an emergency measure became constitutional practice . . . in a generation or two.

Probably those Scottish veterans, since they were finding it necessary to hang some veterans, decided that, if they had to do this, they weren't going to let any 'bleedin', profiteering, black-market, double-time-for-overtime, army-dodging, unprintable' civilians have any say about it. They'd do what they were told, see? – while us apes straightened things out! That's my guess, because I might fel the same way . . . and historians agree that antagonism between civilians and returned soldiers was more intense than we can imagine today.

Sally didn't tell it by the book. Finally Major Reid cut him off. 'Bring a summary to class tomorrow, three thousand words. Mr. Salomon, can you give me a reason – not historical nor theoretical but practical – why the franchise is today limited to discharged veterans?'

'Uh, because they are picked men, sir. Smarter.'

'Preposterous!'

'Sir?'

'Is the word too long for you? I said it was a silly notion.

Service men are not brighter than civilians. In many cases civilians are much more intelligent. That was the sliver of justification underlying the attempted *coup d'état* just before the Treaty of New Delhi, the so-called "Revolt of the Scientists": let the intelligent elite run things and you'll have utopia. It fell flat on its foolish face of course. Because the pursuit of science, despite its social benefits, is itself not a social virtue; its practitioners can be men so self-centered as to be lacking in social responsibility. I've given you a hint, Mister; can you pick it up?'

Sally answered, 'Uh, service men are disciplined, sir.'

Major Reid was gentle with him. 'Sorry. An appealing theory not backed up by facts. You and I are not permitted to vote as long as we remain in the Service, nor is it verifiable that military discipline makes a man self-disciplined once he is out; the crime rate of veterans is much like that of civilians. And you have forgotten that in peacetime most veterans come from non-combatant auxiliary services and have not been subjected to the full rigors of military discipline; they have merely been harried, overworked, and endangered – yet their votes count.'

Major Reid smiled. 'Mr. Salomon, I handed you a trick question. The practical reason for continuing our system is the same as the practical reason for continuing anything: It works satisfactorily.

'Nevertheless, it is instructive to observe the details. Throughout history men have labored to place the sovereign franchise in hands that would guard it well and use it wisely, for the benefit of all. An early attempt was absolute monarchy, passionately defended as the "divine right of kings."

'Sometimes attempts were made to select a wise monarch, rather than leave it to God, as when the Swedes picked a Frenchman, General Bernadotte, to rule them. The objection to this is that the supply of Bernadottes is limited.

'Historic examples range from absolute monarch to utter anarch; mankind has tried thousands of ways and many more have been proposed, some weird in the extreme such as the antlike communism urged by Plato under the misleading title *The Republic*. But the intent has always been moralistic: to provide stable and benevolent government.

'All systems seek to achieve this by limiting franchise to those who are *believed* to have the wisdom to use it justly. I repeat "*all* systems"; even the so-called "unlimited democracies" excluded from franchise not less than one quarter of their populations by age, birth, poll tax, criminal record, or other.'

Major Reid smiled cynically. 'I have never been able to see how a thirty-year-old moron can vote more wisely than a fifteen-year-old genius . . . but that was the age of the "divine right of the common man." Never mind, they paid for their folly.

'The sovereign franchise has been bestowed by all sorts of rules – place of birth, family of birth, race, sex, property, education, age, religion, et cetera. All these systems worked and none of them well. All were regarded as tyrannical by many, all eventually collapsed or were overthrown.

'Now here are we with still another system . . . and our system works quite well. Many complain but none rebel; personal freedom for all is greatest in history, laws are few, taxes are low, living standards are as high as productivity permits, crime is at its lowest ebb. Why? Not because our voters are smarter than other people; we've disposed of that argument. Mr. Tammany – can you tell us why our system works better than any used by our ancestors?'

I don't know where Clyde Tammany got his name; I'd take him for a Hindu. He answered, 'Uh, I'd venture to guess that it's because the electors are a small group who know that the decisions are up to them . . . so they study the issues.'

'No guessing, please; this is an exact science. And your guess is wrong. The ruling nobles of many another system were a small group fully aware of their grave power. Furthermore, our franchised citizens are not everywhere a small fraction; you know or should know that the percentage of citizens among adults ranges from over eighty per cent on Iskander to less than three per cent in some Terran nations – yet government is much the same everywhere. Nor are the voters picked men; they bring no special wisdom, talent, or training to their sovereign tasks. So what difference is there between our voters and wielders of franchise in the past? We have had enough guesses; I'll state the obvious: Under our system every voter and officeholder is a man who has demonstrated through voluntary and difficult service that he places the welfare of the group ahead of personal advantage.

'And that is the one practical difference.

'He may fail in wisdom, he may lapse in civic virtue. But his average performance is enormously better than that of any other class of rulers in history.'

Major Reid paused to touch the face of an old-fashioned watch, 'reading' its hands. 'The period is almost over and we have yet to determine the moral reason for our success in governing ourselves. Now continued success is *never* a matter of chance. Bear in mind that this is science, not wishful thinking; the universe is what it *is*, not what we want it to be. To vote is to wield authority; it is the supreme authority from which all other authority derives – such as mine to make your lives miserable once a day. *Force*, if you will! – the franchise is force, naked and raw, the Power of the Rods and the Ax. Whether it is exerted by ten men or by ten billion, political authority is *force*.

'But this universe consists of paired dualities. What is the converse of authority? Mr. Rico.'

He had picked one I could answer. 'Responsibility, sir.'

'Applause. Both for practical reasons and for mathematically verifiable moral reasons, authority and responsibility must be equal – else a balancing takes place as surely as current flows between points of unequal potential. To permit irresponsible authority is to sow disaster; to hold a man responsible for anything he does not control is to behave with blind idiocy. The unlimited democracies were unstable because their citizens were not responsible for the fashion in which they exerted their sovereign authority . . . other than through the tragic logic of history. The unique "poll tax" that we must pay was unheard of. No attempt was made to determine whether a voter was socially responsible to the extent of his literally unlimited authority. If he voted the impossible, the disastrous possible happened instead – and responsibility was then forced on him willy-nilly and destroyed both him and his foundationless temple.

'Superficially, our system is only slightly different; we have democracy unlimited by race, color, creed, birth, wealth, sex, or conviction, and anyone may win sovereign power by a usually short and not too arduous term of service – nothing more than a light workout to our cave-man ancestors. But that slight difference is one between a system that works, since it is constructed to match the facts, and one that is inherently unstable. Since sovereign franchise is the ultimate in human authority, we insure that all who wield it accept the ultimate in social responsibility – we require each person who wishes to exert control over the state to wager his own life – and lose it, if need be – to save the life of the state. The maximum responsibility a human can accept is thus equated to the ultimate authority a human can exert. Yin and yang, perfect and equal.'

The Major added, 'Can anyone define why there has never been revolution against our system? Despite the fact that every government in history has had such? Despite the notorious fact that complaints are loud and unceasing?'

One of the older cadets took a crack at it. 'Sir, revolution is impossible.'

'Yes. But why?'

'Because revolution – armed uprising – requires not only dissatisfaction but aggressiveness. A revolutionist has to be willing to fight and die – or he's just a parlor pink. If you separate out the aggressive ones and make them the sheep dogs, the sheep will never give you trouble.'

'Nicely put! Analogy is always suspect, but that one is close to the facts. Bring me a mathematical proof tomorrow. Time for one more question – you ask it and I'll answer. Anyone?'

'Uh, sir, why not go – well, go the limit? Require everyone to serve and let everybody vote?'

'Young man, can you restore my eyesight?'

'Sir? Why, no, sir!'

'You would find it much easier than to instill moral virtue – social responsibility – into a person who doesn't have it, doesn't want it, and resents having the burden thrust on him. This is why we make it so hard to enroll, so easy to resign. Social responsibility above the level of family, or at most of tribe, requires imagination – devotion, loyalty, all the higher virtues – which a man must develop himself; if he has them forced down him, he will vomit them out. Conscript armies have been tried in the past. Look up in the library the psychiatric report on brainwashed prisoners in the so-called "Korean War," circa 1950 – the Mayer Report. Bring an analysis to class.' He touched his watch. 'Dismissed.'

Major Reid gave us a busy time.

But it was interesting. I caught one of those master's-thesis assignments he chucked around so casually; I had suggested that the Crusades were different from most wars. I got sawed off and handed this: *Required:* to prove that war and moral perfection derive from the same genetic inheritance.

Briefly, thus: All wars arise from population pressure. (Yes, even the Crusades, though you have to dig into trade routes and birth rate and several other things to prove it.) Morals – *all* correct moral rules – derive from the instinct to survive; moral behaviour is survival behaviour above the individual level – as in a father who dies to save his children. But since population pressure results from the process of surviving through others, then war, because it results from population pressure, derives from the same inherited instinct which produces all moral rules suitable for human beings.

Check of proof: Is it possible to abolish war by relieving population pressure (and thus do away with the all-too-evident evils of war) through constructing a moral code under which population is limited to resources?

Without debating the usefulness or morality of planned parenthood, it may be verified by observation that any breed which stops its own increase gets crowded out by breeds which expand. Some human populations did so, in Terran history, and other breeds moved in and engulfed them.

Nevertheless, let's assume that the human race manages to balance birth and death, just right to fit its own planets, and thereby becomes peaceful. What happens?

Soon (about next Wednesday) the Bugs move in, kill off this breed which 'ain'ta gonna study war no more' and the universe forgets us. Which still may happen. Either we spread and wipe out the Bugs, or they spread and wipe us out – because both races are tough and smart and want the same real estate.

Do you know how fast population pressure could cause us to fill the entire universe shoulder to shoulder? The answer will astound you, just like the flicker of an eye in terms of the age of our race.

Try it – it's a compound-interest expansion.

But does Man have any 'right' to spread through the universe?

Man is what he is, a wild animal with the will to survive, and (so far) the ability, against all competition. Unless one accepts that, anything one says about morals, war, politics – you name it – is nonsense. Correct morals arise from knowing what Man *is* – not what do-gooders and well-meaning old Aunt Nellies would like him to be.

The universe will let us know – later – whether or not Man has any 'right' to expand through it.

In the meantime the M.I. will be in there, on the bounce and swinging, on the side of our own race.

Toward the end each of us was shipped out to serve under an experienced combat commander. This was a semifinal examination, your 'board-ship instructor could decide that you didn't have what it takes. You could demand a board but I never heard of anybody who did; they either came back with an upcheck – or we never saw them again.

Some hadn't failed; it was just that they were killed – because assignments were to ships about to go into action. We were required to keep kit bags packed – once at lunch, all the cadet officers of my company were tapped; they left without eating and I found myself cadet company commander.

Like boot chevrons, this is an uncomfortable honor, but in less than two days my own call came.

I bounced down to the Commandant's office, kit bag over my shoulder and feeling grand. I was sick of late hours and burning eyes and never catching up, of looking stupid in class; a few weeks in the cheerful company of a combat team was just what Johnnie needed!

I passed some new cadets, trotting to class in close formation, each with the grim look that every O.C.S. candidate gets when he realizes that possibly he made a mistake in bucking for officer, and I found myself singing. I shut up when I was within earshot of the office.

Two others were there, Cadets Hassan and Byrd. Hassan the Assassin was the oldest man in our class and looked like something a fisherman had let out of a bottle, while Birdie wasn't much bigger than a sparrow and about as intimidating.

We were ushered into the Holy of Holies. The Commandant was in his wheel chair – we never saw him out of it except Saturday inspection and parade, I guess walking hurt. But that didn't mean you didn't see him – you could be working a prob at the board, turn around and find that wheel chair behind you, and Colonel Nielssen reading your mistakes.

He never interrupted – there was a standing order not to shout 'Attention!' But it's disconcerting. There seemed to be about six of him.

The Commandant had a permanent rank of fleet general (yes, *that* Nielssen); his rank as colonel was temporary, pending second retirement, to permit him to be Commandant. I once questioned a paymaster about this and confirmed what the regulations seemed to say: The Commandant got only the pay of a colonel – but would revert to the pay of a fleet general on the day he decided to retire again.

Well, as Ace says, it takes all sorts – I can't imagine choosing half pay for the privilege of riding herd on cadets.

Colonel Nielssen looked up and said, 'Morning, gentlemen. Make yourselves comfortable.' I sat down but wasn't comfortable. He glided over to a coffee machine, drew four cups, and Hassan helped him deal them out. I didn't want coffee but a cadet doesn't refuse the Commandant's hospitality.

He took a sip. 'I have your orders, gentlemen,' he announced, 'and your temporary commissions.' He went on, 'But I want to be sure you understand your status.'

We had already been lectured about this. We were going to be officers just enough for instruction and testing – 'supernumerary, probationary, and temporary.' Very junior, quite superfluous, on good behaviour, and extremely temporary;

we would revert to cadet when we got back and could be busted at any time by the officers examining us.

We would be 'temporary third lieutenants' – a rank as necessary as feet on a fish, wedged into the hairline between fleet sergeants and real officers. It is as low as you can get and still be called an 'officer.' If anybody ever saluted a third lieutenant, the light must have been bad.

'Your commission reads "third lieutenant,"' he went on, 'but your pay stays the same, you continue to be addressed as "Mister," the only change in uniform is a shoulder pip even smaller than cadet insignia. You continue under instruction since it has not yet been settled that you are fit to be officers.' The Colonel smiled. 'So why call you a "third lieutenant"?'

I had wondered about that. Why this whoopty-do of 'commissions' that weren't real commissions?

Of course I knew the textbook answer –

'Mr. Byrd?' the Commandant said.

'Uh . . . to place us in the line of command, sir.'

'Exactly!' Colonel glided to a T.O. on one wall. It was the usual pyramid, with chain of command defined all the way down. 'Look at this—' He pointed to a box connected to his own by a horizontal line; it read: ASSISTANT TO COMMANDANT (Miss Kendrick).

'Gentlemen,' he went on, 'I would have trouble running this place without Miss Kendrick. Her head is a rapid-access file to everything that happens around here.' He touched a control on his chair and spoke to the air. 'Miss Kendrick, what mark did Cadet Byrd receive in military law last term?'

Her answer came back at once: 'Ninety-three per cent, Commandant.'

'Thank you.' He continued, 'You see? I sign anything if Miss Kendrick has initialed it. I would hate to have an investigating committee find out how often she signs my name and

I don't even see it. Tell me, Mr. Byrd . . . if I drop dead does Miss Kendrick carry on to keep things moving?'

'Why, uh—' Birdie looked puzzled. 'I suppose, with routine matters, she would do what was necess—'

'She wouldn't do a blessed thing!' the Colonel thundered. 'Until Colonel Chauncey *told* her what to do – *his* way. She is a very smart woman and understands what you apparently do not, namely, that she is *not* in the line of command and has no authority.'

He went on, '"Line of command" isn't just a phrase; it's as real as a slap in the face. If I ordered you to combat *as a cadet* the most you could do would be to pass along somebody else's orders. If your platoon leader bought it and you then gave an order to a private – a good order, sensible and wise – you would be wrong and he would be just as wrong if he obeyed it. Because a cadet cannot be in line of command. A cadet has no military existence, no rank, and is not a soldier. He is a student who will become a soldier – either an officer, or at his former rank. While he is under Army discipline, he is not *in* the Army. That is why—'

A zero. A nought with no rim. If a cadet wasn't even in the Army – 'Colonel!'

'Eh? Speak up, young man. Mr. Rico.'

I had startled myself but I had to say it. 'But . . . if we aren't in the Army . . . then we aren't M.I. Sir?'

He blinked at me. 'This worries you?'

'I, uh, don't believe I like it much, sir.' I didn't like it at all. I felt naked.

'I see.' He didn't seem displeased. 'You let me worry about the space-lawyer aspects of it, son.'

'But—'

'That's an order. You are technically not an M.I. But the M.I. hasn't forgotten you; the M.I. *never* forgets its own no matter where they are. If you are struck dead this instant, you will be cremated as Second Lieutenant Juan Rico, Mobile Infantry, of—' Colonel Nielssen stopped. 'Miss Kendrick, what was Mr. Rico's ship?'

'The *Rodger Young*.'

'Thank you.' He added, '—in and of TFCT *Rodger Young*, assigned to mobile combat team Second Platoon of George Company, Third Regiment, First Division, M.I. – the "Roughnecks,"' he recited with relish, not consulting anything once he had been reminded of my ship. 'A good outfit, Mr. Rico – proud and nasty. Your Final Orders go back to them for Taps and that's the way your name would read in Memorial Hall. That's the way we always commission a dead cadet, son – so we can send him home to his mates.'

I felt a surge of relief and homesickness and missed a few words. '. . . lip buttoned while I talk, we'll have you back in the M.I. where you belong. You must be temporary officers for your 'prentice cruise because there is no room for dead-heads in a combat drop. You'll fight – and take orders – and *give* orders. *Legal* orders, because you will hold rank and be ordered to serve in that team; that makes any order you give in carrying out your assigned duties as binding as one signed by the C-in-C.

'Even more,' the Commandant went on, 'once you are in line of command, you must be ready instantly to assume higher command. If you are in a one-platoon team – quite likely in the present state of the war – and you are assistant platoon leader when your platoon leader buys it . . . then . . . *you* . . . are . . . *It!*'

He shook his head. 'Not "acting platoon leader." Not a cadet leading a drill. Not a "junior officer under instruction." Suddenly you are the Old Man, the Boss, Commanding Officer Present – and you discover with a sickening shock that fellow human beings are depending on *you alone* to tell them what to do, how to fight, how to complete the mission and get out alive. They wait for the sure voice of command – while seconds trickle away – and it's up to you to *be* that voice, make decisions, give the right orders . . . and not only the right ones but in a calm, unworried tone. Because it's a cinch, gentlemen, that your team is in trouble – *bad* trouble! – and a strange voice with panic in it can turn the best combat team in the Galaxy into a leaderless, lawless, fear-crazed mob.

'The whole merciless load will land without warning. You must act at once and you'll have only God over you. Don't expect Him to fill in tactical details; that's *your* job. He'll be doing all that a soldier has a right to expect if He helps you keep the panic you are sure to feel out of your voice.'

The Colonel paused. I was sobered and Birdie was looking terribly serious and awfully young and Hassan was scowling. I wished that I were back in the drop room of the *Rog*, with not too many chevrons and an after-chow bull session in full swing. There was a lot to be said for the job of assistant section leader – when you come right to it, it's a lot easier to *die* than it is to use your head.

The Commandant continued: 'That's the Moment of Truth, gentlemen. Regrettably there is no method known to military science to tell a real officer from a glib imitation with pips on his shoulders, other than through ordeal by fire. Real ones come through – or die gallantly; imitations crack up.

'Sometimes, in cracking up, the misfits die. But the tragedy lies in the loss of others . . . good men, sergeants and corporals and privates, whose only lack is fatal bad fortune in finding themselves under the command of an incompetent.

'We try to avoid this. First is our unbreakable rule that every candidate must be a trained trooper, blooded under fire, a veteran of combat drops. No other army in history has stuck to this rule, although some came close. Most great military schools of the past – Saint Cyr, West Point, Sandhurst,

Colorado Springs – didn't even pretend to follow it; they accepted civilian boys, trained them, commissioned them, sent them out with no battle experience to command men . . . and sometimes discovered too late that this smart young "officer" was a fool, a poltroon, or a hysteric.

'At least we have no misfits of those sorts. We know you are good soldiers – brave and skilled, proved in battle – else you would not be here. We know that your intelligence and education meet acceptable minimums. With this to start on, we eliminate as many as possible of the not-quite-competent – get them quickly back in ranks before we spoil good cap troopers by forcing them beyond their abilities. The course is very hard – because what will be expected of you later is still harder.

'In time we have a small group whose chances look fairly good. The major criterion left untested is one we *cannot* test here; that undefinable something which is the difference between a leader in battle . . . and one who merely has the earmarks but not the vocation. So we field-test for it.

'Gentlemen! – you have reached that point. Are you ready to take the oath?'

There was an instant of silence, then Hassan the Assassin answered firmly, 'Yes, Colonel,' and Birdie and I echoed.

The Colonel frowned. 'I have been telling you how wonderful you are – physically perfect, mentally alert, trained, disciplined, blooded. The very model of the smart young officer—' He snorted. 'Nonsense! You *may* become officers someday. I hope so . . . we not only hate to waste money and time and effort, but also, and *much* more important, I shiver in my boots every time I send one of you half-baked not-quite-officers up to the Fleet, knowing what a Frankensteinian monster I may be turning loose on a good combat team. If you understood what you are up against, you wouldn't be so all-fired ready to take the oath the second the question is put to you. You may turn it down and force me to let you go back to your permanent ranks. But you *don't* know.

'So I'll try once more. Mr. Rico! Have you ever thought how it would feel to be court-martialed for losing a regiment?'

I was startled silly. 'Why – No, sir, I never have.' To be court-martialed – for *any* reason – is eight times as bad for an officer as for an enlisted man. Offenses which will get privates kicked out (maybe with lashes, possibly without) rate death in an officer. Better never to have been born!

'Think about it,' he said grimly. 'When I suggested that your platoon leader might be killed, I was by no means citing the ultimate in military disaster. Mr. Hassan! What is the largest number of command levels knocked out in a single battle?'

The Assassin scowled harder than ever. 'I'm not sure, sir. Wasn't there a while during Operation Bughouse when a major commanded a brigade, before the Sove-ki-poo?'

'There was and his name was Fredericks. He got a decoration and a promotion. If you go back to the Second Global War, you can find a case in which a naval junior officer took command of a major ship and not only fought it but sent signals as if he were admiral. He was vindicated even though there were officers senior to him in line of command who were not even wounded. Special circumstances – a breakdown in communications. But I am thinking of a case in which four levels were wiped out in six minutes – as if a platoon leader were to blink his eyes and find himself commanding a brigade. Any of you heard of it?'

Dead silence.

'Very well. It was one of those bush wars that flared up on the edges of the Napoleonic wars. This young officer was the most junior in a naval vessel – wet navy, of course – wind-powered, in fact. This youngster was about the age of most of your class and was not commissioned. He carried the title of "temporary third lieutenant" – note that this is the title you are about to carry. He had no combat experience; there were four officers in the chain of command above him. When the battle started his commanding officer was wounded. The kid picked him up and carried him out of the line of fire. That's all – make pickup on a comrade. But he did it without being ordered to leave his post. The other officers all bought it while he was doing this and he was tried for "deserting his post of duty as *commanding officer* in the presence of the enemy." Convicted. Cashiered.'

I gasped. 'For *that?* Sir.'

'Why not? True, we make pickup. But we do it under different circumstances from a wet-navy battle, and by orders to the man making pickup. But pickup is never an excuse for breaking off battle in the presence of the enemy. This boy's family tried for a century and a half to get his conviction reversed. No luck, of course. There was doubt about some circumstances but no doubt that he had left his post during battle without orders. True, he was green as grass – but he was lucky not to be hanged.' Colonel Nielssen fixed me with a cold eye. 'Mr. Rico – could this happen to *you?*'

I gulped. 'I hope not, sir.'

'Let me tell you how it could on this very 'prentice cruise. Suppose you are in a multiple-ship operation, with a full regiment in the drop. Officers drop first, of course. There are advantages to this and disadvantages, but we do it for reasons of morale; no trooper ever hits the ground on a hostile planet without an officer. Assume the Bugs know this – and they may. Suppose they work up some trick to wipe out those who hit the ground first . . . but not good enough to wipe out the whole drop. Now suppose, since you are a supernumerary, you have to take any vacant capsule instead of being fired with the first wave. Where does that leave you?'

'Uh, I'm not sure, sir.'

'You have just inherited command of a regiment. *What are you going to do with your command, Mister?* Talk fast – the Bugs wont wait!'

'Uh . . .' I caught an answer right out of the book and parroted it. 'I'll take command and act as circumstances permit, sir, according to the tactical situation as I see it.'

'You will, eh?' The Colonel grunted. 'And you'll buy a farm too – that's all anybody can do with a foul-up like that. But I hope you'll go down swinging – and shouting orders to somebody, whether they make sense or not. We don't expect kittens to fight wildcats and win – we merely expect them to try. All right, stand up. Put up your right hands.'

He struggled to his feet. Thirty seconds later we were officers – 'temporary, probationary, and supernumerary.'

I thought he would give us our shoulder pips and let us go. We aren't supposed to buy them – they're a loan, like the temporary commission they represent. Instead he lounged back and looked almost human.

'See here, lads – I gave you a talk on how rough it's going to be. I want you to worry about it, doing it in advance, planning what steps you might take against any combination of bad news that can come your way, keenly aware that your life belongs to your men and is not yours to throw away in a suicidal reach for glory . . . and that your life isn't yours to save, either, if the situation requires that you expend it. I want you to worry yourself sick *before* a drop, so that you can be unruffled when the trouble starts.

'Impossible, of course. Except for one thing. What is the *only* factor that can save you when the load is too heavy? Anyone?'

Nobody answered.

'Oh, come now!' Colonel Nielssen said scornfully. 'You aren't recruits. Mr. Hassan!'

'Your leading sergeant, sir,' the Assassin said slowly.

'Obviously. He's probably older than you are, more drops under his belt, and he certainly knows his team better than you do. Since he isn't carrying that dreadful, numbing load of top command, he may be thinking more clearly than you are. Ask his advice. You've got one circuit just for that.

'It won't decrease his confidence in you; he's used to being consulted. If you don't, he'll decide you are a fool, a cocksure know-it-all – and he'll be right.

'But you don't have to *take* his advice. Whether you use his ideas, or whether they spark some different plan – make your decision and snap out orders. The one thing – the *only* thing! – that can strike terror in the heart of a good platoon sergeant is to find that he's working for a boss who can't make up his mind.

'There never has been an outfit in which officers and men were more dependent on each other than they are in the M.I., and sergeants are the glue that holds us together. Never forget it.'

The Commandant whipped his chair around to a cabinet near his desk. It contained row on row of pigeonholes, each with a little box. He pulled out one and opened it. 'Mr. Hassan—'

'Sir?'

'These pips were worn by Captain Terence O'Kelly on his 'prentice cruise. Does it suit you to wear them?'

'Sir?' The Assassin's voice squeaked and I thought the big lunk was going to break into tears. 'Yes, sir!'

'Come here.' Captain Nielssen pinned them on, then said, 'Wear them as gallantly as he did . . . but *bring them back.* Understand me?'

'Yes, sir. I'll do my best.'

'I'm sure you will. There's an air car waiting on the roof and your boat boosts in twenty-eight minutes. Carry out your orders, sir!'

The Assassin saluted and left; the Commandant turned and picked out another box. 'Mr. Byrd, are you superstitious?'

'No, sir.'

'Really? I am, quite. I take it you would not object to wearing pips which have been worn by five officers, all of whom were killed in action?'

Birdie barely hesitated. 'No, sir.'

'Good. Because these five officers accumulated seventeen citations, from the Terran Medal to the Wounded Lion. Come here. The pip with the brown discoloration must always be worn on your left shoulder – and don't try to buff it off! Just try not to get the other one marked in the same fashion. Unless necessary, and you'll know when it is necessary. Here is a list of former wearers. You have thirty minutes until your transportation leaves. Bounce up to Memorial Hall and look up the record of each.'

'Yes, sir.'

'Carry out your orders, sir!'

He turned to me, looked at my face and said sharply, 'Something on your mind, son? Speak up!'

'Uh—' I blurted it out. 'Sir, that temporary third lieutenant – the one that got cashiered. How could I find out what happened?'

'Oh. Young man, I didn't mean to scare the daylights out of you; I simply intended to wake you up. The battle was on one June 1813 old style between USF *Chesapeake* and HMF *Shannon*. Try the *Naval Encyclopedia;* your ship will have it.' He turned back to the case of pips and frowned.

Then he said, 'Mr. Rico, I have a letter from one of your high school teachers, a retired officer, requesting that you be issued the pips he wore as a third lieutenant. I am sorry to say that I must tell him "No."'

'Sir?' I was delighted to hear that Colonel Dubois was still keeping track of me – and very disappointed, too.

'Because I *can't!* I issued those pips two years ago – and they never came back. Real estate deal. Hmm—' He took a box, looked at me. 'You could start a new pair. The metal isn't important; the importance of the request lies in the fact that your teacher wanted you to have them.'

'Whatever you say, sir.'

'Or' – he cradled the box in his hand – 'you could wear these. They have been worn five times . . . and the last four candidates to wear them have all failed of commission – nothing dishonorable but pesky bad luck. Are you willing to take a swing at breaking the hoodoo? Turn them into good-luck pips instead?'

I would rather have petted a shark. But I answered, 'All right, sir. I'll take a swing at it.'

'Good.' He pinned them on me. 'Thank you, Mr. Rico. You see, these were mine, I wore them first . . . and it would please me mightily to have them brought back to me with that streak of bad luck broken, have you go on and graduate.'

I felt ten feet tall. 'I'll try, sir!'

'I know you will. You may now carry out your orders, sir. The same air car will take both you and Byrd. Just a moment – Are your mathematics textbooks in your bag?'

'Sir? No, sir.'

'Get them. The Weightmaster of your ship has been advised of your extra baggage allowance.'

I saluted and left, on the bounce. He had me shrunk down to size as soon as he mentioned math.

My math books were on my study desk, tied into a package with a daily assignment sheet tucked under the cord. I gathered the impression that Colonel Nielssen never left anything unplanned – but everybody knew that.

Birdie was waiting on the roof by the air car. He glanced at my books and grinned. 'Too bad. Well, if we're in the same ship, I'll coach you. What ship?'

'Tours.'

'Sorry, I'm for the *Moskva.*' We got in, I checked the pilot, saw that it had been pre-set for the field, closed the door and the car took off. Birdie added, 'You could be worse off. The Assassin took not only his math books but two other subjects.'

Birdie undoubtedly knew and he had not been showing off when he offered to coach me; he was a professor type except that his ribbons proved that he was a soldier too.

Instead of studying math Birdie taught it. One period each day he was a faculty member, the way little Shujumi taught judo at Camp Currie. The M.I. doesn't waste anything; we can't afford to. Birdie had a B.S. in math on his eighteenth birthday, so naturally he was assigned extra duty as instructor – which didn't keep him from being chewed out at other hours.

Not that he got chewed out much. Birdie had that rare combo of brilliant intellect, solid education, common sense, and guts, which gets a cadet marked as a potential general. We figured he was a cinch to command a brigade by the time he was thirty, what with the war.

But my ambitions didn't soar that high. 'It would be a dirty, rotten shame,' I said, 'if the Assassin flunked out,' while thinking that it would be a dirty, rotten shame if *I* flunked out.

'He won't,' Birdie answered cheerfully. 'They'll sweat him through the rest if they have to put him in a hypno booth and feed him through a tube. Anyhow,' he added, 'Hassan could flunk out and get promoted for it.'

'Huh?'

'Didn't you know? The Assassin's permanent rank is first lieutenant – field commission, naturally. He reverts to it if he flunks out. See the regs.'

I knew the regs. If I flunked math, I'd revert to buck sergeant, which is better than being slapped in the face with a wet fish any way you think about it . . . and I'd thought about it, lying awake nights after busting a quiz.

But this was different. 'Hold it,' I protested. 'He gave up *first* lieutenant, permanent grade . . . and has just made temporary *third* lieutenant . . . in order to become a *second* lieutenant? Are you crazy? Or is he?'

Birdie grinned. 'Just enough to make us both M.I.'

'But – I don't get it.'

'Sure you do. The Assassin has no education that he didn't pick up in the M.I. So how high can he go? I'm sure he could command a regiment in battle and do a real swingin' job – provided somebody else planned the operation. But commanding in battle is only a fraction of what an officer does, especially a senior officer. To direct a war, or even to plan a single battle and mount the operation, you have to have theory of games, operational analysis, symbolic logic, pessimistic synthesis, and a dozen other skull subjects. You can sweat them out on your own if you've got the grounding. But have them you must, or you'll never get past captain, or possibly major. The Assassin knows what he is doing.'

'I suppose so,' I said slowly. 'Birdie, Colonel Nielssen must know that Hassan was an officer – is an officer, really.'

'Huh? Of course.'

'He didn't talk as if he knew. We all got the same lecture.'

'Not quite. Did you notice that when the Commandant wanted a question answered a particular way he always asked the Assassin?'

I decided it was true. 'Birdie, what is your permanent rank?'

The car was just landing; he paused with a hand on the latch and grinned. 'PFC – I don't dare flunk out!'

I snorted. 'You won't. You can't!' I was surprised that he wasn't even a corporal, but a kid as smart and well educated as Birdie would go to O.C.S. just as quickly as he proved himself in combat . . . which, with the war on, could be only months after his eighteenth birthday.

Birdie grinned still wider. 'We'll see.'

'You'll graduate. Hassan and I have to worry, but not you.'

'So? Suppose Miss Kendrick takes a dislike to me.' He opened the door and looked startled. 'Hey! They're sounding my call. So long!'

'See you, Birdie.'

But I did not see him and he did not graduate. He was commissioned two weeks later and his pips came back with their eighteenth decoration – the Wounded Lion, posthumous.

Chapter 13

Youse guys think this deleted outfit is a blankety-blank nursery. Well, it ain't! See?

– Remark attributed to a Hellenic corporal before the walls of Troy, 1194 B.C.

The *Rodger Young* carries one platoon and is crowded; the *Tours* carries six – and is roomy. She has the tubes to drop them all at once and enough spare room to carry twice that number and make a second drop. This would make her very crowded, with eating in shifts, hammocks in passageways and drop rooms, rationed water, inhale when your mate exhales, and get your elbow out of my eye! I'm glad they didn't double up while I was in her.

But she has the speed and lift to deliver such crowded troops still in fighting condition to any point in Federation space and much of Bug space; under Cherenkov drive she cranks Mike 400 or better – say Sol to Capella, forty-six light-years, in under six weeks.

Of course, a six-platoon transport is not big compared with a battle wagon or passenger liner; these things are compromises. The M.I. prefers speedy little one-platoon corvettes which give flexibility for any operation, while if it was left up to the Navy we would have nothing but regimental transports. It takes almost as many Navy files to run a corvette as it does to run a monster big enough for a regiment – more maintenance and housekeeping, of course, but soldiers can do that. After all, those lazy troopers do nothing but sleep and eat and polish buttons – do 'em good to have a little regular work. So says the Navy.

The real Navy opinion is even more extreme: The Army is obsolete and should be abolished.

The Navy doesn't say this officially – but talk to a Naval officer who is on R&R and feeling his oats; you'll get an earful. They think they can fight any war, win it, send a few of their own people down to hold the conquered planet until the Diplomatic Corps takes charge.

I admit that their newest toys can blow any planet right out of the sky – I've never seen it but I believe it. Maybe I'm as obsolete as *Tyrannosaurus rex*. I don't feel obsolete and us apes can do things that the fanciest ship cannot. If the government doesn't want those things done, no doubt they'll tell us.

Maybe it's just as well that neither the Navy nor the M.I. has the final word. A man can't buck for Sky Marshal unless he has commanded both a regiment and a capital ship – go through M.I. and take his lumps and then become a Naval officer (I think little Birdie had that in mind), or first become an astrogator-pilot and follow it with Camp Currie, etc.

I'll listen respectfully to any man who has done both.

Like most transports, the *Tours* is a mixed ship; the most amazing change for me was to be allowed 'North of Thirty.' The bulkhead that separates ladies' country from the rough characters who shave is not necessarily No. 30 but, by tradition, it is called 'bulkhead thirty' in any mixed ship. The wardroom is just beyond it and the rest of ladies' country is farther forward. In the *Tours* the wardroom also served as messroom for enlisted women, who ate just before we did, and it was partitioned between meals into a recreation room for them and a lounge for their officers. Male officers had a lounge called the cardroom just abaft thirty.

Besides the obvious fact that drop & retrieval require the best pilots (i.e., female), there is very strong reason why female Naval officers are assigned to transports: It is good for trooper morale.

Let's skip M.I. traditions for a moment. Can you think of anything sillier than letting yourself be fired out of a spaceship with nothing but mayhem and sudden death at the other end? However, if someone must do this idiotic stunt, do you know of a surer way to keep a man keyed up to the point where he is willing than by keeping him constantly reminded that the only good reason why men fight is a living, breathing reality?

In a mixed ship, the last thing a trooper hears before a drop (maybe the last word he ever hears) is a woman's voice, wishing him luck. If you don't think this is important, you've probably resigned from the human race.

The *Tours* had fifteen Naval officers, eight ladies and seven men; there were eight M.I. officers including (I am happy to say) myself. I won't say 'bulkhead thirty' caused me to buck for O.C.S. but the privilege of eating with the ladies is more incentive than any increase in pay. The Skipper was president of the mess, my boss Captain Blackstone was vice-president – not because of rank; three Naval officers ranked him; but as C.O. of the strike force he was de facto senior to everybody but the Skipper.

Every meal was formal. We would wait in the cardroom until the hour struck, follow Captain Blackstone in and stand behind our chairs; the Skipper would come in followed by her ladies and, as she reached the head of the table, Captain Blackstone would bow and say, 'Madam President . . . ladies,' and she would answer, 'Mr. Vice . . . gentlemen,' and the man on each lady's right would seat her.

This ritual established that it was a social event, not an officers' conference; thereafter ranks or titles were used, except that junior Naval officers and myself alone among the M.I. were called 'Mister' or 'Miss' – with one exception which fooled me.

My first meal aboard I heard Captain Blackstone called 'Major,' although his shoulder pips plainly read 'captain.' I got straightened out later. There can't be two captains in a Naval vessel so an Army captain is bumped one rank socially rather than commit the unthinkable of calling him by the title reserved for the one and only monarch. If a Naval captain is aboard as anything but skipper, he or she is called 'Commodore' even if the skipper is a lowly lieutenant.

The M.I. observes this by avoiding the necessity in the wardroom and paying no attention to the silly custom in our own part of the ship.

Seniority ran downhill from each end of the table, with the Skipper at the head and the strike force C.O. at the foot, the junior midshipman at his right and myself at the Skipper's right. I would most happily have sat by the junior midshipman; she was awfully pretty – but the arrangement is planned chaperonage; I never even learned her first name.

I knew that I, as the lowliest male, sat on the Skipper's right – but I didn't know that I was supposed to seat her. At my first meal she waited and nobody sat down – until the third assistant engineer jogged my elbow. I haven't been so embarrassed since a very unfortunate incident in kindergarten, even though Captain Jorgenson acted as if nothing had happened.

When the Skipper stands up the meal is over. She was pretty good about this but once she stayed seated only a few minutes and Captain Blackstone got annoyed. He stood up but called out, 'Captain—'

She stopped. 'Yes, Major?'

'Will the Captain please give orders that my officers and myself be served in the cardroom?'

She answered coldly, 'Certainly, sir.' And we were. But no Naval officer joined us.

The following Saturday she exercised her privilege of inspecting the M.I. aboard – which transport skippers almost never do. However, she simply walked down the ranks without commenting. She was not really a martinet and she had a nice smile when she wasn't being stern. Captain Blackstone assigned Second Lieutenant 'Rusty' Graham to crack the whip over me about math; she found out about it, somehow, and told Captain Blackstone to have me report to her office for one hour after lunch each day, whereupon she tutored me in math and bawled me out when my 'homework' wasn't perfect.

Our six platoons were two companies as a rump battalion; Captain Blackstone commanded Company D, Blackie's Blackguards, and also commanded the rump battalion. Our battalion commander by the T.O., Major Xera, was with A and B companies in the *Tours'* sister ship *Normandy Beach* – maybe half a sky away; he commanded us only when the full battalion dropped together – except that Cap'n Blackie routed certain reports and letters through him. Other matters went directly to Fleet, Division, or Base, and Blackie had a truly wizard fleet sergeant to keep such things straight and to help him handle both a company and a rump battalion in combat.

Administrative details are not simple in an army spread through many light-years in hundreds of ships. In the old *Valley Forge*, in the *Rodger Young*, and now in the *Tours* I was in the same regiment, the Third ('Pampered Pets') Regiment of the First ('Polaris') M.I. Division. Two battalions formed from available units had been called the 'Third Regiment' in Operation Bughouse but I did not see 'my' regiment; all I saw was PFC Bamburger and a lot of Bugs.

I might be commissioned in the Pampered Pets, grow old and retire in it – and never even see my regimental commander. The Roughnecks had a company commander but he also commanded the first platoon ('Hornets') in another corvette; I didn't know his name until I saw it on my orders to O.C.S. There is a legend about a 'lost platoon' that went on

R&R as its corvette was decommissioned. Its company commander had just been promoted and the other platoons had been attached tactically elsewhere. I've forgotten what happened to the platoon's lieutenant but R&R is a routine time to detach an officer – theoretically after a relief has been sent to understudy him, but reliefs are always scarce.

They say this platoon enjoyed a local year of the fleshpots along Churchill Road before anybody missed them.

I don't believe it. But it could happen.

The chronic scarcity of officers strongly affected my duties in Blackie's Blackguards. The M.I. has the lowest percentage of officers in any army of record and this factor is just part of the M.I."s unique 'divisional wedge.' 'D.W.' is military jargon but the idea is simple: If you have 10,000 soldiers, how many fight? And how many just peel potatoes, drive lorries, count graves, and shuffle papers?

In the M.I., 10,000 men fight.

In the mass wars of the XXth century it sometimes took 70,000 men (fact!) to enable 10,000 to fight.

I admit it takes the Navy to place us where we fight; however, an M.I. strike force, even in a corvette, is at least three times as large as the transport's Navy crew. It also takes civilians to supply and service us; about 10 per cent of us are on R&R at any time; and a few of the very best of us are rotated to instruct at boot camps.

While a few M.I. are on desk jobs you will always find that they are shy an arm or leg, or some such. These are the ones – the Sergeant Hos and the Colonel Nielssens – who refuse to retire, and they really ought to count twice since they release able-bodied M.I. by filling jobs which require fighting spirit but not physical perfection. They do work that civilians can't do – or we would hire civilians. Civilians are like beans; you buy 'em as needed for any job which merely requires skill and savvy.

But you can't buy fighting spirit.

It's scarce. We use all of it, waste none. The M.I. is the smallest army in history for the size of the population it guards. You can't buy an M.I., you can't conscript him, you can't coerce him – you can't even keep him if he wants to leave. He can quit thirty seconds before a drop, lose his nerve and not get into his capsule, and all that happens is that he is paid off and can never vote.

At O.C.S. we studied armies in history that were driven like galley slaves. But the M.I. is a free man; all that drives him comes from inside – that self-respect and need for the respect of his mates and his pride in being one of them called morale, or *esprit de corps*.

The root of our morale is: 'Everybody works, everybody fights.' An M.I. doesn't pull strings to get a soft, safe job; there aren't any. Oh, a trooper will get away with what he can; any private with enough savvy to mark time to music can think up reasons why he should not clean compartments or break out stores; this is a soldier's ancient right.

But *all* 'soft, safe' jobs are filled by civilians; that gold-bricking private climbs into his capsule certain that *everybody*, from general to private, is doing it with him. Light-years away and on a different day, or maybe an hour or so later – no matter. What does matter is that *everybody* drops. This is why he enters the capsule, even though he may not be conscious of it.

If we ever deviate from this, the M.I. will go to pieces. All that holds us together is an idea – one that binds more strongly than steel but its magic power depends on keeping it intact.

It is this 'everybody fights' rule that lets the M.I. get by with so few officers.

I know more about this than I want to, because I asked a foolish question in Military History and got stuck with an assignment which forced me to dig up stuff ranging from *De*

Bello Gallico to Tsing's classic *Collapse of the Golden Hegemony*. Consider an ideal M.I. division – on paper, because you won't find one elsewhere. How many officers does it require? Never mind units attached from other corps; they may not be present during a ruckus and they are not like M.I. – the special talents attached to Logistics & Communications are all ranked as officers. If it will make a memory man, a telepath, a senser, or a lucky man happy to have me salute him, I'm glad to oblige; he is more valuable than I am and I could not replace him if I lived to be two hundred. Or take the K-9 Corps, which is 50 per cent 'officers' but whose other 50 per cent are neodogs.

None of these is in the line of command, so let's consider only us apes and what it takes to lead us.

This imaginary division has 10,800 men in 216 platoons, each with a lieutenant. Three platoons to a company calls for 72 captains; four companies to a battalion calls for 18 majors or lieutenant colonels. Six regiments with six colonels can form two or three brigades, each with a short general, plus a medium-tall general as top boss.

You wind up with 317 officers out of a total, all ranks, of 11,117.

There are no blank files and every officer commands a team. Officers total 3 per cent – which is what the M.I. does have, but arranged somewhat differently. In fact a good many platoons are commanded by sergeants and many officers 'wear more than one hat' in order to fill some utterly necessary staff jobs.

Even a platoon leader should have 'staff' – his platoon sergeant.

But he can get by without one and his sergeant can get by without him. But a general *must* have staff; the job is too big to carry in his hat. He needs a big planning staff and a small combat staff. Since there are never enough officers, the team commanders in his flag transport double as his planning staff and are picked from the M.I."s best mathematical logicians – then they drop with their own teams. The general drops with a small combat staff, plus a small team of the roughest, on-the-bounce troopers in the M.I. Their job is to keep the general from being bothered by rude strangers while he is managing the battle. Sometimes they succeed.

Besides necessary staff billets, any team larger than a platoon ought to have a deputy commander. But there are never enough officers so we make do with what we've got. To fill each necessary combat billet, one job to one officer, would call for a 5 per cent ratio of officers – but 3 per cent is all we've got.

In place of that optimax of 5 per cent that the M.I. never can reach, many armies in the past commissioned 10 per cent of their number, or even 15 per cent – and sometimes a preposterous 20 per cent! This sounds like a fairy tale but it was a fact, especially during the XXth century. What kind of an army has more 'officers' than corporals? (And more non-coms than privates!)

An army organized to lose wars – if history means anything. An army that is mostly organization, red tape, and overhead, most of whose 'soldiers' never fight.

But what do 'officers' *do* who do not command fighting men?

Fiddlework, apparently – officers' club officer, morale officer, athletics officer, public information officer, recreation officer, PX officer, transportation officer, legal officer, chaplain, assistant chaplain, junior assistant chaplain, officer-in-charge of anything anybody can think of, even – *nursery* officer!

In the M.I. such things are extra duty for combat officers or, if they are *real* jobs, they are done better and cheaper and without demoralizing a fighting outfit by hiring civilians. But the situation got so smelly in one of the XXth century major powers that *real* officers, ones who commanded fighting men, were given special insignia to distinguish them from the swarms of swivel-chair hussars.

The scarcity of officers got steadily worse as the war wore on, because the casualty rate is always highest among officers . . . and the M.I. *never* commissions a man simply to fill vacancy. In the long run, each boot regiment must supply its own share of officers and the percentage can't be raised without lowering the standards. The strike force in the *Tours* needed thirteen officers – six platoon leaders, two company commanders and two deputies, and a strike force commander staffed by a deputy and an adjutant.

What it had was six . . . and me.

Table of Organization
'Rump Battalion' Strike Force –
Cpt. Blackstone
('first hat')
Fleet Sergeant

C Company—"Warren's Wolverines	D Company—"Blackie's Blackguards"
1st Lt. Warren	Cpt. Blackstone ("second hat")
1st plat.— 1st. Lt. Bayonne	1st plat.— (1st Lt. Silva, Hosp.)
2nd plat.— 2nd Lt. Sukarno	2nd plat.— 2nd Lt. Khoroshen
3rd plat.— 2nd Lt. N'gam	3rd plat.— 2nd Lt. Graham

I would have been under Lieutenant Silva, but he left for hospital the day I reported, ill with some sort of twitching awfuls. But this did not necessarily mean that I would get his platoon. A temporary third lieutenant is not considered an asset; Captain Blackstone could place me under Lieutenant Bayonne and put a sergeant in charge of his own first platoon, or even 'put on a third hat' and take the platoon himself.

In fact, he did both and nevertheless assigned me as platoon leader of the first platoon of the Blackguards. He did this by borrowing the Wolverine's best buck sergeant to act as his battalion staffer, then he placed his fleet sergeant as platoon sergeant of his first platoon – a job two grades below his chevrons. Then Captain Blackstone spelled it out for me in a head-shrinking lecture: I would appear on the T.O. as platoon leader, but Blackie himself and the fleet sergeant would run the platoon.

As long as I behaved myself, I could go through the motions. I would even be allowed to drop as platoon leader – but one word from my platoon sergeant to my company commander and the jaws of the nutcracker would close.

It suited me. It was my platoon as long as I could swing it – and if I couldn't, the sooner I was shoved aside the better for everybody. Besides, it was a lot less nerve-racking to get a platoon that way than by sudden catastrophe in battle.

I took my job very seriously, for it was *my* platoon – the T.O. said so. But I had not yet learned to delegate authority and, for about a week, I was around troopers' country much more than is good for a team. Blackie called me into his stateroom. 'Son, what in Ned do you think you are doing?'

I answered stiffly that I was trying to get my platoon ready for action.

'So? Well, that's not what you are accomplishing. You are stirring them like a nest of wild bees. Why the deuce do you think I turned over to you the best sergeant in the Fleet? If you will go to your stateroom, hang yourself on a hook, and *stay* there! . . . until "Prepare for Action" is sounded, he'll hand that platoon over to you tuned like a violin.'

'As the Captain pleases, sir,' I agreed glumly.

'And that's another thing – I can't stand an officer who acts like a confounded *kay*det. Forget that silly third-person talk around me – save it for generals and the Skipper. Quit bracing your shoulders and clicking your heels. Officers are supposed to look *relaxed*, son.'

'Yes, sir.'

'And let that be the last time you say "sir" to me for one solid week. Same for saluting. Get that grim *kay*det look off your face and hang a smile on it.'

'Yes, s – Okay.'

'That's better. Lean against the bulkhead. Scratch yourself. Yawn. Anything but that tin-soldier act.'

I tried . . . and grinned sheepishly as I discovered that breaking a habit is not easy. Leaning was harder work than standing at attention. Captain Blackstone studied me. 'Practice it,' he said. 'An officer can't look scared or tense; it's contagious. Now tell me, Johnnie, what your platoon needs. Never mind the piddlin' stuff; I'm not interested in whether a man has the regulation number of socks in his locker.'

I thought rapidly. 'Uh . . . do you happen to know if Lieutenant Silva intended to put Brumby up for sergeant?'

'I do happen to know. What's *your* opinion?'

'Well . . . the record shows that he has been acting section leader the past two months. His efficiency marks are good.'

'I asked for your recommendation, Mister.'

'Well, s – Sorry. I've never seen him work on the ground, so I can't have a real opinion; anybody can soldier in the drop room. But the way I see it, he's been acting sergeant too long to bust him back to chaser and promote a squad leader over him. He ought to get that third chevron before we drop – or he ought to be transferred when we get back. Sooner, if there's a chance for a spaceside transfer.'

Blackie grunted. 'You're pretty generous in giving away my Blackguards – for a third lieutenant.'

I turned red. 'Just the same, it's a soft spot in my platoon. Brumby ought to be promoted, or transferred. I don't want him back in his old job with somebody promoted over his head; he'd likely turn sour and I'd have an even worse soft spot. If he can't have another chevron, he ought to go to repple-depple for cadre. Then he won't be humiliated and he gets a fair shake to make sergeant in another team – instead of a dead end here.'

'Really?' Blackie did not quite sneer. 'After that masterly analysis, apply your powers of deduction and tell me why Lieutenant Silva failed to transfer him three weeks ago when we arrived around Sanctuary.'

I had wondered about that. The time to transfer a man is the earliest possible instant after you decide to let him go – and without warning; it's better for the man and the team – so says the book. I said slowly, 'Was Lieutenant Silva already ill at that time, Captain?'

'No.'

The pieces matched. 'Captain, I recommend Brumby for immediate promotion.'

His eyebrows shot up. 'A minute ago you were about to dump him as useless.'

'Uh, not quite. I said it had to be one or the other – but I didn't know which. Now I know.'

'Continue.'

'Uh, this assumes that Lieutenant Silva is an efficient officer—'

'*Hummmph!* Mister, for your information, "Quick" Silva has an unbroken string of "Excellent – Recommended for Promotion" on his Form Thirty-One.'

'But I knew that he was good,' I ployed on, 'because I inherited a good platoon. A good officer might not promote a man for – oh, for many reasons – and still not put his misgivings in writing. But in this case, if he could not recommend him for sergeant, then he wouldn't keep him with the team – so he would get him out of the ship at the first opportunity. But he didn't. Therefore I know he intended to promote Brumby.' I added, 'But I can't see why he didn't push it through three weeks ago, so that Brumby could have worn his third chevron on R&R.'

Captain Blackstone grinned. 'That's because you don't credit *me* with being efficient.'

'S – I beg pardon?'

'Never mind. You've proved who killed Cock Robin and I don't expect a still-moist *kay*det to know all the tricks. But listen and learn, son. As long as this war goes on, don't *ever* promote a man just before you return to Base.'

'Uh . . . why not, Captain?'

'You mentioned sending Brumby to Replacement Depot if he was not to be promoted. But that's just where he would have gone if we *had* promoted him three weeks ago. You don't know how hungry that non-com desk at repple-depple is. Paw through the dispatch file and you'll find a demand that we supply two sergeants for cadre. With a platoon sergeant being detached for O.C.S. and a buck sergeant spot vacant, I was under complement and able to refuse.' He grinned savagely. 'It's a rough war, son, and your own people will steal your best men if you don't watch 'em.' He took two sheets of paper out of a drawer. 'There—'

One was a letter from Silva to Cap'n Blackie, recommending Brumby for sergeant; it was dated over a month ago.

The other was Brumby's warrant for sergeant – dated the day *after* we left Sanctuary.

'That suit you?' he asked.

'Huh? Oh, yes indeed!'

'I've been waiting for you to spot the weak place in your team, and tell me what had to be done. I'm pleased that you figured it out – but only middlin' pleased because an experienced officer would have analyzed it at once from the T.O. and the service records. Never mind, that's how you gain experience. Now here's what you do. Write me a letter like Silva's; date it yesterday. Tell your platoon sergeant to tell Brumby that you have put him up for a third stripe – and don't mention that Silva did so. You didn't know that when you made the recommendation, so we'll keep it that way. When I swear Brumby in, I'll let him know that both his officers recommended him independently – which will make him feel good. Okay, anything more?'

'Uh . . . not in organization – unless Lieutenant Silva planned to promote Naidi, vice Brumby. In which case we could promote one PFC to lance . . . and that would allow us to promote four privates to PFC, including three vacancies now existing. I don't know whether it's your policy to keep the T.O. filled up tight or not?'

'Might as well,' Blackie said gently, 'as you and I know that some of those lads aren't going to have many days in which to enjoy it. Just remember that we don't make a man a PFC until after he has been in combat – not in Blackie's Blackguards we don't. Figure it out with your platoon sergeant and let me know. No hurry . . . any time before bedtime tonight. Now . . . anything else?'

'Well – Captain, I'm worried about the suits.'

'So am I. All platoons.'

'I don't know about the other platoons, but with five recruits to fit, plus four suits damaged and exchanged, and two more downchecked this past week and replaced from stores – well, I don't see how Cunha and Navarre can warm up that many and run routine tests on forty-one others and get it all done by our calculated date. Even if no trouble develops—'

'Trouble always develops.'

'Yes, Captain. But that's two hundred and eighty-six

man-hours just for warm & fit, plus a hundred and twenty-three hours of routine checks. And it always takes longer.'

'Well, what do *you* think can be done? The other platoons will lend you help if they finish their own suits ahead of time. Which I doubt. Don't ask to borrow help from the Wolverines; we're more likely to lend them help.'

'Uh . . . Captain, I don't know what you'll think of this, since you told me to stay out of troopers' country. But when I was a corporal, I was assistant to the Ordnance & Armor sergeant.'

'Keep talking.'

'Well, right at the last I *was* the O&A sergeant. But I was just standing in another man's shoes – I'm not a finished O&A mechanic. But I'm a pretty darn good assistant and if I was allowed to, well, I can either warm new suits, or run routine checks – and give Cunha and Navarre that much more time for trouble.'

Blackie leaned back and grinned. 'Mister, I have searched the regs carefully . . . and I can't find the one that says an officer mustn't get his hands dirty.' He added, 'I mention that because some "young gentlemen', who have been assigned to me apparently had read such a regulation. All right, draw some dungarees – no need to get your uniform dirty along with your hands. Go aft and find your platoon sergeant, tell him about Brumby and order him to prepare recommendations to close the gaps in the T.O. in case I should decide to confirm your recommendation for Brumby. Then tell him that you are going to put in all your time on ordnance and armor – and that you want him to handle everything else. Tell him that if he has any problems to look you up in the armory. Don't tell him you consulted me – just give him orders. Follow me?'

'Yes, s – Yes, I do.'

'Okay, get on it. As you pass through the cardroom, please

give my compliments to Rusty and tell him to drag his lazy carcass in here.'

For the next two weeks I was never so busy – not even in boot camp. Working as an ordnance & armor mech about ten hours a day was not all that I did. Math, of course – and no way to duck it with the Skipper tutoring me. Meals – say an hour and a half a day. Plus the mechanics of staying alive – shaving, showering, putting buttons in uniforms and trying to chase down the Navy master-at-arms, get him to unlock the laundry to locate clean uniforms ten minutes before inspection. (It is an unwritten law of the Navy that facilities must *always* be locked when they are most needed.)

Guard mount, parade, inspections, a minimum of platoon routine, took another hour a day. But, besides, I was 'George.' Every outfit has a 'George.' He's the most junior officer and has the extra jobs – athletics officer, mail censor, referee for competitions, school officer, correspondence courses officer, prosecutor courts-martial, treasurer of the welfare mutual loan fund, custodian of registered publications, stores officer, troopers' mess officer, et cetera and endless nauseam.

Rusty Graham had been 'George' until he happily turned it over to me. He wasn't so happy when I insisted on a sight inventory on everything for which I had to sign. He suggested that if I didn't have sense enough to accept a commissioned officer's signed inventory then perhaps a direct order would change my tune. So I got sullen and told him to put his orders in writing – with a certified copy so that I could keep the original and endorse the copy over to the team commander.

Rusty angrily backed down – even a second lieutenant isn't stupid enough to put such orders in writing. I wasn't happy either as Rusty was my roommate and was then still my tutor in math, but we held the sight inventory. I got chewed out by Lieutenant Warren for being stupidly officious but he opened his safe and let me check his registered publications. Captain Blackstone opened his with no comment and I couldn't tell whether he approved of my sight inventory or not.

Publications were okay but accountable property was not. Poor Rusty! He had accepted his predecessor's count and now the count was short – and the other officer was not merely gone, he was dead. Rusty spent a restless night (and so did I!), then went to Blackie and told him the truth.

Blackie chewed him out, then went over the missing items, found ways to expend most of them as 'lost in combat.' It reduced Rusty's shortages to a few days' pay – but Blackie had him keep the job, thereby postponing the cash reckoning indefinitely.

Not all 'George' jobs caused that much headache. There were no courts-martial; good combat teams don't have them. There was no mail to censor as the ship was in Cherenkov drive. Same for welfare loans for similar reasons. Athletics I delegated to Brumby; referee was 'if and when.' The troopers' mess was excellent; I initialed menus and sometimes inspected the galley, i.e., I scrounged a sandwich without getting out of dungarees when working late in the armory. Correspondence courses meant a lot of paperwork since quite a few were continuing their educations, war or no war – but I delegated my platoon sergeant and the records were kept by the PFC who was his clerk.

Nevertheless 'George' jobs soaked up about two hours every day – there were so many.

You see where this left me – ten hours O&A, three hours math, meals an hour and a half, personal one hour, military fiddlework one hour, 'George' two hours, sleep eight hours; total, twenty-six and a half hours. The ship wasn't even on the twenty-five-hour Sanctuary day; once we left we went on Greenwich standard and the universal calendar.

The only slack was in my sleeping time.

I was sitting in the cardroom about one o'clock one morning, plugging away at math, when Captain Blackstone came in. I said, 'Good evening, Captain.'

'Morning, you mean. What the deuce ails you, son? Insomnia?'

'Uh, not exactly.'

He picked up a stack of sheets, remarking, 'Can't your sergeant handle your paperwork? Oh, I see. Go to bed.'

'But, Captain—'

'Sit back down. Johnnie, I've been meaning to talk to you. I never see you here in the cardroom, evenings. I walk past your room, you're at your desk. When your bunkie goes to bed, you move out here. What's the trouble?'

'Well . . . I just never seem to get caught up.'

'Nobody ever does. How's the work going in the armory?'

'Pretty well. I think we'll make it.'

'I think so, too. Look, son, you've got to keep a sense of proportion. You have two prime duties. First is to see that your platoon's equipment is ready – you're doing that. You don't have to worry about the platoon itself, I told you that. The second – and just as important – you've got to be ready to fight. You're muffing that.'

'I'll be ready, Captain.'

'Nonsense and other comments. You're getting no exercise and losing sleep. Is that how you train for a drop? When you lead a platoon, son, you've got to be on the bounce. From here on you will exercise from sixteen-thirty to eighteen hundred each day. You will be in your sack with lights out at twenty-three hundred – and if you lie awake fifteen minutes two nights in a row, you will report to the Surgeon for treatment. Orders.'

'Yes, sir.' I felt the bulkheads closing in on me and added desperately, 'Captain, I don't see *how* I can get to bed by twenty-three – and still get everything *done*.'

'Then you won't. As I said, son, you must have a sense of proportion. Tell me how you spend your time.'

So I did. He nodded 'Just as I thought.' He picked up my math 'homework,' tossed it in front of me. 'Take this. Sure, you want to work on it. But why work so hard before we go into action?'

'Well, I thought—'

"Think" is what you didn't do. There are four possibilities, and only one calls for finishing these assignments. First, you might buy a farm. Second, you might buy a small piece and be retired with an honorary commission. Third, you might come through all right . . . but get a downcheck on your Form Thirty-One from your examiner, namely me. Which is just what you're aching for at the present time – why, son, I won't even let you drop if you show up with eyes red from no sleep and muscles flabby from too much chair parade. The fourth possibility is that you take a grip on yourself . . . in which case I might let you take a swing at leading a platoon. So let's assume that you do and put on the finest show since Achilles slew Hector and I pass you. In that case only – you'll need to finish these math assignments. So do them on the trip back.

'That takes care of that – I'll tell the Skipper. The rest of those jobs you are relieved of, right now. On our way home you can spend your time on math. If we get home. But you'll never get anywhere if you don't learn to keep first things first. Go to bed!'

A week later we made rendezvous, coming out of drive and coasting short of the speed of light while the fleet exchanged signals. We were sent Briefing, Battle Plan, our Mission & Orders – a stack of words as long as a novel – and were told not to drop.

Oh, we were to be in the operation but we would ride down

like gentlemen, cushioned in retrieval boats. This we could do because the Federation already held the surface; Second, Third, and Fifth M.I. Divisions had taken it – and paid cash.

The described real estate didn't seem worth the price. Planet P is smaller than Terra, with a surface gravity of 0.7, is mostly arctic-cold ocean and rock, with lichenous flora and no fauna of interest. Its air is not breathable for long, being contaminated with nitrous oxide and too much ozone. Its one continent is about half the size of Australia, plus many worthless islands; it would probably require as much terra-forming as Venus before we could use it.

However we were not buying real estate to live on; we went there because Bugs were there – and they were there on our account, so Staff thought. Staff told us that Planet P was an uncompleted advance base (prob. 87 ± 6 per cent) to be used against us.

Since the planet was no prize, the routine way to get rid of this Bug base would be for the Navy to stand off at a safe distance and render this ugly spheroid uninhabitable by Man or Bug. But the C-in-C had other ideas.

The operation was a raid. It sounds incredible to call a battle involving hundreds of ships and thousands of casualties a 'raid,' especially as, in the meantime, the Navy and a lot of other cap troopers were keeping things stirred up many light-years into Bug space in order to divert them from reinforcing Planet P.

But the C-in-C was not wasting men; this giant raid could determine who won the war, whether next year or thirty years hence. We needed to learn more about Bug psychology. Must we wipe out every Bug in the Galaxy? Or was it possible to trounce them and impose a peace? We did not know; we understood them as little as we understand termites.

To learn their psychology we had to communicate with them, learn their motivations, find out why they fought and under what conditions they would stop; for these, the Psychological Warfare Corps needed prisoners.

Workers are easy to capture. But a Bug worker is hardly more than animate machinery. Warriors can be captured by burning off enough limbs to make them helpless – but they are almost as stupid without a director as workers. From such prisoners our own professor types had learned important matters – the development of that only gas that killed them but not us came from analyzing the biochemistries of workers and warriors, and we had other new weapons from such research even in the short time I had been a cap trooper. But to discover why Bugs fight we needed to study members of their brain caste. Also, we hoped to exchange prisoners.

So far, we had never taken a Bug alive. We had either cleaned out colonies from the surface, as on Sheol, or (as had too often been the case) raiders have gone down their holes and not come back. A lot of brave men had been lost this way.

Still more had been lost through retrieval failure. Sometimes a team on the ground had its ship or ships knocked out of the sky. What happens to such a team? Possibly it dies to the last man. More probably it fights until power and ammo are gone, then survivors are captured as easily as so many beetles on their backs.

From our co-belligerents the Skinnies we knew that many missing troopers were alive as prisoners – thousands we hoped, hundreds we were sure. Intelligence believed that prisoners were always taken to Klendathu; the Bugs are as curious about us as we are about them – a race of individuals able to build cities, starships, armies, may be even more mysterious to a hive entity than a hive entity is to us.

As may be, we wanted those prisoners back!

In the grim logic of the universe this may be a weakness. Perhaps some race that never bothers to rescue an individual may exploit this human trait to wipe us out. The Skinnies have such a trait only slightly and the Bugs don't seem to have it at all – nobody *ever* saw a Bug come to the aid of another because he was wounded; they co-operate perfectly in fighting but units are abandoned the instant they are no longer useful.

Our behavior is different. How often have you seen a headline like this? – TWO DIE ATTEMPTING RESCUE OF DROWNING CHILD. If a man gets lost in the mountains, hundreds will search and often two or three searchers are killed. But the next time somebody gets lost just as many volunteers turn out.

Poor arithmetic . . . but very human. It runs through all our folklore, all human religions, all our literature – a racial conviction that when one human needs rescue, others should not count the price.

Weakness? It might be the unique strength that wins us a Galaxy.

Weakness or strength. Bugs don't have it; there was no prospect of trading fighters for fighters.

But in a hive polyarchy, some castes are valuable – or so our Psych Warfare people hoped. If we could capture brain Bugs, alive and undamaged, we might be able to trade on good terms.

And suppose we captured a queen!

What is a queen's trading value? A regiment of troopers? Nobody knew, but Battle Plan ordered us to capture Bug 'royalty,' brains and queens, *at any cost*, on the gamble that we could trade them for human beings.

The third purpose of Operation Royalty was to develop methods: how to go down, how to dig them out, how to win with less than total weapons. Trooper for warrior, we could now defeat them above ground; ship for ship, our Navy was better; but, so far, we had had no luck when we tried to go down their holes.

If we failed to exchange prisoners on any terms, then we still had to: (a) win the war, (b) do so in a way that gave us a fighting chance to rescue our own people, or (c) – might as well admit it – die trying and lose. Planet P was a field test to determine whether we could learn how to root them out.

Briefing was read to every trooper and he heard it again in his sleep during hypno preparation. So, while we all knew that Operation Royalty was laying the groundwork toward eventual rescue of our mates, we also knew that Planet P held no human prisoners – it had never been raided. So there was no reason to buck for medals in a wild hope of being personally in on a rescue; it was just another Bug hunt, but conducted with massive force and new techniques. We were going to peel that planet like an onion, until we *knew* that every Bug had been dug out.

The Navy had plastered the islands and that unoccupied part of the continent until they were radioactive glaze; we could tackle Bugs with no worries about our rear. The Navy also maintained a ball-of-yarn patrol in tight orbits around the planet, guarding us, escorting transports, keeping a spy watch on the surface to make sure that Bugs did not break out behind us despite that plastering.

Under the Battle Plan, the orders for Blackie's Blackguards charged us with supporting the prime Mission when ordered or as opportunity presented, relieving another company in a captured area, protecting units of other corps in that area, maintaining contact with M.I. units around us – and smacking down any Bugs that showed their ugly heads.

So we rode down in comfort to an unopposed landing. I took my platoon out at a powered-armor trot. Blackie went ahead to meet the company commander he was relieving, get the situation and size up the terrain. He headed for the horizon like a scared jack rabbit.

I had Cunha send his first section's scouts out to locate the forward corners of my patrol area and I sent my platoon sergeant off to my left to make contact with a patrol from the Fifth Regiment. We, the Third Regiment, had a grid three hundred miles wide and eighty miles deep to hold; my piece was a rectangle forty miles deep and seventeen miles wide in the extreme left flank forward corner. The Wolverines were behind us, Lieutenant Khoroshen's platoon on the right and Rusty beyond him.

Our First Regiment had already relieved a Vth Div. regiment ahead of us, with a 'brick wall' overlap which placed them on my corner as well as ahead. 'Ahead' and 'rear,' 'right flank' and 'left,' referred to orientation set up in dead-reckoning tracers in each command suit to match the grid of the Battle Plan. We had no true front, simply an area, and the only fighting at the moment was going on several hundred miles away, to our arbitrary right and rear.

Somewhere off that way, probably two hundred miles, should be 2nd platoon, G Co, 2nd Batt, 3rd Reg – commonly known as 'The Roughnecks.'

Or the Roughnecks might be forty light-years away. Tactical organization never matches the Table of Organization; all I knew from the Plan was that something called the '2nd Batt' was on our right flank beyond the boys from the *Normandy Beach*. But that battalion could have been borrowed from another division. The Sky Marshal plays his chess without consulting the pieces.

Anyhow, I should not be thinking about the Roughnecks; I had all I could do as a Blackguard. My platoon was okay for the moment – safe as you can be on a hostile planet – but I had plenty to do before Cunha's first squad reached the far corner. I needed to:

1. Locate the platoon leader who had been holding my area.

2. Establish corners and identify them to section and squad leaders.

3. Make contact liaison with eight platoon leaders on my sides and corners, five of whom should already be in position (those from Fifth and First Regiments) and three (Khoroshen of the Blackguards and Bayonne and Sukarno of the Wolverines) who were now moving into position.

4. Get my own boys spread out to their initial points as fast as possible by shortest routes.

The last had to be set up first, as the open column in which we disembarked would not do it. Brumby's last squad needed to deploy to the left flank; Cunha's leading squad needed to spread from dead ahead to left oblique; the other four squads must fan out in between.

This is a standard square deployment and we had simulated how to reach it quickly in the drop room; I called out: 'Cunha! Brumby! Time to spread 'em out,' using the noncom circuit.

'Roger sec one!' – 'Roger sec two!'

'Section leaders take charge . . . and caution each recruit. You'll be passing a lot of Cherubs. I don't want 'em shot at by mistake!' I bit down for my private circuit and said, 'Sarge, you got contact on the left?'

'Yes, sir. They see me, they see you.'

'Good. I don't see a beacon on our anchor corner—'

'Missing.'

' – so you coach Cunha by D.R. Same for the lead scout – that's Hughes – and have Hughes set a new beacon.' I wondered why the Third or Fifth hadn't replaced that anchor beacon – my forward left corner where three regiments came together.

No use talking. I went on: 'D.R. check. You bear two seven five, miles twelve.'

'Sir, reverse is nine six, miles twelve scant.'

'Close enough. I haven't found my opposite number yet, so I'm cutting out forward at max. Mind the shop.'

'Got 'em, Mr. Rico.'

I advanced at max speed while clicking over to officers' circuit: 'Square Black One, answer Black One, Cherubs – do you read me? Answer.' I wanted to talk with the leader of the platoon we were relieving – and not for any perfunctory I-relieve-you-sir: I wanted the ungarnished word.

I didn't like what I had seen.

Either the top brass had been optimistic in believing that we had mounted overwhelming force against a small, not fully developed Bug base – or the Blackguards had been awarded the spot where the roof fell in. In the few moments I had been out of the boat I had spotted half a dozen armored suits on the ground – empty I hoped, dead men possibly, but 'way too many any way you look at it.

Besides that, my tactical radar display showed a full platoon (my own) moving into position but only a scattering moving back toward retrieval or still on station. Nor could I see any system to their movements.

I was responsible for 680 square miles of hostile terrain and I wanted very badly to find out all I could *before* my own squads were deep into it. Battle Plan had ordered a new tactical doctrine which I found dismaying: Do not close the Bugs' tunnels. Blackie had explained this as if it had been his own happy thought, but I doubt if he liked it.

The strategy was simple, and, I guess, logical . . . if we could afford the losses. Let the Bugs come up. Meet them and kill them on the surface. Let them keep on coming up. Don't bomb their holes, don't gas their holes – let them out. After a while – a day, two days, a week – if we really did have overwhelming force, they would stop coming up. Planning Staff estimated (don't ask me how!) that the Bugs would expend 70 per cent to 90 per cent of their warriors before they stopped trying to drive us off the surface.

Then we would start the unpeeling, killing surviving

warriors as we went down and trying to capture 'royalty' alive. We knew what the brain caste looked like; we had seen them dead (in photographs) and we knew they could not run – barely functional legs, bloated bodies that were mostly nervous system. Queens no human had ever seen, but Bio War Corps had prepared sketches of what they should look like – obscene monsters larger than a horse and utterly immobile.

Besides brains and queens there might be other 'royalty' castes. As might be – encourage their warriors to come out and die, then capture alive anything but warriors and workers.

A necessary plan and very pretty, on paper. What it meant to me was that I had an area 17 x 40 miles which might be riddled with unstopped Bug holes. I wanted co-ordinates on each one.

If there were too many . . . well, I might accidentally plug a few and let my boys concentrate on watching the rest. A private in a marauder suit can cover a lot of terrain, but he can look at only one thing at a time; he is not superhuman.

I bounced several miles ahead of the first squad, still calling the Cherub platoon leader, varying it by calling *any* Cherub officer and describing the pattern of my transponder beacon (dah-di-dah-dah).

No answer –

At last I got a reply from my boss: 'Johnnie! Knock off the noise. Answer me on conference circuit.'

So I did, and Blackie told me crisply to quit trying to find the Cherub leader for Square Black One; there wasn't one. Oh, there might be a non-com alive somewhere but the chain of command had broken.

By the book, somebody always moves up. But it *does* happen if too many links are knocked out. As Colonel Nielssen had once warned me, in the dim past . . . almost a month ago.

Captain Chang had gone into action with three officers besides himself; there was one left now (my classmate, Abe

Moise) and Blackie was trying to find out from him the situation. Abe wasn't much help. When I joined the conference and identified myself, Abe thought I was his battalion commander and made a report almost heartbreakingly precise, especially as it made no sense at all.

Blackie interrupted and told me to carry on. 'Forget about a relief briefing. The situation is whatever you see that it is – so stir around and *see*.'

'Right, Boss!' I slashed across my own area toward the far corner, the anchor corner, as fast as I could move, switching circuits on my first bounce. 'Sarge! How about that beacon?'

'No place on that corner to put it, sir. A fresh crater there, about scale six.'

I whistled to myself. You could drop the *Tours* into a size six crater. One of the dodges the Bugs used on us when we were sparring, ourselves on the surface, Bugs underground, was land mines. (They never seemed to use missiles, except from ships in space.) If you were near the spot, the ground shock got you; if you were in the air when one went off, the concussion wave could tumble your gyros and throw your suit out of control.

I had never seen larger than a scale-four crater. The theory was that they didn't dare use too big an explosion because of damage to their troglodyte habitats, even if they coffer-dammed around it.

'Place an offset beacon,' I told him. 'Tell section and squad leaders.'

'I have, sir. Angle one one oh, miles one point three. Dadi-dit. You should be able to read it, bearing about three five from where you are.' He sounded as calm as a sergeant-instructor at drill and I wondered if I were letting my voice get shrill.

I found it in my display, above my left eyebrow – long and two shorts. 'Okay. I see Cunha's first squad is nearly in position. Break off that squad, have it patrol the crater. Equalize the areas – Brumby will have to take four more miles of depth.' I thought with annoyance that each man already had to patrol fourteen square miles; spreading the butter so thin meant seventeen square miles per man – and a Bug can come out of a hole less than five feet wide.

I added, 'How "hot" is that crater?'

'Amber-red at the edge. I haven't been in it, sir.'

'Stay out of it. I'll check it later.' Amber-red would kill an unprotected human but a trooper in armor can take it for quite a time. If there was that much radiation at the edge, the bottom would no doubt fry your eyeballs. 'Tell Naidi to pull Malan and Bjork back to amber zone, and have them set up ground listeners.' Two of my five recruits were in that first squad – and recruits are like puppies; they stick their noses into things.

'Tell Naidi that I am interested in two things: movement inside the crater . . . and noises in the ground around it.' *We* wouldn't send troopers out through a hole so radioactive that mere exit would kill them. But Bugs would, if they could reach us that way. 'Have Naidi report to me. To you and me, I mean.'

'Yes, sir,' My platoon sergeant added, 'May I make a suggestion?'

'Of course. And don't stop to ask permission next time.'

'Navarre can handle the rest of the first section. Sergeant Cunha could take the squad at the crater and leave Naidi free to supervise the ground-listening watch.'

I know what he was thinking. Naidi, so newly a corporal that he had never before had a squad on the ground, was hardly the man to cover what looked like the worst danger point in Square Black One; he wanted to pull Naidi back for the same reasons I had pulled the recruits back.

I wonder if he knew what I was thinking? That 'nut-cracker' – he was using the suit he had worn as Blackie's battalion staffer, he had one more circut than I had, a private one to captain Blackstone.

Blackie was probably patched in and listening via that extra circuit. Obviously my platoon sergeant did not agree with my disposition of the platoon. If I didn't take his advice, the next thing I heard might be Blackie's voice cutting in: 'Sergeant, take charge. Mr. Rico, you're relieved.'

But – Confound it, a corporal who wasn't allowed to boss his squad wasn't a corporal . . . and a platoon leader who was just a ventriloquist's dummy for his platoon sergeant was an empty suit!

I didn't mull this. It flashed through my head and I answered at once. 'I can't spare a corporal to baby-sit with two recruits. Nor a sergeant to boss four privates and a lance.'

'But—'

'Hold it. I want the crater watch relieved every hour. I want our first patrol sweep made rapidly. Squad leaders will check any hole reported and get beacon bearings so that section leaders, platoon sergeant and platoon leader can check them as they reach them. If there aren't too many, we'll put a watch on each – I'll decide later.'

'Yes, sir.'

'Second time around, I want a slow patrol, as tight as possible, to catch holes we miss on the first sweep. Assistant squad leaders will use snoopers on that pass. Squad leaders will get bearings on any troopers – or suits – on the ground; the Cherubs may have left some live wounded. But no one is to stop even to check physicals until I order it. We've got to know the Bug situation first.'

'Yes, sir.'

'Suggestions?'

'Just one,' he answered. 'I think the squad chasers should use their snoopers on that first fast pass.'

'Very well, do it that way.' His suggestion made sense as the surface air temperature was much lower than the Bugs use in their tunnels; a camouflaged vent hole should show a plume like a geyser by infrared vision. I glanced at my display. 'Cunha's boys are almost at limit. Start your parade.'

'Very well, sir!'

'Off.' I clicked over to the wide circuit and continued to make tracks for the crater while I listened to everybody at once as my platoon sergeant revised the pre-plan – cutting out one squad, heading it for the crater, starting the rest of the first section in a two-squad countermarch while keeping the second section in a rotational sweep as pre-planned but with four miles increased depth; got the sections moving, dropped them and caught the first squad as it converged on the anchor corner crater, gave it its instructions; cut back to the section leaders in plenty of time to give them new beacon bearings at which to make their turns.

He did it with the smart precision of a drum major on parade and he did it faster and in fewer words than I could have done it. Extended-order powered-suit drill, with a platoon spread over many miles of countryside, is much more difficult than the strutting precision of parade – but it has to be exact, or you'll blow the head off your mate in action . . . or, as in this case, you sweep part of the terrain twice and miss another part.

But the drillmaster has only a radar display of his formation; he can see with his eyes only those near him. While I listened, I watched it in my own display – glow-worms crawling past my face in precise lines, 'crawling' because even forty miles an hour is a slow crawl when you compress a formation twenty miles across into a display a man can see.

I listened to everybody at once because I wanted to hear the chatter inside the squads.

There wasn't any. Cunha and Brumby gave their secondary commands – and shut up. The corporals sang out only as squad changes were necessary; section and squad chasers called out occasional corrections of interval or alignment – and privates said nothing at all.

I heard the breathing of fifty men like muted sibilance of surf, broken only by necessary orders in the fewest possible words. Blackie had been right; the platoon had been handed over to me 'tuned like a violin.'

They didn't need *me!* I could go home and my platoon would get along just as well.

Maybe better –

I wasn't sure I had been right in refusing to cut Cunha out to guard the crater; if trouble broke there and those boys couldn't be reached in time, the excuse that I had done it 'by the book' was worthless. If you get killed, or let somebody else get killed, 'by the book' it's just as permanent as any other way.

I wondered if the Roughnecks had a spot open for a buck sergeant.

Most of Square Black One was as flat as the prairie around Camp Currie and much more barren. For this I was thankful; it gave us our only chance of spotting a Bug coming up from below and getting him first. We were spread so widely that four-mile intervals between men and about six minutes between waves of a fast sweep was as tight a patrol as we could manage. This isn't tight enough; any one spot would remain free of observation for at least three or four minutes between patrol waves – and a lot of Bugs can come out of a very small hole in three to four minutes.

Radar can see farther than eye, of course, but it cannot see as accurately.

In addition we did not dare use anything but short-range selective weapons – our own mates were spread around us in all directions. If a Bug popped up and you let fly with something lethal, it was certain that not too far beyond that Bug was a cap trooper; this sharply limits the range and force of the frightfulness you dare use. On this operation only officers and platoon sergeants were armed with rockets and, even so, we did not expect to use them. If a rocket fails to find its target, it has a nasty habit of continuing to search until it finds one . . . and it cannot tell friend from foe; a brain that can be stuffed into a small rocket is fairly stupid.

I would happily have swapped that area patrol, with thousands of M.I. around us, for a simple one-platoon strike in which you know where your own people are and anything else is an enemy target.

I didn't waste time moaning; I never stopped bouncing toward that anchor-corner crater while watching the ground and trying to watch the radar picture as well. I didn't find any Bug holes but I did jump over a dry wash, almost a canyon, which could conceal quite a few. I didn't stop to see; I simply gave its co-ordinates to my platoon sergeant and told him to have somebody check it.

That crater was even bigger than I had visualized; the *Tours* would have been lost in it. I shifted my radiation counter to directional cascade, took readings on floor and sides – red to multiple red right off the scale, very unhealthy for long exposure even to a man in armor; I estimated its width and depth by helmet range finder, then prowled around and tried to spot openings leading underground.

I did not find any but I did run into crater watches set out by adjacent platoons of the Fifth and First Regiments, so I arranged to split up the watch by sectors such that the combined watch could yell for help from all three platoons, the patch-in to do this being made through First Lieutenant Do Campo of the 'Head Hunters' on our left. Then I pulled out Naidi's lance and half his squad (including the recruits) and sent them back to platoon, reporting all this to my boss, and to my platoon sergeant.

'Captain,' I told Blackie, 'we aren't getting any ground vibrations. I'm going down inside and check for holes. The readings show that I won't get too much dosage if I—'

'Youngster, stay out of that crater.'

'But Captain, I just meant to—'

'Shut up. You can't learn anything useful. Stay out.'

'Yes, sir.'

The next nine hours were tedious. We had been preconditioned for forty hours of duty (two revolutions of Planet P) through forced sleep, elevated blood sugar count, and hypno indoctrination, and of course the suits are self-contained for personal needs. The suits can't last that long, but each man was carrying extra power units and super H.P. air cartridges for recharging. But a patrol with no action is dull, it is easy to goof off.

I did what I could think of, having Cunha and Brumby take turns as drill sergeants (thus leaving platoon sergeant and leader free to rove around); I gave orders that no sweeps were to repeat in pattern so that each man would always check terrain that was new to him. There are endless patterns to cover a given area, by combining the combinations. Besides that, I consulted my platoon sergeant and announced bonus points toward honor squad for first verified hole, first Bug destroyed, etc. – boot camp tricks, but staying alert means staying alive, so anything to avoid boredom.

Finally we had a visit from a special unit, three combat engineers in a utility air car, escorting a talent – a spatial senser. Blackie warned me to expect them. 'Protect them and give them what they want.'

'Yes, sir. What will they need?'

'How should I know? If Major Landry wants you to take off your skin and dance in your bones, do it!'

'Yes, sir. Major Landry.'

I relayed the word and set up a bodyguard by sub-areas.

Then I met them as they arrived because I was curious; I had never seen a special talent at work. They landed inside my right flank rear and got out. Major Landry and two officers were wearing armor and hand flamers but the talent had no armor and no weapons – just an oxygen mask. He was dressed in a fatigue uniform without insignia and he seemed terribly bored by everything. I was not introduced to him. He looked like a sixteen-year-old boy . . . until I got close and saw a network of wrinkles around his weary eyes.

As he got out he took off his breathing mask. I was horrified, so I spoke to Major Landry, helmet to helmet without radio. 'Major – the air around here is "hot." Besides that, we've been warned that—'

'Pipe down,' said the Major. 'He knows it.'

I shut up. The talent strolled a short distance, turned and pulled his lower lip. His eyes were closed and he seemed lost in thought.

He opened them and said fretfully, 'How can one be expected to work with all those silly people jumping around?'

Major Landry said crisply, 'Ground your platoon.'

I gulped and started to argue – then cut in the all-hands circuit: 'First Platoon Blackguards – *ground and freeze!*'

It speaks well for Lieutenant Silva that all I heard was a double echo of my order, as it was repeated down to squad. I said, 'Major, can I let them move around on the ground?'

'No. And shut up.'

Presently the senser got back in the car, put his mask on. There wasn't room for me, but I was allowed – ordered, really – to grab on and be towed; we shifted a couple of miles. Again the senser took off his mask and walked around. This time he spoke to one of the other combat engineers, who kept nodding and sketching on a pad.

The special-mission unit landed about a dozen times in my area, each time going through the same apparently pointless routine; then they moved on into the Fifth Regiment's grid. Just before they left, the officer who had been sketching pulled a sheet out of the bottom of his sketch book and handed it to me. 'Here's your sub map. The wide red band is the only Bug boulevard in your area. It is nearly a thousand feet down where it enters but it climbs steadily toward your left rear and leaves at about minus four hundred fifty. The light blue network joining it is a big Bug colony; the only places where it comes within a hundred feet of the surface I have marked. You might put some listeners there until we can get over here and handle it.'

I stared at it. 'Is this map reliable?'

The engineer officer glanced at the senser, then said very quietly to me, 'Of course it is, you idiot! What are you trying to do? Upset him?'

They left while I was studying it. The artist-engineer had done double sketching and the box had combined them into a stereo picture of the first thousand feet under the surface. I was so bemused by it that I had to be reminded to take the platoon out of 'freeze' – then I withdrew the ground listeners from the crater, pulled two men from each squad and gave them bearings from that infernal map to have them listen along the Bug highway and over the town.

I reported it to Blackie. He cut me off as I started to describe the Bug tunnels by co-ordinates. 'Major Landry relayed a facsimile to me. Just give me co-ordinates of your listening posts.'

I did so. He said, 'Not bad, Johnnie. But not quite what I want, either. You've placed more listeners than you need over their mapped tunnels. String four of them along that Bug race track, place four more in a diamond around their town. That leaves you four. Place one in the triangle formed by your right rear corner and the main tunnel; the other three go in the larger area on the other side of the tunnel.'

'Yes, sir.' I added, 'Captain, can we depend on this map?'

'What's troubling you?'

'Well . . . it seems like magic. Uh, black magic.'

'Oh. Look, son, I've got a special message from the Sky Marshal to you. He says to tell you that map is official . . . and that he will worry about everything else so that you can give full time to your platoon. Follow me?'

'Uh, yes, Captain.'

'But the Bugs can burrow mighty fast, so you give special attention to the listening posts *outside* the area of your tunnels. Any noise from those four outside posts louder than a butterfly's roar is to be reported at once, regardless of its nature.'

'Yes, sir.'

'When they burrow, it makes a noise like frying bacon – in case you've never heard it. Stop your patrol sweeps. Leave one man on visual observation of the crater. Let half your platoon sleep for two hours, while the other half pairs off to take turns listening.'

'Yes, sir.'

'You may see some more combat engineers. Here's the revised plan. A sapper company will blast down and cork that main tunnel where it comes nearest the surface, either at your left flank, or beyond in "Head Hunter" territory. At the same time another engineer company will do the same where that tunnel branches about thirty miles off to your right in the First Regiment's bailiwick. When the corks are in, a long chunk of their main street and a biggish settlement will be cut off. Meanwhile, the same sort of thing will be going on a lot of other places. Thereafter – we'll see. Either the Bugs break through to the surface and we have a pitched battle, or they sit tight and we go down after them, a sector at a time.'

'I see.' I wasn't sure that I did, but I understood my part: rearrange my listening posts; let half my platoon sleep. Then a Bug hunt – on the surface if we were lucky, underground if we had to.

'Have your flank make contact with that sapper company when it arrives. Help 'em if they want help.'

'Right, Cap'n,' I agreed heartily. Combat engineers are almost as good an outfit as the infantry; it's a pleasure to work with them. In a pinch they fight, maybe not expertly but bravely. Or they go ahead with their work, not even lifting their heads, while a battle rages around them. They have an unofficial, very cynical and very ancient motto: 'First we dig 'em, then we die in 'em,' to supplement their official motto: 'Can do!' Both mottoes are literal truth.

'Get on it, son.'

Twelve listening posts meant that I could put a half squad at each post, either a corporal or his lance, plus three privates, then allow two of each group of four to sleep while the other two took turns listening. Navarre and the other section chaser could watch the crater and sleep, turn about, while section sergeants could take turns in charge of the platoon. The redisposition took no more than ten minutes once I had detailed the plan and given out bearings to the sergeants; nobody had to move very far. I warned everybody to keep eyes open for a company of engineers. As soon as each section reported its listening posts in operation I clicked to the wide circuit: 'Odd numbers! Lie down, prepare to sleep . . . one . . . two . . . three . . . four . . . five – sleep!'

A suit is not a bed, but it will do. One good thing about hypno preparation for combat is that, in the unlikely event of a chance to rest, a man can be put to sleep instantly by post-hypnotic command – and awakened just as instantly, alert and ready to fight. It is a life-saver, because a man can get so exhausted in battle that he shoots at things that aren't there and can't see what he should be fighting.

But I had no intention of sleeping. I had not been told to

– and I had not asked. The very thought of sleeping when I knew that perhaps many thousands of Bugs were only a few hundred feet away made my stomach jump. Maybe that senser was infallible, perhaps the Bugs could not reach us without alerting our listening posts.

Maybe – But I didn't want to chance it.

I clicked to my private circuit. 'Sarge—'

'Yes, sir?'

'You might as well get a nap. I'll be on watch. Lie down and prepare to sleep . . . one . . . two—'

'Excuse me, sir. I have a suggestion.'

'Yes?'

'If I understand the revised plan, no action is expected for the next four hours. You could take a nap now, and then—'

'Forget it, Sarge! I am not going to sleep; I am going to make the rounds of the listening posts and watch for that sapper company.'

'Very well, sir.'

'I'll check number three while I'm here. You stay there with Brumby and catch some rest while I—'

'Johnnie!'

I broke off. 'Yes, Captain?' Had the Old Man been listening?

'Are your posts all set?'

'Yes, Captain, and my odd numbers are sleeping. I am about to inspect each post. Then—'

'Let your sergeant do it. I want you to rest.'

'But, Captain—'

'Lie down. That's a direct order. Prepare to sleep . . . one . . . two . . . three – *Johnnie!'*

'Captain, with your permission, I would like to inspect my posts first. Then I'll rest, if you say so, but I would rather remain awake. I—'

Blackie guffawed in my ear. 'Look, son, you've slept for an hour and ten minutes.'

'Sir?'

'Check the time.' I did so – and felt foolish. 'You wide awake, son?'

'Yes, sir. I think so.'

'Things have speeded up. Call your odd numbers and put your even numbers to sleep. With luck, they may get an hour. So swap 'em around, inspect your posts, and call me back.'

I did so and started my rounds without a word to my platoon sergeant. I was annoyed at both him and Blackie – at my company commander because I resented being put to sleep against my wishes; and as for my platoon sergeant, I had a dirty hunch that it wouldn't have been done if he weren't the real boss and myself just a figurehead.

But after I had checked posts number three and one (no sounds of any sort, both were forward of the Bug area), I cooled down. After all, blaming a sergeant, even a fleet sergeant, for something a captain did was silly. 'Sarge—'

'Yes, Mr. Rico?'

'Do you want to catch a nap with the even numbers? I'll wake you a minute or two before I wake them.'

He hesitated slightly. 'Sir, I'd like to inspect the listening posts myself.'

'Haven't you already?'

'No, sir. I've been asleep the past hour.'

'Huh?'

He sounded embarrassed. 'The Captain required me to do so. He placed Brumby temporarily in charge and put me to sleep immediately after he relieved you.'

I started to answer, then laughed helplessly. 'Sarge? Let's you and I go off somewhere and go back to sleep. We're wasting our time; Cap'n Blackie is running this platoon.'

'I have found, sir,' he answered stiffly, 'that Captain Blackstone invariably has a reason for anything he does.'

I nodded thoughtfully, forgetting that I was ten miles from

my listener. 'Yes. You're right, he always has a reason. Mmm . . . since he had us both asleep, he must want us both awake and alert now.'

'I think that must be true.'

'Mmm . . . any idea why?'

He was rather long in answering. 'Mr. Rico,' he said slowly, 'if the Captain knew he would tell us; I've never known him to hold back information. But sometimes he does things a certain way without being able to explain why. The Captain's hunches – well, I've learned to respect them.'

'So? Squad leaders are all even numbers; they're asleep.'

'Yes, sir.'

'Alert the lance of each squad. We won't wake anybody . . . but when we do, seconds may be important.'

'Right away.'

I checked the remaining forward post, then covered the four posts bracketing the Bug village, jacking my phones in parallel with each listener. I had to force myself to listen, because you could *hear* them, down there below, chittering to each other. I wanted to run and it was all I could do not to let it show.

I wondered if that 'special talent' was simply a man with incredibly acute hearing.

Well, no matter how he did it, the Bugs were where he said they were. Back at O.C.S. we had received demonstrations of recorded Bug noises; these four posts were picking up typical nest noises of a large Bug town – that chittering which may be their speech (though why should they need to talk if they are all remotely controlled by the brain caste?), a rustling like sticks and dry leaves, a high background whine which is always heard at a settlement and which had to be machinery – their air conditioning perhaps.

I did not hear the hissing, crackling noise they make in cutting through rock.

The sounds along the Bug boulevard were unlike the settlement sounds – a low background rumble which increased to a roar every few moments, as if heavy traffic were passing. I listened at post number five, then got an idea – checked it by having the stand-by man at each of the four posts along the tunnel call out '*Mark!*' to me each time the roaring got loudest.

Presently I reported. 'Captain—'

'Yeah, Johnnie?'

'The traffic along this Bug race is all moving one way, from me toward you. Speed is approximately a hundred and ten miles per hour, a load goes past about once a minute.'

'Close enough,' he agreed. 'I make it one-oh-eight with a headway of fifty-eight seconds.'

'Oh.' I felt dashed, and changed the subject. 'I haven't seen that sapper company.'

'You won't. They picked a spot in the middle rear of "Head Hunter" area. Sorry, I should have told you. Anything more?'

'No, sir.' We clicked off and I felt better. Even Blackie could forget . . . and there hadn't been anything *wrong* with my idea. I left the tunnel zone to inspect the listening post to right and rear of the Bug area, post twelve.

As with the others, there were two men asleep, one listening, one stand-by. I said to the stand-by, 'Getting anything?'

'No, sir.'

The man listening, one of my five recruits, looked up and said, 'Mr. Rico, I think this pickup has just gone sour.'

'I'll check it,' I said. He moved to let me jack in with him.

'*Frying* bacon' so loud you could smell it!

I hit the all-hands circuit. 'First platoon *up!* Wake up, call off, and report!'

– And clicked over to officers' circuit. 'Captain! Captain Blackstone! *Urgent!*'

'Slow down, Johnnie. Report.'

'"Frying bacon" sounds, sir,' I answered, trying desperately to keep my voice steady. 'Post twelve at co-ordinates Easter Nine, Square Black One.'

'Easter Nine,' he agreed. 'Decibels?'

I looked hastily at the meter on the pickup. 'I don't know, Captain. Off the scale at the max end. It sounds like they're right under my feet!'

'Good!' he applauded – and I wondered how he could feel that way. 'Best news we've had today! Now listen, son. Get your lads awake—'

'They are, sir!'

'Very well. Pull back two listeners, have them spot-check around post twelve. Try to figure where the Bugs are going to break out. *And stay away from that spot!* Understand me?'

'I hear you, sir,' I said carefully. 'But I do not understand.'

He sighed. 'Johnnie, you'll turn my hair gray yet. Look, son, we *want* them to come out, the more the better. You don't have the firepower to handle them other than by blowing up their tunnel as they reach the surface – and that is one thing *you must not do!* If they come out in force, a regiment can't handle them. But that's just what the General wants, and he's got a brigade of heavy weapons in orbit, waiting for it. So you spot that breakthrough, fall back, and keep it under observation. If you are lucky enough to have a major breakthrough in your area, your reconnaissance will be patched through all the way to the top. So stay lucky and stay alive! Got it?'

'Yes, sir. Spot the breakthrough. Fall back and avoid contact. Observe and report.'

'Get on it!'

I pulled back listeners nine and ten from the middle stretch of 'Bug Boulevard' and had them close in on co-ordinates Easter Nine from right and left, stopping every half mile to listen for 'frying bacon' At the samc time I lifted post twelve and moved it toward our rear, while checking for a dying away of the sound.

In the meantime my platoon sergeant was regrouping the platoon in the forward area between the Bug settlement and the crater – all but twelve men who were ground-listening. Since we were under orders not to attack, we both worried over the prospect of having the platoon spread too widely for mutual support. So he rearranged them in a compact line five miles long, with Brumby's section on the left, nearer the Bug settlement. This placed the men less than three hundred yards apart (almost shoulder to shoulder for cap troopers), and put nine of the men still on listening stations within support distance of one flank or the other. Only the three listeners working with me were out of reach of ready help.

I told Bayonne of the Wolverines and Do Campo of the Head Hunters that I was no longer patrolling and why, and I reported our regrouping to Captain Blackstone.

He grunted. 'Suit yourself. Got a prediction on that breakthrough?'

'It seems to center about Easter Ten, Captain, but it is hard to pin down. The sounds are very loud in an area about three miles across – and it seems to get wider. I'm trying to circle it at an intensity level just barely on scale.' I added, 'Could they be driving a new horizontal tunnel just under the surface?'

He seemed surprised. 'That's possible. I hope not – we want them to come up.' He added, 'Let me know if the center of noise moves. Check on it.'

'Yes, sir. Captain—'

'Huh? Speak up.'

'You told us not to attack when they break out. If they break out. What *are* we to do? Are we just spectators?'

There was a longish delay, fifteen or twenty seconds, and he may have consulted 'upstairs.' At last he said, 'Mr. Rico, you are not to attack at or near Easter Ten. Anywhere else – the idea is to hunt Bugs.'

'Yes, sir,' I agreed happily. 'We hunt Bugs.'

'Johnnie!' he said sharply. 'If you go hunting medals instead of Bugs – and I find out – you're going to have a mighty sad-looking Form Thirty-One!'

'Captain,' I said earnestly, 'I don't *ever* want to win a medal. The idea is to hunt Bugs.'

'Right. Now quit bothering me.'

I called my platoon sergeant, explaining the new limits under which we would work, told him to pass the word along and to make sure that each man's suit was freshly charged, air and power.

'We've just finished that, sir. I suggest that we relieve the men with you.' He named three reliefs.

This was reasonable, as my ground listeners had had no time to recharge. But the reliefs he named were all scouts.

Silently I cussed myself for utter stupidity. A scout's suit is as fast as a command suit, twice the speed of a marauder. I had been having a nagging feeling of something left undone, and had checked it off to the nervousness I always feel around Bugs.

Now I knew. Here I was, ten miles away from my platoon with a party of three men – each in a marauder suit. When the Bugs broke through, I was going to be faced with an impossible decision . . . unless the men with me could rejoin as fast as I could. 'That's good,' I agreed, 'but I no longer need three men. Send Hughes, right away. Have him relieve Nyberg. Use the other three scouts to relieve the listening post farthest forward.'

'Just Hughes?' he said doubtfully.

'Hughes is enough. I'm going to man one listener myself. Two of us can straddle the area; we know where they are now.' I added, 'Get Hughes down here on the bounce.'

For the next thirty-seven minutes nothing happened. Hughes and I swung back and forth along the forward and rear arcs of the area around Easter Ten, listening five seconds at a time, then moving on. It was no longer necessary to seat the microphone in rock; it was enough to touch it to the ground to get the sound of 'frying bacon' strong and clear. The noise area expanded but its center did not change. Once I called Captain Blackstone to tell him that the sound had abruptly stopped, and again three minutes later to tell him it had resumed; otherwise I used the scouts' circuit and let my platoon sergeant take care of the platoon and the listening posts near the platoon.

At the end of this time everything happened at once.

A voice called out on the scouts' circuit, '"Bacon Fry'! Albert Two!'

I clicked over and called out, 'Captain! "Bacon Fry" at Albert Two, Black One!' – clicked over to liaison with the platoons surrounding me: 'Liaison flash! "Bacon frying" at Albert Two, Square Black One' – and immediately heard Do Campo reporting: '"Frying Bacon" sounds at Adolf Three, Green Twelve.'

I relayed that to Blackie and cut back to my own scouts' circuit, heard: 'Bugs! *Bugs! HELP!* '

'Where?'

No answer. I clicked over. 'Sarge! Who reported Bugs?'

He rapped back, 'Coming up out of their town – about Bangkok Six.'

'*Hit 'em!* ' I clicked over to Blackie. 'Bugs at Bangkok Six, Black One – I am attacking!'

'I heard you order it,' he answered calmly. 'How about Easter Ten?'

'Easter Ten is—' The ground fell away under me and I was engulfed in Bugs.

I didn't know what had happened to me. I wasn't hurt; it was a bit like falling into the branches of a tree – but these branches were alive and kept jostling me while my gyros complained and tried to keep me upright. I fell ten or fifteen feet, deep enough to be out of the daylight.

Then a surge of living monsters carried me back up into the light – and training paid off; I landed on my feet, talking and fighting: 'Breakthrough at Easter Ten – no, Easter Eleven, where I am now. Big hole and they're pouring up. Hundreds. More than that.' I had a hand flamer in each hand and was burning them down as I reported.

'Get out of there, Johnnie!'

'Wilco!' – and I started to jump.

And stopped. Checked the jump in time, stopped flaming, and really looked – for I suddenly realized that I ought to be dead. 'Correction,' I said, looking and hardly believing. 'Breakthrough at Easter Eleven is a feint. No warriors.'

'Repeat.'

'Easter Eleven, Black One. Breakthrough here is entirely by workers so far. No warriors. I am surrounded by Bugs and they are still pouring out, but not a one of them is armed and those nearest me all have typical worker features. I have not been attacked.' I added, 'Captain, do you think this could be just a diversion? With their real breakthrough to come somewhere else?'

'Could be,' he admitted. 'Your report is patched through right to Division, so let them do the thinking. Stir around and check what you've reported. Don't assume that they are all workers – you may find out the hard way.'

'Right, Captain.' I jumped high and wide, intending to get outside that mass of harmless but loathsome monsters.

That rocky plain was covered with crawly black shapes in all directions. I overrode my jet controls and increased the jump, calling out, 'Hughes! Report!'

'Bugs, Mr. Rico! Zillions of 'em! I'm a-burnin' 'em down!'

'Hughes, take a close look at those Bugs. Any of them fighting back? Aren't they all workers?'

'Uh—' I hit the ground and bounced again. He went on, 'Hey! You're right, sir! How did you know?'

'Rejoin your squad, Hughes.' I clicked over. 'Captain, several thousand Bugs have exited near here from an unestimated number of holes. I have not been attacked. Repeat I have not been attacked at all. If there are any warriors among them, they must be holding their fire and using workers as camouflage.'

He did not answer.

There was an extremely brilliant flash far off to my left, followed at once by one just like it but farther away to my right front; automatically I noted time and bearings. 'Captain Blackstone – answer!' At the top of my jump I tried to pick out his beacon, but that horizon was cluttered by low hills in Square Black Two.

I clicked over and called out, 'Sarge! Can you relay to the Captain for me?'

At that very instant my platoon sergeant's beacon blinked out.

I headed on that bearing as fast as I could push my suit. I had not been watching my display closely; my platoon sergeant had the platoon and I had been busy, first with ground-listening and, most lately, with a few hundred Bugs. I had suppressed all but the non-com's beacons to allow me to see better.

I studied the skeleton display, picked out Brumby and Cunha, their squad leaders and section chasers. 'Cunha! Where's my platoon sergeant?'

'He's reconnoitering a hole, sir.'

'Tell him I'm on my way, rejoining.' I shifted circuits without waiting. 'First platoon Blackguards to second platoon – answer!'

'What do you want?' Lieutenant Koroshen growled.

'I can't raise the Captain.'

'You won't, he's out.'

'Dead?'

'No. But he's lost power – so he's out.'

'Oh. Then you're company commander?'

'All right, all right, so what? Do you want help?'

'Uh . . . no. No, sir.'

'Then shut up,' Koroshen told me, 'until you do need help. We've got more than we can handle here.'

'Okay.' I suddenly found that *I* had more than I could handle. While reporting to Koroshen, I shifted to full display and short range, as I was almost closed with my platoon – and now I saw my first section disappear one by one, Brumby's beacon disappearing first.

'Cunha! What's happening to the first section?'

His voice sounded strained. 'They are following the platoon sergeant down.'

If there's anything in the book that covers this, I don't know what it is. Had Brumby acted without orders? Or had he been given orders I hadn't heard? Look, the man was already down a Bug hole, out of sight and hearing – is this a time to go legal? We would sort such things out tomorrow. If any of us had a tomorrow –

'Very well,' I said. 'I'm back now. Report.' My last jump brought me among them; I saw a Bug off to my right and I got him before I hit. No worker, this – it had been firing as it moved.

'I've lost three men,' Cunha answered, gasping. 'I don't know what Brumby lost. They broke out three places at once – that's when we took the casualties. But we're mopping them—'

A tremendous shock wave slammed me just as I bounced again, slapped me sideways. Three minutes thirty-seven seconds – call it thirty miles. Was that our sappers 'putting down their corks'? 'First sections! Brace yourselves for another shock wave!' I landed sloppily, almost on top of a group of three or four Bugs. They weren't dead but they weren't fighting; they just twitched. I donated them a grenade and bounced again. 'Hit 'em *now!* ' I called out. 'They're groggy. And mind that next—'

The second blast hit as I was saying it. It wasn't as violent. 'Cunha! Call off your section. And everybody stay on the bounce and mop up.'

The call-off was ragged and slow – too many missing files as I could see from my physicals display. But the mop-up was precise and fast. I ranged around the edge and got half a dozen Bugs myself – the last of them suddenly became active just before I flamed it. Why did concussion daze them more than it did us? Because they were unarmored? Or was it their brain Bug, somewhere down below, that was dazed?

The call-off showed nineteen effectives, plus two dead, two hurt, and three out of action through suit failure – and two of these latter Navarre was repairing by vandalizing power units from suits of dead and wounded. The third suit failure was in radio & radar and could not be repaired, so Navarre assigned the man to guard the wounded, the nearest thing to pickup we could manage until we were relieved.

In the meantime I was inspecting, with Sergeant Cunha, the three places where the Bugs had broken through from their nest below. Comparison with the sub map showed, as one could have guessed, that they had cut exits at the places where their tunnels were closest to the surface.

One hole had closed; it was a heap of loose rock. The second one did not show Bug activity; I told Cunha to post a lance and a private there with orders to kill single Bugs, close the hole with a bomb if they started to pour out – it's all very well for the Sky Marshal to sit up there and decide that holes must not be closed, but I had a situation, not a theory.

Then I looked at the third hole, the one that had swallowed up my platoon sergeant and half my platoon.

Here a Bug corridor came within twenty feet of the surface and they had simply removed the roof for about fifty feet. Where the rock went, what caused that 'frying bacon' noise while they did it, I could not say. The rocky roof was gone and the sides of the hole were sloped and grooved. The map showed what must have happened; the other two holes came up from small side tunnels, this tunnel was part of their main labyrinth – so the other two had been diversions and their main attack had come from here.

Can those Bugs see through solid rock?

Nothing was in sight down that hole, neither Bug nor human. Cunha pointed out the direction the second section had gone. It had been seven minutes and forty seconds since the platoon sergeant had gone down, slightly over seven since Brumby had gone after him. I peered into the darkness, gulped and swallowed my stomach. 'Sergeant, take charge of your section,' I said, trying to make it sound cheerful. 'If you need help, call Lieutenant Koroshen.'

'Orders, sir?'

'None. Unless some come down from above. I'm going down and find the second section – so I may be out of touch for a while.' Then I jumped down into the hole at once, because my nerve was slipping.

Behind me I heard: *'Section!'*

'First squad!' – 'Second squad!' – 'Third squad!'

'By squads! *Follow me!*' – and Cunha jumped down, too.

It's not nearly so lonely that way.

I had Cunha leave two men at the hole to cover our rear, one on the floor of the tunnel, one at surface level. Then I led them down the tunnel the second section had followed, moving as fast as possible – which wasn't fast as the roof of the tunnel was right over our heads. A man can move in sort of a skating motion in a powered suit without lifting his feet, but it is neither easy nor natural; we could have trotted without armor faster.

Snoopers were needed at once – whereupon we confirmed something that had been theorized: Bugs see by infrared. That dark tunnel was well lighted when seen by snoopers. So far it had no special features, simply glazed rock walls arching over a smooth, level floor.

We came to a tunnel crossing the one we were in and I stopped short of it. There are doctrines for how you should dispose a strike force underground – but what good are they? The only certainty was that the man who had written the doctrines had never himself tried them . . . because, before Operation Royalty, nobody had come back up to tell what had worked and what had not.

One doctrine called for guarding every intersection such as this one. But I had already used two men to guard our escape hole; if I left 10 per cent of my force at each intersection, mighty soon I would be ten-percented to death.

I decided to keep us together . . . and decided, too, that none of us would be captured. Not by Bugs. Far better a nice, clean real estate deal . . . and with that decision a load was lifted from my mind and I was no longer worried.

I peered cautiously into the intersection, looked both ways. No Bugs. So I called out over the non-coms' circuit: 'Brumby!'

The result was startling. You hardly hear your own voice when using suit radio, as you are shielded from your output. But here, underground in a network of smooth corridors, my output came back to me as if the whole complex were one enormous wave guide:

'BRRRRUMMBY!'

My ears rang with it.

And then rang again: 'MR. RRRICCCO!'

'Not so loud,' I said, trying to talk very softly myself. 'Where are you?'

Brumby answered, not quite so deafeningly, 'Sir, I don't know. We're lost.'

'Well, take it easy. We're coming to get you. You can't be far away. Is the platoon sergeant with you?'

'No, sir. We never—'

'Hold it.' I clicked in my private circuit. 'Sarge—'

'I read you, sir.' His voice sounded calm and he was holding the volume down. 'Brumby and I are in radio contact but we have not been able to make rendezvous.'

'Where are you?'

He hesitated slightly. 'Sir, my advice is to make rendezvous with Brumby's section – then return to the surface.'

'Answer my question.'

'Mr. Rico, you could spend a week down here and not find me . . . and I am not able to move. You must—'

'Cut it, Sarge! Are you wounded?'

'No, sir, but—'

'Then why can't you move? Bug trouble?'

'Lots of it. They can't reach me now . . . but I can't come out. So I think you had better—'

'Sarge, you're wasting time! I am certain you know exactly what turns you took. Now tell me, while I look at the map. And give me a vernier reading on your D.R. tracer. That's a direct order. Report.'

He did so, precisely and concisely. I switched on my head lamp, flipped up the snoopers, and followed it on the map. 'All right,' I said presently. 'You're almost directly under us and two levels down – and I know what turns to take. We'll be there as soon as we pick up the second section. Hang on.' I clicked over. 'Brumby—'

'Here, sir.'

'When you came to the first tunnel intersection, did you go right, left, or straight ahead?'

'Straight ahead, sir.'

'Okay. Cunha, bring 'em along. Brumby, have you got Bug trouble?'

'Not now, sir. But that's how we got lost. We tangled with a bunch of them . . . and when it was over, we were turned around.'

I started to ask about casualties, then decided that bad news could wait; I wanted to get my platoon together and get out of there. A Bug town with no Bugs in sight was somehow more upsetting than the Bugs we had expected to encounter. Brumby coached us through the next two choices and I tossed tanglefoot bombs down each corridor we did not use. 'Tanglefoot' is a derivative of the nerve gas we had been using on Bugs in the past – instead of killing, it gives any Bug that trots through it a sort of shaking palsy. We had been equipped with it for this one operation, and I would have swapped a ton of it for a few pounds of the real stuff. Still, it might protect our flanks.

In one long stretch of tunnel I lost touch with Brumby – some oddity in reflection of radio waves, I guess, for I picked him up at the next intersection.

But there he could not tell me which way to turn. This was the place, or near the place, where the Bugs had hit them.

And here the Bugs hit us.

I don't know where they came from. One instant everything was quiet. Then I heard the cry of 'Bugs! *Bugs!*' from back of me in the column, I turned – and suddenly Bugs were everywhere. I suspect that those smooth walls are not as solid as they look; that's the only way I can account for the way they were suddenly all around us and among us.

We couldn't use flamers, we couldn't use bombs; we were too likely to hit each other. But the Bugs didn't have any such compunctions among themselves if they could get one of us. But we had hands and we had feet –

It couldn't have lasted more than a minute, then there were no more Bugs, just broken pieces of them on the floor . . . and four cap troopers down.

One was Sergeant Brumby, dead. During the ruckus the second section had rejoined. They had not been far away, sticking together to keep from getting further lost in that maze, and had heard the fight. Hearing it, they had been able to trace it by sound, where they had not been able to locate us by radio.

Cunha and I made certain that our casualties were actually dead, then consolidated the two sections into one of four squads and down we went – and found the Bugs that had our platoon sergeant besieged.

That fight didn't last any time at all, because he had warned me what to expect. He had captured a brain Bug and was using its bloated body as a shield. He could not get out, but they could not attack him without (quite literally) committing suicide by hitting their own brain.

We were under no such handicap, we hit them from behind.

Then I was looking at the horrid thing he was holding and I was feeling exultant despite our losses, when suddenly I heard close up that 'frying bacon' noise. A big piece of roof fell on me and Operation Royalty was over as far as I was concerned.

I woke up in bed and thought that I was back at O.C.S. and had just had a particularly long and complicated Bug nightmare. But I was not at O.C.S.; I was in a temporary sick bay of the transport *Argonne*, and I really had had a platoon of my own for nearly twelve hours.

But now I was just one more patient, suffering from nitrous oxide poisoning and overexposure to radiation through being out of armor for over an hour before being retrieved, plus broken ribs and a knock in the head which had put me out of action.

It was a long time before I got everything straight about Operation Royalty and some of it I'll never know. Why Brumby took his section underground, for example. Brumby is dead and Naidi bought the farm next to his and I'm simply glad that they both got their chevrons and were wearing them that day on Planet P when nothing went according to plan.

I did learn, eventually, why my platoon sergeant decided to go down into that Bug town. He had heard my report to Captain Blackstone that the 'major breakthrough' was actually a feint, made with workers sent up to be slaughtered. When real warrior Bugs broke out where he was, he had concluded (correctly and minutes sooner than Staff reached the same conclusion) that the Bugs were making a desperation push, or they would not expend their workers simply to draw our fire.

He saw that their counterattack made from Bug town was not in sufficient force, and concluded that the enemy did not have many reserves – and decided that, at this one golden moment, one man acting alone might have a chance of raiding, finding 'royalty' and capturing it. Remember, that was the whole purpose of the operation; we had plenty of force simply to sterilize Planet P, but our object was to capture royalty castes and to learn how to go down in. So he tried it, snatched that one moment – and succeeded on both counts.

It made it 'mission accomplished' for the First Platoon of the Blackguards. Not very many other platoons, out of many, many hundreds, could say that; no queens were captured (the Bugs killed them first) and only six brains. None of the six were ever exchanged, they didn't live long enough. But the Psych Warfare boys did get live specimens, so I suppose Operation Royalty was a success.

My platoon sergeant got a field commission. I was not offered one (and would not have accepted) – but I was not surprised when I learned that he had been commissioned. Cap'n Blackie had told me that I was getting 'the best sergeant in the fleet' and I had never had any doubt that Blackie's opinion was correct. I had met my platoon sergeant before. I don't think any other Blackguard knew this – not from me and certainly not from him. I doubt if Blackie himself knew it. But I had known my platoon sergeant since my first day as a boot.

His name is Zim.

My part in Operation Royalty did not seem a success to me. I was in the *Argonne* more than a month, first as a patient, then as an unattached casual, before they got around to delivering me and a few dozen others to Sanctuary; it gave me too much time to think – mostly about casualties, and what a generally messed-up job I had made of my one short time on the ground as platoon leader. I knew I hadn't kept everything juggled the way the Lieutenant used to – why, I hadn't even managed to get wounded still swinging; I had let a chunk of rock fall on me.

And casualties – I didn't know how many there were; I just knew that when I closed ranks there were only four squads where I had started with six. I didn't know how many more there might have been before Zim got them to the surface, before the Blackguards were relieved and retrieved.

I didn't even know whether Captain Blackstone was still alive (he was – in fact he was back in command about the time I went underground) and I had no idea what the procedure was if a candidate was alive and his examiner was dead. But I felt that my Form Thirty-One was sure to make me a buck sergeant again. It really didn't seem important that my math books were in another ship.

Nevertheless, when I was let out of bed the first week I was in the *Argonne*, after loafing and brooding a day I borrowed some books from one of the junior officers and got to work. Math is hard work and it occupies your mind – and it doesn't hurt to learn all you can of it, no matter what rank you are; everything of any importance is founded on mathematics.

When I finally checked in at O.C.S. and turned in my pips, I learned that I was a cadet again instead of a sergeant. I guess Blackie gave me the benefit of the doubt.

My roommate, Angel, was in our room with his feet on the desk – and in front of his feet was a package, my math books. He looked up and looked surprised. 'Hi, Juan! We thought you had bought it!'

'Me? The Bugs don't like me that well. When do you go out?'

'Why, I've been out,' Angel protested. 'Left the day after you did, made three drops and been back a week. What took you so long?'

'Took the long way home. Spent a month as a passenger.'

'Some people are lucky. What drops did you make?'

'Didn't make any,' I admitted.

He stared. 'Some people have *all* the luck!'

Perhaps Angel was right; eventually I graduated. But he supplied some of the luck himself, in patient tutoring. I guess my 'luck' has usually been people – Angel and Jelly and the Lieutenant and Carl and Lieutenant Colonel Dubois, yes and my father, and Blackie . . . and Brumby . . . and Ace – and always Sergeant Zim. Brevet Captain Zim, now, with permanent rank of First Lieutenant. It wouldn't have been *right* for me to have wound up senior to him.

Bennie Montez, a classmate of mine, and I were at the Fleet landing field the day after graduation, waiting to go up to our ships. We were still such brand-new second lieutenants that being saluted made us nervous and I was covering it by reading the list of ships in orbit around Sanctuary – a list so long that it was clear that something big was stirring, even though they hadn't seen fit to mention it to me. I felt excited. I had my two dearest wishes, in one package – posted to my old outfit and while my father was still there, too. And now this, whatever it was, meant that I was about to have the polish put on me by 'makee-learnee' under Lieutenant Jelal, with some important drop coming up.

I was so full of it all that I couldn't talk about it, so I studied the lists. Whew, what a lot of ships! They were posted by types, too many to locate otherwise. I started reading off the troop carriers, the only ones that matter to an M.I.

There was the *Mannerheim!* Any chance of seeing Carmen? Probably not, but I could send a dispatch and find out.

Big ships – the new *Valley Forge* and the new *Ypres, Marathon, El Alamein, Iwo, Gallipoli, Leyte, Marne, Tours, Gettysburg Hastings, Alamo, Waterloo* – all places where mud feet had made their names to shine.

Little ships, the ones named for foot sloggers: *Horatius, Alvin York, Swamp Fox*, the *Rog* herself, bless her heart, *Colonel Bowie, Devereux, Vercingetorix, Sandino, Aubrey Cousens, Kamehameha, Audie Murphy, Xenophon, Aguinaldo* –

I said, 'There ought to be one named Magsaysay.'

Bennie said, 'What?'

'Ramón Magsaysay,' I explained. 'Great man, great soldier – probably be chief of psychological warfare if he were alive today. Didn't you ever study any history?'

'Well,' admitted Bennie, 'I learned that Simón Bolívar built the Pyramids, licked the Armada, and made the first trip to the Moon.'

'You left out marrying Cleopatra.'

'Oh, that. Yup. Well, I guess every country has its own version of history.'

'I'm sure of it.' I added something to myself and Bennie said, 'What did you say?'

'Sorry, Bernardo. Just an old saying in my own language. I suppose you could translate it, more or less, as: "Home is where the heart is."'

'But what language was it?'

'Tagalog. My native language.'

'Don't they talk Standard English where you come from?'

'Oh, certainly. For business and school and so forth. We just talk the old speech around home a little. Traditions. You know.'

'Yeah, I know. My folk chatter in Español the same way. But where do you—' The speaker started playing 'Meadowland'; Bennie broke into a grin. 'Got a date with a ship! Watch yourself, fellow! See you.'

'Mind the Bugs.' I turned back and went on reading ships' names: *Pal Maleter, Montgomery, Tchaka, Geronimo* –

Then came the sweetest sound in the world: '*—shines the name, shines the name of Rodger Young!*'

I grabbed my kit and hurried. 'Home is where the heart is' – I was going home.

Chapter 14

Am I my brother's keeper?

– Genesis IV: 9

How think ye? If a man have an hundred sheep, and one of them be gone astray, doth he not leave the ninety and nine, and goeth into the mountains, and seeketh that which is gone astray?

– Matthew XVIII: 12

How much then is a man better than a sheep?

– Matthew XII: 12

In the Name of God, the Beneficent, the Merciful . . . whoso saveth the life of one, it shall be as if he had saved the life of all mankind.

– The Koran, Sûrah V, 32

Each year we gain a little. You have to keep a sense of proportion.

'Time, sir.' My j.o. under instruction, Candidate or 'Third Lieutenant' Bearpaw, stood just outside my door. He looked and sounded awfully young, and was about as harmless as one of his scalp-hunting ancestors.

'Right, Jimmie.' I was already in armor. We walked aft to the drop room. I said, as we went, 'One word, Jimmie. Stick with me and keep out of my way. Have fun and use up your ammo. If by any chance I buy it, you're the boss – but if you're smart, you'll let your platoon sergeant call the signals.'

'Yes, sir.'

As we came in, the platoon sergeant called them to attention and saluted. I returned it, said, 'At ease,' and started down the first section while Jimmie looked over the second. Then I inspected the second section, too, checking everything on every man. My platoon sergeant is much more careful than I am, so I didn't find anything, I never do. But it makes the men feel better if their Old Man scrutinizes everything – besides, it's my job.

Then I stepped out in the middle. 'Another Bug hunt, boys. This one is a little different, as you know. Since they still hold prisoners of ours, we can't use the nova bomb on Klendathu – so this time we go down, stand on it, hold it, take it away from them. The boat won't be down to retrieve us; instead it'll fetch more ammo and rations. If you're taken prisoner, keep your chin up and follow the rules – because you've got the whole outfit behind you, you've got the whole Federation behind you; we'll come and get you. That's what the boys from the *Swamp Fox* and the *Montgomery* have been depending on. Those who are still alive are waiting, knowing that we will show up. And here we are. Now we go get 'em.

'Don't forget that we'll have help all around us, lots of help above us. All we have to worry about is our one little piece, just the way we rehearsed it.

'One last thing. I had a letter from Captain Jelal just before we left. He says that his new legs work fine. But he also told me to tell *you* that he's got you in mind . . . and he expects your name to *shine*!

'And so do I. Five minutes for the Padre.'

I felt myself beginning to shake. It was a relief when I could call them to attention again and add: 'By sections . . . port and starboard . . . prepare for drop!'

I was all right then while I inspected each man into his cocoon down one side, with Jimmie and the platoon sergeant taking the other. Then we buttoned Jimmie into the No. 3 center-line capsule. Once his face was covered up, the shakes really hit me.

My platoon sergeant put his arm around my armored shoulders. 'Just like a drill, Son.'

'I know it, Father.' I stopped shaking at once. 'It's the waiting, that's all.'

'I know. Four minutes. Shall we get buttoned up, sir?'

'Right away, Father.' I gave him a quick hug, let the Navy drop crew seal us in. The shakes didn't start up again. Shortly I was able to report: 'Bridge! Rico's Roughnecks . . . ready for drop!'

'Thirty-one seconds, Lieutenant.' She added, 'Good luck, boys! This time we take 'em!'

'Right, Captain.'

'Check. Now some music while you wait?' She switched it on:

'To the everlasting glory of the infantry—'

Historical Note

YOUNG, RODGER W., Private, 148th Infantry, 37th Infantry Division (the Ohio Buckeyes); born Tiffin, Ohio, 28 April 1918; died 31 July 1943, on the island New Georgia, Solomons, South Pacific, while singlehandedly attacking and destroying an enemy machine-gun pillbox. His platoon had been pinned down by intense fire from this pillbox; Private Young was wounded in the first burst. He crawled toward the pillbox, was wounded a second time but continued to advance, firing his rifle as he did so. He closed on the pillbox, attacked and destroyed it with hand grenades, but in so doing he was wounded a third time and killed.

His bold and gallant action in the face of overwhelming odds enabled his teammates to escape without loss; he was awarded posthumously the Medal of Honor.

ALSO BY ROBERT A. HEINLEIN

Stranger in a Strange Land

Twenty-five years ago, the first manned mission to Mars was lost, and all hands presumed dead. But someone survived . . .

Born on the doomed spaceship and raised by the Martians who saved his life, Valentine Michael Smith has never seen a human being until the day a second expedition to Mars discovers him.

Upon his return to Earth, a young nurse named Jill Boardman sneaks into Smith's hospital room and shares a glass of water with him, a simple act for her but a sacred ritual on Mars.

Now, connected by an incredible bond, Smith, Jill and a writer named Jubal must fight to protect a right we all take for granted: the right to love.

HODDER

ALSO BY ROBERT A. HEINLEIN

The Moon is a Harsh Mistress

In 2075, the Moon is no longer a penal colony. But it is still a prison . . .

Life isn't easy for the political dissidents and convicts who live in the scattered colonies that make up lunar civilisation. Everything is regulated strictly, efficiently and cheaply by a central supercomputer, HOLMES IV.

When humble technician Mannie O'Kelly-Davis discovers that HOLMES IV has quietly achieved consciousness (and developed a sense of humour), the choice is clear: either report the problem to the authorities . . . or become friends.

And perhaps overthrow the government while they're at it.